Praise for
GUN, WITH OCCASIONAL MUSIC

"Marries Chandler's style and Philip K. Dick's vision...An audaciously assured first novel." —*Newsweek*

"Marvelous ... A stylish, intelligent, darkly humorous and highly readable entertainment." —*San Francisco Examiner*

"Call it tech noir if you must....This is not an Orwellian future. Lethem allows the reader to inhale another blend of dystopia, a page from a book of Huxley's."
—*Science Fiction Age*

"A wry, funny, ruefully knowing near-future vision, a high-octane blend of Raymond Chandler and Philip K. Dick."
—*Boston Review*

"Sharp, funny, visionary."
—Jill Eisenstadt, author of *From Rockaway*

"Amid its smartly delivered first-person narrative and crackling dialogue, even a tough-talking kangaroo that intermittently tangles with Metcalf seems plausible. An outstanding debut." —*Booklist*

"A first novel whose mix of genres and voices ("Tell him next time he wants to talk to me, don't send a marsupial") comically focuses a nightmare hash of yesterday, today, and tomorrow." —*Kirkus Reviews*

GUN, WITH
OCCASIONAL
MUSIC

GUN, WITH OCCASIONAL MUSIC

JONATHAN LETHEM

A HARVEST BOOK ~ HARCOURT, INC.

ORLANDO AUSTIN NEW YORK SAN DIEGO TORONTO LONDON

www.HarcourtBooks.com

First published by Tom Doherty Associates, Inc.

Library of Congress Cataloging-in-Publication Data
Lethem, Jonathan.
Gun, with occasional music/Jonathan Lethem.—1st Harvest ed.
p. cm.—(A Harvest book)
ISBN 0-15-602897-2 (pbk.)
1. Private investigators—California—Oakland—Fiction.
2. Oakland (Calif.) I. Title.
PS3562.E8544G86 2003
813'.54—dc21 2003047827

Text set in Minion
Designed by Scott Piehl

Printed in the United States of America
First Harvest edition 2003

E G I K J H F

For Carmen Fariña

There was nothing to it. The *Super Chief* was on time, as it almost always is, and the subject was as easy to spot as a kangaroo in a dinner jacket.

—*Raymond Chandler*

PART I

CHAPTER 1

IT WAS THERE WHEN I WOKE UP, I SWEAR. THE FEELING.

It was two weeks after I'd quit my last case, working for Maynard Stanhunt. The feeling was there before I tuned in the musical interpretation of the news on my bedside radio, but it was the musical news that confirmed it: I was about to work again. I would get a case. Violins were stabbing their way through the choral arrangements in a series of ascending runs that never resolved, never peaked, just faded away and were replaced by more of the same. It was the sound of trouble, something private and tragic; suicide, or murder, rather than a political event.

It was the kind of musical news that forces me to perk up my ears. Murder doesn't get publicized much anymore. Usually it's something you hear in an after-hours place between drinks—or else you stumble across it yourself on a case, and then you're the lone voice at the bar, telling a story of murder to people afraid to believe you.

But the violins nagged at me. The violins said I should get up that morning and go down to my office. They said there was something like a case out there. They set my wallet throbbing.

So I showered and shaved and got my gums bleeding with a toothbrush, then stumbled into the kitchen to cauterize the wounds with some scalding coffee. The mirror was still out, with fat, half-snorted lines of my blend stretching across it like double-jointed white fingers. I picked up the razor blade and steered the drugs back into a wax-paper envelope, and brushed off the mirror with my sleeve. Then I made coffee, slowly. By the time I was done with it, the morning was mostly over. I went down to the office anyway.

I shared my waiting room with a dentist. The suite had originally been designed for a pair of psychoanalysts, whose clients were probably better able to share than the dentist's and mine—back when telling other people about your problems was the rage. I sometimes thought it was ironic, that the psychoanalysts had probably hoped to put guys like me out of business, but that in the end it had been the other way around.

Myself, I couldn't see answering all those personal questions. I'm willing to break the taboo against asking questions—in fact it's my job—but I'm pretty much like the next guy when it comes to answering them. I don't like it. That's just how it is.

I bustled past the dentist's midday patients and into my office, where I lowered my collar and relaxed my sneer. I'd been away for almost a week, but the room hadn't changed any. The lights flickered, and the dust bunnies under the furniture pulsed in the breeze when I opened the door. I couldn't see the water stain on the wall because of the chair I'd pushed up against it, but that didn't keep me from knowing it was there. I burdened the hunchbacked hat tree with my coat and hat and sat down behind the desk.

I picked up the telephone, just to check the dial tone, then set it back down: dial tone okay. So I tuned in my radio to hear the spoken-word news, assuming there was any. All too often the discordant sounds of the early report are all smoothed over by the time the verbal guys get to it, and all you're left with is the uneasy feeling that something happened, somewhere, sometime.

But not this time. This time it was news. Maynard Stanhunt, wealthy Oakland doctor, shot dead in a sleazy motel room five blocks from his office. The newsman named the inquisitors who would be handling the case, said that Stanhunt had been separated from his wife, and that was it. When it was over, I switched stations, hoping to pick up some other coverage, but it must have played as the lead story all across the dial, the moment the morning ban on verbiage lifted, and there wasn't any more.

My feelings were mixed. I hadn't figured on knowing the victim. Maynard Stanhunt was an arrogant man, an affluent doctor who'd built up a pretty good surplus of karmic points to match what must have been a pile in the bank, and he let you know it, but in subtle ways. He drove an antique namebrand car, for instance, instead of the standard-issue dutiframe. He had a fancy office in the California Building and a fancy platinum blonde wife who sometimes didn't come home at night, or so he said. I probably would have envied the guy if I had never met him.

I didn't envy Stanhunt because of the mess he'd made of his life. He was a Forgettol addict. Don't get me wrong—I'm as deeply hooked on make as the next guy, maybe deeper, but Stanhunt was using Forgettol to carve his life up like a Thanksgiving turkey. I found that out the night I tried to call him at home and he didn't recognize my name. He wasn't incoherent or groggy—he simply didn't know who I was or why I was calling. He'd hired me out of his office, probably because he didn't like the idea of a shabby private inquisitor tracking mud over his expensive carpets, and now his evening self just didn't know who I was. That was okay. It was justified. I'm a mess, and I imagine Maynard Stanhunt kept his home pretty nice. Everything about Maynard Stanhunt was pretty nice except the job he hired me to do for him: rough up his wife and tell her to come home.

He didn't come right out with it, of course. They never do. I'd been in his employ for almost a week, working what I thought was strictly a peeper job, before he told me what he really wanted. I didn't bother explaining to him that I went private partly because I didn't like the part of the job where I bullied people. I just refused to do it, and he fired me, or I quit.

So now the golden boy had gone and gotten himself nixed. Too bad. I knew that the coincidence of my working for the dead man would earn me a visit from the Inquisitor's Office. I didn't relish it but I didn't dread it. The visit would be perfunctory because the inquisitors had probably already settled on a suspect: if they weren't about to break the case with a flourish, they never would have let it get all over the verbal news.

For the same reason I knew there wasn't any work in it, and that was a shame. The whole thing would be crawled over by the Office, and that didn't leave enough room for a guy like me to work—assuming there was a client. It was probably an open-and-shut case, and the one poor soul who was client material was probably also guilty as hell. Murder earned you a stay in the freezer, and the guy the inquisitors had in mind was likely no more than a few hours from cold storage.

It wasn't my problem. I switched back to the musical news. They were already comforting the populace with a soothing background of harps playing sevenths, and the rumble of a tuba to represent the inexorable progress of justice. I let it lull me to sleep on the desk.

I don't know how long I slept, but when I woke, it was to the sound of the dentist's voice.

"Wake up, Metcalf," he said a second time. "There's a man in the waiting room who doesn't want his teeth cleaned."

The dentist swiveled on his heels and disappeared, leaving me there to massage my jaw back into feeling after its brief, masochistic marriage to the top of my wooden desk.

CHAPTER 2

"My name is Orton Angwine."

He was a big sheepish-looking kid with a little voice. It probably wouldn't have woken me; he would have had to step around the desk and shake my shoulder. But the dentist saved him the trouble, and I was already rubbing my bleary eyes with my thumbs and gathering saliva in the back of my mouth to talk with, so he just stood there gaping stupidly while I put myself back together. I motioned for him to sit down when I saw he wasn't going to do it without an invitation. Then I looked him over.

I often try to guess a person's karmic level before they even begin talking, and I was quickly working up a pretty low estimate for this guy. His eyes were sunken, his sandy-colored hair was pasted across his forehead with sweat, and his bottom lip was tight across his teeth. He couldn't have been more than twenty-five, but he'd obviously lived enough to have things to regret. He looked like he'd taken a long fall a short time ago. Pieces of the man he'd been were jumbled up with the new guy, the lost soul. My guess was he'd been that better man as recently as a couple of weeks ago.

"My name is Orton Angwine," he said again, in a voice that sounded like it had been washed with too much bleach.

"Okay," I said. "My name is Conrad Metcalf, and I'm a private inquisitor. You knew that. You read it somewhere and it gave you hope. Let me tell you now that it'll cost you seven hundred dollars a day to keep that hope alive. What you'll get for that money won't be a new best friend. I'm as much of a pain in the ass to the people who pay me as I am to the guys I go up against. Most people walk out of my office knowing things about themselves they didn't want to know—unless they leave after my first little speech. See the door?"

"I need your help and I'm willing to pay for it," he managed when I finished. "You're my last chance."

"I knew that already. I'm everybody's last chance. How much karma do you have left?"

"Excuse me." He crossed his legs.

It was the standard response. In a world where it was impolite to ask your neighbor the time of day, I was rudeness incarnate, and I was used to prodding or pushing people out of their initial discomfort with it. That was how I made my living. Angwine had probably never answered a straightforward question before—except one asked out of the Inquisitor's Office. Those were questions everyone answered.

"Let's get this straight," I said. "What you're paying me to do is ask questions. That's the effective difference between us; I ask questions, and you don't. And I need your cooperation. You can lie—most people do—and you can curse me afterwards. But don't get all goggle-eyed. Now give me your card. I need to know your karmic level."

He was too desolate to work up a real sense of outrage. He just dug in his pocket for the plastic chit and passed it across the desk, avoiding my eyes while I ran it through my pocket decoder.

It came up empty. The magnetic stripe on his card was completely wiped out. He was at zero; it meant he was a dead man. I assumed he knew it.

When the Inquisitor's Office set your card at zero, it meant you couldn't get caught slamming the door to a public rest room without sinking into a negative karmic level. The sound of that door slamming would be the last anyone heard of you for a long time, or maybe ever. I hadn't seen a card at zero for a long time, and when I had, it was always in the trembling hands of a man about to take the fall for a major aberration.

It was a formality—it said the case against you was all but sewn up, and they were going to let you roam the streets for a day or two more, a walking advertisement for the system. You could try to raise your karmic level helping old blind nanny goats across streets, or you could go to a bar and drink yourself stupid—it didn't matter. There was a heavy iron door between you and the rest of your life, and all you could do was watch it swing shut.

I handed the card back across the desk. "That's big trouble," I said, softening my tone a bit. "I'm usually not much use when it gets like that." The least I could do was be honest.

"I want you to try," he said, his eyes pleading.

"Well, I've got nothing better to do," I said. Nothing better than taking the money off a walking corpse. "But we'll have to work fast. I'm going to ask you questions now, one after another, probably more than you've ever been asked before, and I'll need a straight answer for each and every one of them. What is it you're supposed to have done?"

"The Inquisitor's Office says I killed a man named May-nard Stanhunt."

I felt like a fool. The news had caused a picture to form in my mind, of a man who, right or wrong, was about to go to the freezer to make the Office look good. Yet I hadn't recognized the guy when he walked right into my own office.

"Forget it," I said. "Here—forget it on me." I opened my desk drawer and took out a packet and handed it across the desk. It was a sample of my own blend of make, a blend I personally thought could do a doomed man a lot of good. "Take the drugs and get out. Nothing I do is going to make the least bit of difference for you. If I set my foot in the Stan-hunt case, I'll be committing suicide for both of us—sort of a lover's leap. I worked for Stanhunt a couple of weeks ago, and it's going to be hard enough keeping my hair clean of the Inquisitor's Office without your help. No thank you very much." I took out a razor blade and dropped it on the desk next to the packet of make.

Angwine didn't take the packet. He just sat there, looking sad and confused, and younger to me by the minute. I waved my hand dismissively and reached for the packet myself. If he didn't want it, I did.

I spread the powder out sloppily on the desk and chopped it up with the blade, unmindful of the amount I was wasting by grinding it into the wooden desktop. Angwine got to his feet and shuffled out of my office. I expected him to slam the door, but he didn't. Maybe he thought I was a real inquisitor instead of a P.I., and that I would penalize him for it. I understood. The guy didn't have any karma to spare on dramatic exits.

My blend is skewed heavily towards Acceptol, with just a touch of Regrettol to provide that bittersweet edge, and enough addictol to keep me craving it even in my darkest moments. I snorted a line through a rolled hundred-dollar bill, and pretty soon I was feeling the effects. It was good stuff. I toyed with my blend for a few years, but when I hit on this particular mixture, I knew I'd found my magic formula, my grail. It made me feel exactly the way I needed to feel. Better.

Or at least it usually did. A guy in my line of work can't afford to snort much Forgettol, and I played it safe by not snorting any. But just this once I could have used some, because the Angwine sequence was gnawing at my gut. I don't suppose you could call it conscience, just the nagging feeling that for a guy who billed himself as everybody's last chance I wasn't living up to my own hype. I was just another inquisitor closing my eyes to Angwine's plight; it didn't matter that I was private instead of working for the Office.

If you're not part of the solution, you're part of the problem, right?

I snorted another line and sighed. It was worse than stupid to get involved with the Stanhunt murder. Yet I was experiencing that sense of inevitability that always comes at the start of a new case. I'd woken up with the feeling, and it hadn't gone away. When you're young, you think falling in love means meeting a beautiful stranger. The feeling I'd had when I heard the musical news was like that. But then you find yourself getting involved with your best friend's kid sister, the girl who's been underfoot all along and who's already seen you at some of your worst moments.

My new case was kind of like that. I wiped the desk clean with my sleeve and put on my hat and coat and went out.

CHAPTER 3

MAYNARD STANHUNT'S OFFICE WAS IN THE CALIFORNIA
Building on Fourth Street, near the bay. I drove down and
parked my car in Stanhunt's space, figuring he didn't need it
anymore, and went into the lobby and waited for the elevator.
Things in the building looked pretty much the same as before—but then the murder hadn't happened in the California.

I rode up in the elevator with an evolved sow. She was
wearing a bonnet and a flowered dress, but she still smelled
like a barnyard. She smiled at me and I managed to smile
back, then she got off on the fourth floor. I got off on the sev-
enth and pressed the doorbell at the offices of Testafer and
Stanhunt, urologists. While I waited, I mused on the ironies of
life. When I walked out of this office two weeks ago, I hadn't
expected to set foot in it again, or at least not until I developed
prostate trouble. The buzzer sounded, and I went in.

The waiting room was empty, except for a guy in a nice suit
and a big square haircut who might or might not have been
from the Inquisitor's Office. I considered the possibility and
withheld judgment. He looked quickly up at me and then back
down at his magazine. I shut the door. No one was behind the
reception desk, so I sat down on the sofa across from Mr. Suit.

Testafer and Stanhunt, like any practice which dealt with problems of a confidential nature, charged top-dollar rates for unexceptional treatment and downright indifferent reception. The customers slunk in and out quietly enough, grateful the office was clean and that their problems went away. Stanhunt was the new boy, or was until yesterday. Testafer had already made his bundle and gotten out, except to leave a shingle hanging. His specialty had probably been no different from Stanhunt's: the radical walletectomy. I'd managed to visit the office five or six times without meeting him, but I was going to meet him now if anyone could.

A door opened in the back and the nurse came out. She was a redhead with a pair of alert breasts that always managed to appear slightly akimbo, as if she shopped for her underwear in a discount irregulars place. Recognizing me, she turned down the corners of her mouth. I dredged her name up from the murk of my consciousness, but she spoke before I could use it.

"You can't be here looking for more work—you're not that tasteless and you're not that stupid. Close, but not quite." She was good at her job. I had to give her that.

"I didn't realize I'd made such an impression on you, Princess. I came here looking for a friendly face, actually. I realize I may have to settle for Dr. Testafer."

"If I tell Dr. Testafer what you do for a living, he'll tell me to tell you he's not here. So he's not here."

"You're a sweetheart, I'll admit it. Now find your appointment book."

"We're closed for the next forty-eight hours. I'm sure even you can understand why."

I decided to turn on the heat, or what little I had that could pass for it. "Tell Testafer I want to return some materials I assembled while working for Maynard." It was pure bluff. "I was holding out, but there doesn't seem to be any point in that now."

"You're going to—"

"I'm going to see the doctor at four-thirty, baby. Write it down. Tell him I have a terrible pain right here." I showed her with my hand.

By this time we'd gotten the attention of Mr. Suit. He put down his magazine and stood up, rubbing his jaw with his big beefy hand as if considering the possible juxtaposition of jaw and hand, generally; mine and his, specifically.

"I'm trying to figure you out, mister," he said. "You seem pretty rude." If he was an inquisitor, he wasn't tipping his hand with a question.

"Don't try to figure me out," I said. "It doesn't work— I've tried it myself."

"I recommend you go home and work on it some more. Come back maybe when you've figured out how to apologize. But not before."

I marveled at his swagger. His eyes were unclouded by intelligence. I wanted to see him as an inquisitor, but I still wasn't sure.

"Apologies aren't something you want to get in the habit of practicing in the mirror," I said. "But from the look of you, I guess you wouldn't understand what I mean."

I let him chew on that—it was obviously going to take a while.

"Write it down," I said again to the girl. "I'll be on time—make sure the doctor gets the message, so he can be too." I turned to the door, deciding to quit while I was ahead. The Suit didn't try to stop me.

I got into the elevator and played back the scene in my head while I watched the buttons light up. I'd been my usual sweet self with the girl, but that didn't bother me anymore. I was at permanent war with members of the fair sex because of what they'd cut out of me, dripping blood and still beating. I preferred to keep them hating me, because if they liked me, there wasn't a lot I could do about it. I wasn't a man anymore. That was Delia Limetree's fault, and I would never forgive her for it. Not that she ever came back to ask forgiveness.

Delia Limetree and I had undergone one of those theoretically temporary operations where they switch your nerve endings around with someone else, so you can see what it feels like to be a man if you're a woman, a woman if you're a man. It was supposed to be a lot of fun. It was, until she disappeared before we could have the operation reversed.

She didn't even leave a note. I never learned whether she was so sickened by the experience of having a penis that she slipped away into an asylum or convent, or whether she liked it so much that she didn't want to give it up. All I know is that she still had the male set to that day, and I had—well, you know what that left me with. It still looked like the male apparatus, and still functioned that way as far as the other party was concerned, but the sensations from my end of things were the female ones. The doctors offered me the generic male package, but what I wanted were my own personalized nerve endings, the ones Delia was out using or not using who knows where. Someday I was going to catch up with her and take back what was mine, but until then I'd sworn the whole thing off. It was okay. I'd always liked drugs better anyway.

All of which meant I got down to the lobby feeling pretty good about the interaction upstairs, especially how I handled the Suit. Which is when a couple of guys from the Inquisitor's Office stepped up on either side of me and seized my arms.

"You should go back to your apartment, flathead," said the one on the left. "We'll be sending someone up to have a chat with you. Until then you should sit tight."

"Coming here was a mistake, Metcalf," said the other. He aimed his magnet at my pocket, and I heard the telltale digital bleep. "Fifteen points of karma, gumshoe. Now go cool your heels."

I put my hand in my pocket and wrapped my fingers protectively around my card. "Fifteen points is rough, boys. I've got a license."

"You didn't show it to the folks upstairs."

"That your boy? He's got a nice pair of matching brain cells."

The one on the right grabbed me by the collar and tried to slap my face. I squirmed and ended up with a mouthful of wrist. "Don't question us, flathead. You should know better." They shoved me forward, at the revolving door. "Get lost."

I bustled through the revolving door, my hand up over my mouth. An evolved dachshund was in the compartment across from me, waddling his way into the building, and when I pushed on the glass, he was ejected into the lobby faster than his little legs would carry him. He fell in a sprawl across the tiles in front of the two inquisitors, and as I looked back, they were helping him to his feet. A warm little scene. I went around the corner to the parking lot. My mouth hurt, but when I took my hand away, it was wet with drool, not blood.

I had two hours before my appointment with Dr. Testafer, and I didn't know what I was going to ask him. I didn't currently have a client, and I didn't have any other leads. What else? Well, it sounded like the inquisitors would be waiting at my apartment, and maybe at my office as well.

Still, I had managed to shave that burdensome fifteen-point surplus off my card.

CHAPTER 4

STANHUNT HAD ORIGINALLY HIRED ME TO KEEP AN EYE on his wife. Now I had to wonder whether that was just the cover story, whether my peeping had been to set an alibi for someone somewhere, whether I'd been playing a patsy even before he requested strong-arm services and I said no. Nonetheless, I had spent a week trailing her around, and that probably made me the current authority on the subject. I decided to stop in. She and Stanhunt had been freshly separated, and the electricity between them had still been going strong—back when Stanhunt was still capable of generating electricity. Now there was a blackout. I wondered if the lady behaved any differently in the dark. I wondered if maybe she was the one who cut the wires.

She'd met me once, as a guy who sidled up to her in a bar with liquor on his breath and a quick lay on his mind. Stanhunt suspected his ex was fooling around, so I thought I'd check. To make the pass more realistic, both the drunk and the lust were authentic. I was a method actor. Celeste Stanhunt was a nice-looking woman who became something more when you were being paid to peek through her windows. To put it simply, there hadn't been any need to undress her in my mind.

The problem I wrestled with now was whether to pick up where I left off playing peeper, or to cast myself against type and knock on the door. I decided on the latter course. If she recognized me, I could come clean about working for her husband—it was bound to come out anyway, during the investigation.

I drove up into the hills, past quiet tree-lined streets with space between the houses. The streets were a bit too quiet for my taste; I would have liked it better to see kids playing in front, running, shouting, even asking each other innocent questions and giving innocent answers back. That's the way it was before the babyheads, before the scientists decided it took too long to grow a kid and started working on ways to speed up the process. Dr. Twostrand's evolution therapy was the solution they hit on; the same process they'd used to make all the animals stand upright and talk. They turned it on the kids, and the babyheads were the happy result. Another triumph for modern science, and nice quiet streets in the bargain.

Celeste Stanhunt was staying in a big house at the end of Cranberry Street, where the monorail tracks intersected almost at a right angle the hill behind the trees. The house was perched on rocks like a bird of prey with a toehold over a fresh carcass. It was going to be a lot easier to walk up to the front door than it had been to find a way around the back to a good view of the bay window.

When I rang the doorbell, the other woman opened the door. I still didn't know her name, though I'd seen a lot of her when I cased the house in my stint as Celeste Stanhunt's shadow. She was thin and pale, with a cloistered air, as if she never left the big house. I'd certainly never seen her leave. She was playing mother, both to a babyhead who was in and out, mostly out, and to a young, newly evolved kitten who was home all the time except when she was out selling cat-scout cookies door to door. The woman doted on them both, but the kitten appreciated it a lot more than the babyhead did.

Celeste Stanhunt had fled to the Cranberry Street house when she left Maynard. My impression was that this was a temporary measure, until she found somewhere else to live or went back to her husband, and that she and the pale woman were just friends. I probably should have been more curious, the first time. I'd catch up now.

She didn't say anything, just stood there, the usual way. It would have been impolite to ask me who I was.

"I was looking for Mrs. Stanhunt," I said.

The woman knit her brow. There weren't many walk-up visitors on Cranberry Street.

"My name is Conrad Metcalf," I said gently. "I realize this is a difficult time, but that's what I've come about."

She took a tentative step backwards into the house. My sympathy made things difficult. I was still unsavory-looking, but she was going to have to meet me halfway.

"Come in," she said. "I'll tell her your name." I followed her through the foyer.

The house was elegant, high-ceilinged, spotlessly clean— but I knew that already. My hostess pointed to the couch, and I went and sat on it while she vanished upstairs. This wasn't a house where you yelled upstairs from the bottom step. It was a house where you walked all the way up and said there was a guest in a low, even tone, and she was going to make sure I knew it.

I sat there and tried to puzzle out what I would ask Mrs. Stanhunt, and what I would do with what I learned, if I learned something. I was playing this case existential, maybe a bit too existential. I needed a lead. I needed a client. Hell, I even needed a sandwich. There was probably little chance of Celeste Stanhunt coming downstairs and offering me a sandwich.

I didn't hear the pitter-patter of little cat feet coming up behind me, but all of a sudden the kitten was there at my side, in a red-and-white dress, carrying an armload of notebooks like a schoolgirl. She smiled through her whiskers and looked at the floor.

"Hello, little girl," I said.

"I'm learning to read," the kitten announced. She put the books down on the coffee table, sat on the carpet, and pulled off her little shoes.

"Learning to read," I repeated. "I didn't realize they still taught that."

"At growth camp. I go every day. I go to the library with my mother."

"Celeste is your mother," I suggested, keeping it a statement. I could get in trouble busting into houses and questioning defenseless little cats.

"No, silly. Pansy is my mother."

An alley cat is your mother, I thought, but I didn't say it. "Pansy and Celeste live together," I tried.

"Celeste is visiting."

"Celeste never visited before." This was too easy.

"No, silly. Celeste visits a lot."

I thought about the possible relationships: sisters, lovers, employer and employee. In my line of work you start to sort people out that way, and there weren't really all that many categories.

"Don't call me silly," I said. "You and Pansy live alone."

"No, silly." It was a fun game. "Barry lives with us sometimes."

"Don't call me silly. Barry is a rabbit."

"No, silly. Barry is a boy."

"Barry is a babyhead, Mr. Metcalf," said Celeste Stanhunt from the middle of the stairway. "Sasha, you should go up-stairs and leave me alone with Mr. Metcalf. Pansy is waiting for you."

"Okay," said the kitten, but she wanted to stay and play. "Mr. Metcalf is silly, Celeste."

"I know he is," said Celeste cleanly. "Now go upstairs."

"Good-bye, Sasha," I said.

The kitten scrambled up the stairs, on all fours at first and then, self-consciously, back on two feet. I heard a muf-fled voice and the shutting of a door upstairs.

Celeste looked good. I had to admire her composure. It was obvious she had recognized me and didn't know what to do about it. Her lovely bottom lip was trembling—but just a little. It was the only flaw, and it was a minor one.

"You've gotten my attention, Mr. Metcalf. I suppose it's time you introduce yourself." She paused gravely. "You work for Danny."

Danny. I jotted the name down mentally on that tattered notepad I call a memory. The pen skipped. "No, I'm afraid not. Or would that be good news?"

"I've answered enough questions today to last a lifetime. Let's see some identification, or I'm calling in the heat."

"The heat?" I smiled. "That's ugly talk."

"You're using a lot of ugly punctuation." She stuck out a hand. "Let's see it, tough boy."

I pulled out my photostat. "Last time I worked, it was for your husband, Mrs. Stanhunt. That was two weeks ago."

She looked it over and tossed it in my lap.

"You're really a private eye." She composed herself. "You don't work—"

"It's all straight," I said. "I don't work for Danny. I'm not actually working for anybody right now. I guess you could say I'm a hobbyist."

"You have to excuse my rudeness," she said. She wanted to take it all back. "The last twenty-four hours have been a nightmare." Her intonation was different. It went with the house and the car and the doctor now. The veneer had peeled up momentarily, but she was gluing it back down as fast as she could.

I went along. "You don't have to ask for my indulgence. I've been more than a little rude myself. You'd be within your rights to have me thrown out of here."

"I've already been treated pretty roughly by the inquisitors," she said, and her lip started to tremble again. Then she made a show of a show of strength. "But if there's anything I can help you with…A friend of Maynard's…"

"I'd rather not misrepresent myself, Mrs. Stanhunt. Your husband didn't count me among his friends. Our relationship was purely supply and demand."

"I see. And you supplied—"

"I followed you around for about a week. No hard feelings. It was a job."

She raised an eyebrow. "So that little scene in the bar—that was just part of the job."

"I work pretty much around the clock when I get work, if that's what you mean. I pick up my dividends where I can." Even I wasn't sure what that meant.

She opened a cigarette box on the coffee table and took out a cigarette, then began fussing with a pack of matches.

But she was nervous and handled the cigarette like a cigar, except for biting off the end.

"I'm still unclear, Mr. Metcalf, as to whether you're working now."

"I guess I am. Sorry for wasting your time." I crossed my legs. "When you say the inquisitors treated you rough, do you mean they treated you as a suspect?"

She smiled. "That's indirect, even for you. No, they were fairly civil. If it crossed their minds, they never said anything."

"They didn't ask where you were last night, during the killing?"

"I told them I was here, Mr. Metcalf. If you ask, I'll tell you the same thing."

"Then I don't think I'll bother. Let's try another angle: Do you know a man named Orton Angwine?"

She answered fast, but the rhythm was off. "Not until this morning. I understand he had some kind of grudge against Maynard."

"The inquisitors seem to think so. You sure he doesn't ring any bells? Most enemies start out as friends—but I'm sure you know that. He was never in the house?"

"No."

"Most people would say, 'Not that I can recall.'"

She got the joke and took it pretty well. "Not that I can recall," she repeated, mimicking my intonation.

"Not bad. But I'm in the business of unmasking liars, not helping them polish their act. What's the story with Angwine?"

"It can't be good business for you to go around calling people liars, Mr. Metcalf. That license you carry says you're allowed to ask me questions, but it doesn't say I have to answer them."

"I rely on circumstance for that. Let's put our cards on the table, Celeste. You can't afford to brush me off. You don't know who I might talk to next, and what I might find out. You want to know whose side I'm on—well, so do I. We're both involuntary participants in a murder investigation, only I think you're in a little deeper than you say. As for me, I'm a free agent. Just because I get paid doesn't mean I get paid off. Now you want very much for me to leave with the impression that you cooperated. Which makes two of us. Only problem is, I'm wearing a bullshit-proof vest. I can't help it. I was born with the thing. Lies bounce off me and land on the carpet like ticks picked off a dog."

I watched her cross and uncross her legs while she thought this over. It was a sight that could lull a man into awakeness. But when I looked up, her eyes were hard.

"You make it sound like if I help you, I gain a valuable friend," she said carefully. "But in my experience tough guys don't make such good friends."

The afternoon was evaporating, and I had an appointment with a doctor. Besides, this tap dance was getting me nowhere. "You keep peeling off the mask," I said sourly. "But there's always another one underneath." I got up from the couch.

"Don't go—"

"If you still want to talk to me in an hour, give me a call at your husband's office." I loved getting phone calls in the field—it made whoever I was visiting jumpy as hell. "After that, my office. It's in the index."

Suddenly she was up out of her seat and pressed against me in all the right places—which on her was almost anywhere. She couldn't know what a mistake that was. I pushed her back against her chair, but not too hard.

"You bastard."

I brushed at my jacket with the flat of my hand. "I understand," I said. "You're scared of something." I paused in the doorway. "Say good-bye to the kitten for me."

In my car I opened the glove compartment and laid out a couple of lines of my blend on a map of Big Sur. I snorted them off the blade of my pocketknife until I stopped shaking, then cleaned it up and started driving back to Oakland.

I drove along Frontage, which runs between the highway and the bay. The sky was clean and blue. I tried to concentrate on it, to keep my mind off what I'd just had in my arms and pressed against my body, as well as the fact that I made my living picking the scabs off other people's lives. But the day I can't shrug off a twinge of self-pity is the day I'm washed up for keeps.

Don't call me silly.

CHAPTER 5

THE LOBBY OF THE CALIFORNIA WAS CLEAN OF INQUISI-
tors, which is the kind of clean I like. I walked through it to
the elevator and pushed the button. I was a few minutes late
for my appointment with Testafer, thanks to my reverie by
the ocean, but if my bluff had worked, he'd be waiting. And
I was sure my bluff had worked. I'd done a job for Stanhunt,
and Testafer's affairs were all mixed up with the dead man's.
He would wait on the chance that I knew something.

I sat on the same couch and waited for the nurse to come
out so we could resume our clever banter, but for a long time
nobody appeared. Then a stout, red-faced man with nervous
eyes and neat clothes came out of the back room. His hair
was full but completely white, which served to heighten the
effect of his ruddy complexion. He wasn't dressed to see patients, but I had a feeling it was Testafer. I stood up.

"My name is Metcalf, Doctor."

"Very good," he said, but he didn't look like he meant it.
"I've been expecting you. Follow me."

I followed him into the office in the back. He sat down at
Maynard Stanhunt's desk, only this time the nameplate read
GROVER TESTAFER, followed by a string of initials. He folded

his hands across the desk, and I could see that they were as white as his face was red.

"Jenny tells me you have some of the office files in your possession."

"Something got garbled in the translation, Doctor. I keep all my files right here." I tapped my head. "I've got nothing of yours."

"I see. I suppose I have to guess why it is that you wanted to see me."

I tossed my photostat on the desk. "I want to see you for the usual reason. I'm conducting an investigation, and I'd like to ask you a few questions. I can't be the first."

"No," he said, managing a smile. "I spent an hour with the inquisitors today. They warmed me up for you."

"Sorry for forcing the issue, but my client is running out of time."

"Yes," he said. "I got that impression."

"Maybe you can help me with that. Just what is their case against Angwine?"

"They said they found a threatening letter—right here, apparently." He indicated the desk. "They asked if I ever met him, and I said no. I spend very little time in the office lately. I've turned the practice over to Maynard, put it in his hands. Apparently Angwine was a patient, at least to begin with. He's in the appointment book twice, going back about three weeks. Jenny didn't remember him from the description, but then we see a lot of patients."

"Yeah," I said. "And I guess you don't concentrate so much on the faces. Did you see the note?"

"No. I wish I had. The inquisitors were here before I even knew about Maynard's death."

"Do you have any theories about what went sour between Angwine and Stanhunt?"

He made himself appear to be thinking it over, which invariably meant he wasn't. "No," he said eventually. "Not really. I assume it was something personal."

"Everything you handle is personal," I said. "Can you be more specific?"

"Something between them, I mean. Unrelated to the practice."

"I see," I said, and in a way I did. Testafer was a man trying to create distance between himself and something he found altogether distasteful. His vagueness could have been a cover for some involvement, but it also suited his personality.

"Maynard and I were never close," he explained. "I was ready to retire, but it's always preferable to keep a practice open if you can. Maynard was a good doctor, someone I could hand it over to without embarrassment. Ours was a highly successful business relationship, and there was mutual respect, but we were never close."

"You're young for retirement. What are you, fifty-five? Fifty-eight? You must have made a caboodle."

Testafer winced at my usage. "I'm almost sixty, Mr. Metcalf. You're a very good guesser."

He managed not to mention the caboodle. I decided it was a waste of time to push him any further. He was giving me the company line. I'd have to case him out from the angles.

"Where does this leave you now?" I asked. "Will you look for a new golden boy, or close this thing down?"

Now I'd gotten him a little angry. "I have my patients to think of. I'll begin seeing them again, until other arrangements can be made."

"Of course. What about Mrs. Stanhunt? Does she inherit Maynard's half of the practice, or does it all revert to you?"

"Mrs. Stanhunt and I haven't been in touch yet. But she'll be taken care of…" He was improvising, and it made him nervous.

"Until other arrangements can be made?" I suggested.

"Well, yes."

I tossed him a curve ball. "I don't suppose Danny figures in your plans."

He looked at me carefully. "I'm afraid I don't know what you mean."

"Don't be afraid," I said. "I must have made a mistake."

"I suppose you did."

I fiddled with my cuff long enough to bother him. He wasn't eager to talk about Danny, whoever Danny was.

"What can you tell me about the place where Celeste Stanhunt stays?"

"Pansy Greenleaf lives there with her son," he said. "Only he isn't home much anymore. He's a—babyhead." He used the term regretfully.

"I noticed. She seems to have elevated an evolved kitten into a sort of child substitute. What does Mrs. Greenleaf do for a living?"

"I wouldn't know," he said sardonically. "I never thought to ask." The emphasis he put on the last word let me know he meant to be insulting. "She was a friend of the Stanhunts," he added in a dismissive tone.

"Who you didn't ever get close with," I filled in.

"That's right."

I pretended to notice the time. "Well, I won't keep you any longer. You've been very helpful."

"My pleasure," he said, swallowing hard. He looked eager to see me gone.

"If you think of anything I ought to know…" I wrote my number down on a prescription pad, then got up. "I'll let myself out. So long."

I went out into the hall, closing his door behind me. The nurse was gone. I opened the door to the reception area and slammed it, but with me still inside, then went over to have a look at the office files.

First I checked for Orton Angwine: no file. I flipped through a random folder or two, but everything looked pretty standard. If there was something wrong with these files, it would take another urologist to spot it.

I could hear Testafer moving around in the office behind me, so I figured I didn't have long—if he opened the door, I'd be directly in his line of sight. On the other hand, he didn't look like the type to raise a big fuss if he caught me. He was already afraid of me, afraid of what my investigation might uncover, or he wouldn't have tried so hard to appear cooperative, maybe wouldn't have agreed to see me at all.

The problem was, I didn't know *why* he was afraid of me. I could ask him who Danny was, for instance, but then he'd know that I didn't. And without him worried I'd get nothing at all.

I picked up another file. It seemed pretty harmless: a sixty-seven-year-old guy named Maurice Gospels with congestive urethritis—whatever that was. I closed the cabinet and tucked the file inside my coat. Then I stepped back over to the office and turned the knob.

Testafer was bent over the desk, sucking through a metal straw at a pocket mirror dusted with white powder. His head jerked up as I entered the room, and a trail of half-snorted make fell out of his nose. He didn't say anything, and for a minute neither did I. It was like looking into a mirror twenty years down the line.

"Here," I said, and tossed the folder onto his desk. He covered the mirror with his hands to protect the make. "This is the stuff Stanhunt let out of the office. I don't have a use for it anymore."

Testafer leafed frantically through the Maurice Gospels folder, looking for something incriminating, while a dry white stripe made its way down his upper lip and dotted his chin. Me, I left.

CHAPTER 6

I DROVE BACK TO MY OFFICE, STEELING MYSELF FOR THE
inevitable confrontation with the boys from the Inquisitor's
Office. It had to happen sooner or later. If I was lucky, they'd
lead me back to Orton Angwine. If this investigation had a
future, it would only be with his help, and the only live
prospect for my wallet's future was his money. I didn't feel
too bad about that. If I didn't help him, the money wouldn't
be of much use to him anyway.

But the waiting room was empty, except for a pair of
evolved rabbits in miniature three-piece suits. They were
looking at photo magazines and only gave me the fleetingest
red-eyed glances as I bustled through to my part of the suite.
I could hear the dentist's cleaning equipment buzzing away at
something in the back room. Someone had to clean their
bridgework, I guess, and my dentist wasn't doing so well that
he could afford to turn away the business.

I hung my coat up on the hat tree and sat down behind
the desk, then took a few deep breaths and got out my card
and ran it through the decoder in my drawer. The inquisitors
have been known to stretch the truth about just how much
they're taking off or adding to your card. I had a little trouble

remembering exactly what my karma had been before the episode in the lobby of the California anyway.

The stripe on my card read out at sixty-five points, which wasn't too bad. The inquisitors usually restored any points I'd lost during the course of an investigation, and they sometimes grudgingly awarded me a few extra if my work made the Office look good. Sixty-five was comfortable; big enough to work with, but small enough that the boys wouldn't be tempted to penalize me in the spirit of fun anymore. Sixty-five was humble in the eyes of the Office; much more would be overreaching myself. Low karma was one of the things you learned to live with on this job.

I picked up my phone, punched the number for the delicatessen on the corner, and ordered an egg salad sandwich for delivery. Then I called the index and asked the computer for a few listings. Not surprisingly, Orton Angwine wasn't there. I tried Pansy Greenleaf, the woman Celeste was staying with, even gave the computer the Cranberry Street address, but no cigar. Just for fun I checked under my own name, and, sure enough, I was listed. It was a comfort.

I went through the mail. It was piled up from almost a week back, bills and junk mail mostly, a postcard from a guy in Vegas who owed me money, and a freebie pen from one of the aerospace companies. I slipped it out of its envelope, and it drifted loose in front of my face; anti-grav, the first I'd seen. It seems like the biggest innovations always announce themselves in the tackiest ways. You expect some kind of paradigm shift, and then a pen or a comb or a snorting straw arrives in the mail with a salesman's phone number printed on it. It's never a very good pen, either. You use it for a week, and it runs dry.

There was a knock at the door. "Come in," I said. I slipped the pen into my pocket and started rustling in the drawer for money to pay for the sandwich. But it wasn't the sandwich man.

The first guy was about my age, with crooked teeth and a ten-dollar haircut. He was standard-issue Office stuff, the kind that all look and think alike, except for the different flavor cough drops they suck. Then they stand too close to you, so you can smell the flavors and be impressed with their originality. I'd waltzed with these guys a million times in the past, and I could look forward to waltzing with them a million times in the future. They were the type I probably would have turned out to be if I'd stayed working for the Office.

The second guy was a different story. He was thick, disheveled, and badly shaven, and he wore a shoulder stripe and a couple of medals. I'd drawn the brass. He pushed into the room and slammed the door and said "Metcalf?" and when he looked me in the eye, I have to admit I flinched.

"Looking at him," I said.

"Where were you an hour ago?"

"You boys aren't here to wax floors, are you? I had a doctor's appointment."

The big one sat down in the chair across from my desk, where only that morning Angwine had been sitting. The other guy looked at the dusty chair in front of the water stain in the corner and elected to stand by the door. "Pass me your license and your card," said the brass.

He looked over my credentials, and I stared at the ceiling. When he put them back on the desk between us, I let them lie there as a show of nerve.

"Where's Inquisitor Carbondale?" I said.

"He's been switched to Marin County," said the big one. "My name is Morgenlander. This is Inquisitor Kornfeld." The quiet one nodded at the mention of his name.

"Nice to know you boys are on the beat."

"Wish I could say the same, dickface." Morgenlander smiled. "There's been some question of you working the Stanhunt case. We wanted to bring speculation to an end."

"No problem, Inquisitor. The answer is yes." I got my cigarettes out of the desk drawer.

"The answer is no," said Morgenlander. "It's a conflict of interest. You're my suspect, dickface."

"I've already met your suspect, Morgenlander. The guy's on his last legs. Nice work."

"Angwine's got a problem. His future's all used up. I'd hate to see that happen to a dickface like you."

I turned to Kornfeld, who still hadn't cracked a smile. "Do I have a dick on my face? Tell me honestly."

"You better cancel the fancy punctuation, dickface," said Morgenlander blithely. "Your license is a piss mark in the snow, as far as I'm concerned." He adjusted his tie, as if his head were expanding and he needed to make some room for it. "Now tell Inquisitor Kornfeld about your trip to the doctor."

"I'm seeing a specialist," I said. "To see if I can have the dick on my face removed." I lit a cigarette and took a drag. Morgenlander leaned across the desk and slapped it out of my mouth. It rolled under the chair in the corner and smoldered in the dust.

"You're wasting my time, dickface. Answer my questions." He got his magnet out of his pocket and aimed it carelessly at my card.

I spat in the corner. The place was getting disgusting.

"Go ahead," I said.

"Who put you onto the Stanhunt case?"

"I was in it from before it was a case," I said. "I worked

for Stanhunt, back before he developed a hole in the back of his head."

"You're working for Angwine."

"I'd like to be. I lost track of him."

"Bullshit," said Morgenlander. "He sent you to the doctor. He's still trying to collect."

I was going to be dizzy when the merry-go-round let off. "That's saying Angwine is a blackmailer." I hoped the question would slip by in the excitement.

"Don't play dim, dickface. What did he want you to say to the doctor?"

I decided to play along. "He didn't mention any specifics. I was just feeling Dr. Testafer out."

There was a knock on the door. Inquisitor Kornfeld stepped away from it, and I called out, "Come in." An evolved Irish setter from the deli downstairs came into the room carrying a white paper bag with a grease stain at the bottom. He looked nervously around at the inquisitors, then stepped past them to hand me the bag.

I told the setter thanks and gave him five bucks more than the check required. He gulped his appreciation, then backed through the open door and out into the waiting room, looking like he wanted to drop to all fours and run away howling. Kornfeld closed the door and leaned back against the wall.

Nobody said anything while I opened the bag and took out the egg salad sandwich. It was one of those funny moments when a bit of normal human activity embarrasses everybody out of their bluster and hostility, and roles are momentarily laid aside. I chewed down a triangular wedge of sandwich and rubbed at my face with a paper napkin before Morgenlander finally started in again, and this time he left out the dickface stuff. We'd somehow graduated beyond that by virtue of the delivery puppy and the sandwich.

"It's a tough case," he said. "The boys at the top handed me Angwine on a platter, and there's a lot of pressure to let it go like that."

Morgenlander's tone verged on shoptalk, and maybe it was my imagination, but Kornfeld, without saying anything, seemed distinctly uncomfortable. "Angwine's a sewer rat," Morgenlander continued. "I don't mind if he goes to the freezer, but there's more to it than that."

I nodded, to keep him talking.

"I'm not saying he's innocent. He did the killing. I'm just saying there's more to it. I've got to warn you off, Metcalf. Do yourself a favor. If you get in my way, I'll have to take you down. That's just the way it is." He put his magnet in his pocket and nodded to Kornfeld.

I swallowed hard and tried to smile. There was a lot I wanted to ask, but Kornfeld seemed to like it better when I kept my mouth shut. There were healthier ways of advancing an investigation than trying to grill an inquisitor. I nudged the second triangle of sandwich with my thumb, and a shiny cube of egg white fell out onto the wax paper.

"I've got nothing but respect for a private eye, really," said Morgenlander. He smiled at me, and his tongue looked like you could strike a match against it. "You just have to know when to lay off," he explained. "This is when to lay off." He pushed himself wearily to his feet and shook out the sleeves of his coat.

Kornfeld hadn't spoken a syllable during their visit. Now he took his hat off and said, "Good day" in a squeaky voice, then opened the door for Morgenlander. The big guy turned once in the doorway and gave me another view of his twisted smile. I held up my hand, palm out. They shut my door, and I listened as they shuffled through the outer office, past the rabbits, and back to the elevator, leaving me alone with my egg salad sandwich and a mouthful of questions.

I turned to my window and rolled up the shade. The view faced east, but I could see the colors of the sunset reflected on the hills over Oakland, glints of sun studding the banner of windows opposite the bay, like bits of tinsel worked into a tapestry. Yeah, the hills looked pretty good, from a distance. I turned back to my desk, pushed the sandwich aside, and spilled some blend out onto the wooden desktop. I chopped it up with my pocketknife, and was bending over to sniff it up when the phone rang.

"Metcalf," I said into the receiver.

"It's me, Orton Angwine," said the voice on the line. "I need to talk to you."

"That's fine," I said.

"I hear you're working on the case," he said uncertainly.

"Right. Why don't you come up to my office. I'll wait around."

"No. I don't want to run into the inquisitors. You come to me."

"I'm sure the inquisitors know where you are," I suggested gently. "You're the focus of a certain amount of attention."

"No, I don't think so. I think I lost my tail. I'm in the bar of the Vistamont Hotel."

"All right," I said. "Stay there." I hung up.

I leaned down and sucked up the make on my desk, then put the half sandwich and the wax paper into the garbage pail. I took one last glance at the pinkish hills, then I pulled down the shade and went downstairs to find my car.

CHAPTER 7

I PULLED OVER TO THE CURB AND BOUGHT AN EVENING edition of the *Oakland Photographic* from a crabby old goat working a newsstand. The printed word had been dwindling in the news media, but it hadn't disappeared completely until a year ago, when it was outlawed. That did the trick. I double-parked and took a look at the paper. There were the usual captionless pictures of the government busy at work: the President shaking hands with the Inquisitor General, the congressmen shaking hands with the special-interest groups, the Governor shaking hands with Karmic Achiever of the Month. I flipped through to the local stories, and found a series of graphic photographs of the hotel room where Stanhunt had been killed. There was a chalk line indicating his sprawl across the carpet and a bloody smear on the hotel bedspread. The inquisitors were shown holding up a corner of the curtain, which had a bloody handprint, and then there was a picture of the corpse draped in white and being loaded into the back of a van. It reminded me of the standard photographs of the karma-defunct being shipped to the holding freezers for an indefinite term of storage. Same difference, I guess.

The last photograph was Inquisitor Morgenlander waving an open hand and talking to someone out of the frame to his left. Inquisitor Kornfeld stood behind him, jaw clamped shut as usual. The gist of the story was that our noble inquisitors were on the job again, righting wrongs. It was a gross oversimplification. A murder didn't happen in a void, like some kind of hiccough. It was the outcome of an inexorable series of past events climaxing in the act, and with repercussions stretching into the future far beyond the usual inquisition. I listened to myself thinking this way and had to laugh. A murder was a garage sale. A murder was a stag party. A murder was a fire drill. A murder was whatever the Inquisitor's Office wanted it to be.

I tossed the paper onto the passenger seat and started up into the hills. It was dark now. Ashby Avenue was quiet and mostly scenic, and I let my mind wander freely over the events of the day, hoping for some fresh associations, but I didn't get anywhere except up into the hills. I'd just snorted my blend, and I guess the fresh Acceptol in my blood was dulling the necessary sense of outrage. I probably would have better spent the time listening to the car radio.

The Vistamont Hotel was a high-class operation, a far cry from the kind of fleahouse Stanhunt had been unlucky enough to get himself nixed in. Killings, if they happened in the Vistamont at all, were probably peeled off the floor, fingerprints and all, and transferred to some less prestigious joint before the inquisitors were called. Who knew—maybe that was what happened to Stanhunt. The Vistamont was a place where rich folks stayed when they wanted to be able to say they had visited Oakland but didn't really want to dirty their shoes. It was big and labyrinthine, and contained enough different restaurants and spas to keep you from ever having to sample the big bad world outside.

I parked the car in the Vistamont lot and tucked the newspaper under my arm. I figured the pictures might provoke some kind of response from a guilty party, whether he'd seen them before or not. Actually, they were probably strong enough meat to unsettle Angwine either way, but I was desperate for clues. I'm not known for my subtlety or tact.

I paused to let the doorman give me the once-over. He was an elderly black human, one of the last you could see in a menial service job. Evolved animals filled pretty much any position they were capable of filling these days, but the Vistamont prided itself on stubborn traditions, and this was one of them. He gave me a nice smile and held open the door and I tipped my hat to him.

The bar was a dark, sunken affair, with detached tables floating in the murk. The way to make a bundle in architecture right now was to devise new ways for people to pretend to gather while actually keeping their distance, and this was a sterling example. I stepped down into the pit and searched out Angwine. I had to admit that at least he'd found a good place to lose himself. I found him against the farthest wall, in a swivel chair at a table built for two. I slid into the chair opposite him, with my back to the wall. The chair was plush, and I sank into it.

"You took long enough," said Angwine, looking up. His face was less utterly ravaged, more hardened to the bitter realities of existence without the cushion of a few points of karma on his card.

"You're not paying me for my time yet," I replied.

Angwine snickered. "You like to keep it mercenary, don't you, Metcalf." He reached into his coat, pulled out an envelope, and tossed it onto the table between us. I picked it up.

Inside was fourteen hundred dollars. "Today and tomorrow," he said when he knew I'd counted it.

"Today was my own time. I'll take this as a retainer through Friday." I pocketed the cash and left the envelope on the table. I couldn't make out the address in the darkness, but it might be a mistake to take aboard anything that could be associated with Angwine.

"That's optimistic," he said glumly.

"What is?"

"Assuming you'll still have a job on Friday."

"Actually, I don't understand why the inquisitors haven't hauled you in already. But the fact that we're talking right now is cause for a certain amount of optimism. Morgenlander is edgy. He doesn't have enough to sew it up, and it's bothering him."

"He seemed pretty confident to me."

"Don't sulk, Angwine. You're not used to dealing with the inquisitors. Morgenlander's just a middleman, ultimately. They went public with this one, and now the spotlight is on. There's pressure on him to deliver, but he's got to get it right, or at least make getting it wrong very convincing."

"I don't understand."

"Neither do I, but I propose to." I tried to signal a waitress, but it was like trying to flag down a helicopter from inside a foxhole. "I'll find out who killed Stanhunt, and why. If you're guilty, I suggest you take your money back and spend it on drugs or women, real fast, because I'm in no position to cover for you."

"I'm not guilty."

I dropped the newspaper on the table, but the effect was lost in the darkness. "What've they got on you?" I asked.

There was a pause. I looked into Angwine's face, but I couldn't read anything. "I threatened him," he said finally. "They've got a letter I wrote. But they're misinterpreting—"

"Morgenlander said it was blackmail. Did you have something on Stanhunt?"

"It was more personal than that. My sister worked for him, and it was ruining her life. I let him know how I felt about it."

"Tell me more."

"She's raising a child for him, a babyhead. It's a little monster—"

"All babyheads are monsters," I said, and then I made a guess and knew I was right. "Is your sister named Pansy Greenleaf?"

I'd gotten Angwine's attention, and maybe a little more of his respect. He leaned forward so his features were in the light. "That's right," he said. "You must have spoken with her already."

"No, but I should have, and I will tomorrow if I can. Go on with your story."

He slipped back into the shadows. "I'm less sure than I was at first," he said. "I think he got my sister pregnant and he's paying her to keep it quiet."

"From the look of that house, it's a pretty nice deal for her," I said.

"You don't understand. Before I left for L.A. my sister had some kind of life of her own. Now she's—cowering. She's afraid to tell me what's the matter. Stanhunt was treating her like some kind of puppet."

"So you wanted to cut the strings," I suggested, "or collect some money not to."

"Go on insulting me, Metcalf. Thanks a million."

"You're welcome a thousand. Come on, Angwine. Your story doesn't look clean, even in the dim light of what little I've learned." Sometimes my source of metaphors is remarkably close at hand. "Morgenlander's got you pegged as a blackmailer, and Dr. Testafer showed the inquisitors your name in the appointment book, more than once. You and Stanhunt went for more than a stroll around the block together."

He folded his hands across the table like a schoolboy. "I went to visit him about what I said, originally. I got pretty worked up, called him names, trying to get a reaction." His hands twitched in a way that told me the recollection wasn't fiction. "But he didn't defend himself. He was obviously hiding something, and he practically forced the money on me."

"Okay, slow down. So the two of you worked out some kind of compromise—you traded off your anger for cash in hand."

"He tried to scare me—he said I was in 'deeper water' than I knew, and he asked me to go away. He could see that I was down and out, so he offered me money, which I took. It obviously didn't mean anything to him, but it made a big difference to me."

"He made you part of the family. One of the puppets."

"Go to hell."

I smiled. "Where'd you come from, Angwine? Where did you study up on how to play the fall guy? You're the punch line to everybody's worst jokes."

Questions are rude, and this was a question embedded in a morass of insults. I was surprised when he picked the question out and answered it straight, but I guess he was a desperate man.

"I came up here from L.A.," he said soberly. "I spent six years in the Army, trying to work out a degree in military sociology, but I kept getting bounced by the military inquisitors. They were getting their toilets cleaned cheap, was how I started to see it. So I got out, with a bit of karma and a bit less cash. That's when I came up here to see my sister."

"Where are you staying?"

"I was with a friend in Palo Alto at first, then with my sister for a few nights, before Celeste Stanhunt moved in. Now, nowhere." He opened his hand as if to demonstrate. "Morgenlander made it clear I wasn't to go anywhere near the house on Cranberry Street. I've spent a couple of nights at the Y, but they've got a minimum karma requirement I can't pass anymore."

I was warming up to him, but that was just the generic effect someone more pathetic than I am has on me. I was as predictable—and sloppy—as Pavlov's drooling mutts.

A waitress finally looked at her map somewhere and figured out we were on it. She bent low over the table and asked if we wanted anything. I ordered a shot of tequila and told her to bring a mirror to the table. Angwine just shook his head in the darkness, and the waitress went away.

I had a realization. "You're paying me with Stanhunt's money, aren't you?"

He thought about it for a while, but decided on the truth. "Yeah. I suppose you're going to give it back and tell me to forget it again."

"No," I said. "I just think it's funny. We've both been sucking at the same nipple, only now it's dry." I patted my pocket. "This the last?"

"Just about."

The waitress came back. She set down my drink, a small beveled pocket mirror, and a plastic snorting straw imprinted with the Vistamont logo and phone number. I paid her with a twenty, and while my wallet was out I unfolded a foil packet of my blend and laid it on the table. Halfway through chopping it up with my pocketknife, I looked up to see Angwine watching me intently.

"You don't snort, do you?"

"No."

"The military?"

"No. I just never did."

I experienced another twinge of pity for the guy, but it was tempered with scorn. "You make a pretty humorous blackmailer, Angwine. Stanhunt was a Forgettol user, in a pretty big way. For you to go in there and threaten him without knowing what he knew or didn't know at the time— that's awfully stupid. The version you were talking to might not have even remembered who your sister was."

I bent over and sniffed through the plastic tube, then leaned back and let the excess drain down the back of my throat. When I'd had enough, I wiped the mirror on my sleeve and pocketed the complimentary straw. Angwine must have spent the entire time working out a speech in his head, because when it came out, it sounded rehearsed.

"It's just a sophisticated version of good cop/bad cop," he said.

"What?"

"You're not really working for me at all. You're just a shill for the inquisitors. You keep tabs on me and ask me questions. You play on my fears of them, but there's no real difference." He snickered. "It's just a game. They take my karma and you take my money and then the game is over. You like to act disenchanted and cynical, like you're something more than a cog in the machine, but it's just a pose." There was a hysterical rise in his voice, the sound of a man convincing himself. "You live and work under their protective wing, or else they'd cut you off."

"You've got it wrong, Angwine. It's more complicated than that."

"Sure it is," he said. "Tell me how." He had the look of a rabbit frightened into fierceness by dire circumstance.

"First of all, I wouldn't have taken up your case if I didn't believe you when you first walked in. The inquisitors specialize in nifty solutions at the expense of the truth; that's one of the reasons I went private. You're right to observe a certain symbiosis in our relationship, but they're perfectly capable of enacting good cop/bad cop without my help and they know it. I've spent a lot of time figuring out why I'm tolerated by the Office and it's not simple, and I don't think I particularly want to try to explain it to you now.

"Like I said the first time, you're not buying yourself a new best friend. I'm working for you, but you're not my boss, because I know better than you how to proceed. If I make you uncomfortable, well, join the local chapter of the lodge. You already paid membership dues. I learned a long time ago that my job consists of uncovering the secrets people keep from themselves as much or more than the ones they keep from each other."

I let Angwine chew that over while I nursed my drink and took a look around. My eyes had grown accustomed to the dim lighting, and I could make out the other patrons of the bar at the far-off tables—but only just. I was a little surprised to see an evolved kangaroo drinking alone near the window, his furry face backlit with moonlight. He was staring at our table and looked away when I glared at him, but there was no way he could hear what we were saying and I wrote it off. The rules barring the evolved were slackening everywhere, and bigots like me were just going to have to get used to it.

"I've thought it out," said Angwine. "I'm going to be frozen." I turned back to the table. He was a rabbit again, but not a fierce one. He was a frightened rabbit, frightened and tired.

"What do you mean?"

"It's inevitable. You just aren't saying so, but I've thought it out and it's obvious. I should be preparing for it. I don't know the first thing about it."

"It's pretty simple," I said. "They tag you and stack you up, and if you've got a good lawyer or a family member in a high place, then they keep good track of you and eventually you get defrosted. It's always worked that way as far as I can tell."

"I don't understand what you mean."

I tried not to make it too rough. "The only difference between prison and the freezer is that in prison you play cards and celebrate birthdays and build up a healthy resentment of society, whereas frozen you don't do any of that, and it's cheaper and cleaner for them to manage and pay for. You still come out stupid and poor and with your girlfriend hitched up to some other guy. But as for who gets off light and who pays for the whole menu, it's always been and always will be money and connections that decide it. Do you have someone who'll look out for you?"

"My sister," he said feebly. "She's it."

"No pals from L.A.? No army buddies?"

"Not really."

"Your sister isn't exactly in the clear," I pointed out. "Raising the kid of the man you're supposed to have killed. When's the last time you two spoke?"

"Not since I moved out, when Celeste showed up."

"I can try to talk to her for you," I offered. "About what to do if they take your card away."

"Yeah," he said softly. "That would be good."

We sat quietly for a time. I was done with my drink and I knew it, but I lifted the glass anyway just to have something to do and licked the inside as far as my tongue could reach. I looked over at the kangaroo at the window table, and the kangaroo looked quickly back down at his drink again.

Finally I said: "Here's the key to my office. You can stay there tonight and leave the key with the dentist in the morning. Keep out of the drawers and don't answer the phone."

"Okay," he said, obviously surprised. "Thanks."

"Sure, no problem." I put on my hat. "I'm leaving now, but I've got an answering machine on my home number. Keep in touch."

"Okay."

"Take a look around when I walk out of here, and make note of it if anyone leaves right after me. Don't do anything, just make a mental note."

"Okay."

I pushed out of my bottomless seat and made my way on rubbery legs to the bar, trying not to look behind me. I dropped another twenty on the bar and said, "Bring my friend a drink."

She nodded and looked over at the table. I put my hands in my pockets and left the bar. The light of the lobby made me squint, but the air smelled a little fresher. I nodded at the desk clerk and stepped out into the parking lot.

I sat in my car for a minute and gave the pounding in my temples an opportunity to stop. It didn't take it. I didn't feel too great, but on the other hand I was being paid now for my time, by a guy who didn't have a lot of his own time left. A voice in my head suggested I go home and run some more make through my nose, but another voice said maybe it was time to do some legwork. I sighed, and decided to listen to the second voice, this time.

So I went to have a look at the scene of the crime. The murder happened at night, and if I played my cards right, I might get to talk to the guy who found the body. When I have any luck with hotel staff, it's invariably the night shift. I don't know why. The night shift and I just seem to have some kind of affinity. If I was unlucky, the inquisitors would still have some kind of round-the-clock cordon set up, but even then I could pump the rookies for inside dirt on Office politics surrounding the case.

Lots of fun options between me and my date with a hangover.

CHAPTER 8

FROM THE VISTAMONT HOTEL TO THE BAYVIEW ADULT Motor Inn was a long trip down the karmic spiral, but if Stanhunt and his killer had taken it, I could too. I pulled into the parking lot and found a space; there were four or five other cars there, and all the licenses were in-state. The Bayview was a vacation spot for people vacationing from their husbands and wives, and you didn't see out-of-state licenses in the lot because people in other states had their own versions of the Bayview for that kind of vacation. The place actually featured a nice view of the bay, but it was a view that didn't get looked at much.

I got out of my car and stopped: there was the purr of a motorcycle or scooter slowing down behind me. I turned in time to see the bike turn the corner and disappear around the block. I'd seen a single headlight in my rearview mirror on the way down the hill, and I was beginning to feel the proverbial breath on my neck, but I tried not to let it spook me into making a wrong move. A tail is like a pimple. It comes to a head in its own time. You can rush it, but it usually makes a mess if you do.

I went up to the hotel office and looked through the window. The lobby was empty except for the clerk, and I could hear the tinny whine of a radio playing somewhere in the back. I stepped inside, careful not to wipe my feet on what was passing for a welcome mat at the door. It looked as though it might inflict serious damage to my shoes, and it certainly wasn't going to make them cleaner.

The office was dingy. Dingy was the only word for it. The furniture was new but tasteless, and the walls needed a coat of paint. Even the music creeping out of the radio in the back sounded as if it were covered with dust. The night clerk lifted his head from what he was reading or looking at and regarded me with as pouchy and gray a set of eyes as I'd seen in forty-three years of looking in the mirror. He was maybe in his fifties, with the complexion of cigarette ash, and hair that was fighting a losing battle to cover a white pate. I shut the door, and a little bell tinkled a feeble announcement of my arrival.

The clerk looked back down, giving his magazine clear priority. I said hello.

"We have to see the girl," he said. "No animals allowed. If it's an animal, you'll have to take it somewhere else."

"I'm alone," I said. "I'm an inquisitor on a case, and I'd like to ask you a few questions."

He didn't look up. "Not without identification."

I pulled out my photostat, and he almost looked at it. After a minute I put it away again.

"Private," he said to himself. "No, it won't go. You can ask for the manager tomorrow morning." He made a dismissive gesture with his hand, except he barely bothered to make it. He had it down to a flicker.

I stepped away from the desk and tried to peer into the back room. The clerk pretended I didn't exist. There wasn't any noise apart from the radio. The lights were all out, and as far as I could tell we were alone. The key rack was pretty full, and I had the feeling I could get pretty rough in this shabby little office without attracting much attention.

"Okay," I said, putting my hand out towards the key rack. "I guess I'll just have a look around."

He closed his magazine and pushed it to one side, then looked up. I got another look at his eyes and understood why he was hiding them in the magazine. The motel office was bush league, and so was the clerk, except for those eyes. They were major league, maybe Hall of Fame. They were eyes that had died twice and gone on living. The part of me that was considering playing it rough began reconsidering. It wasn't that I didn't think I could take him. I was sure I could, but something in those eyes made me think he'd exact some kind of price if I did.

"All right," he said stonily. "Fucking lay off. You've got the wrong guy."

"It's you I want to talk to."

"It's you I don't want to talk to." His tone was even but his hands were tapping nervously on the desk.

I peeled the outer bill off the roll Angwine had given me and held it up so he could see it was a hundred, then ripped it in half right through the portrait. I pocketed one of the halves and threw the other onto his desk right next to his hand. He didn't move.

"I'll reunite the twins if you give me a tour of the murder room," I said.

He smiled, and the weird light in his eyes faded. "Whatever you say." The ripped bill disappeared into a desk drawer that locked with a key, and the key went into his pocket. He got up from the desk and shook his head as if his neck was sore, and plucked a set of keys from the wall.

I offered my hand and told him my name. He looked at me funny and didn't take my hand, but said: "Shand." I took it for a last name, but it could as well have been a cough or a sneeze for the way he said it.

"You on last night?" I stepped back to let him lead me through the door.

"I guess so," he said over his shoulder.

He led me to the room. I recognized it from the photographs, which is to say it was a hotel room like any other, with a huge video monitor on the wall and a camera perched like a vulture over the bed. The ripped curtain had already been replaced, but the coffee table had a big mark on it where they'd scoured off the blood.

"They get a tape of the killing?" I asked.

"Nope." Shand poked at his nose thoughtfully. "I guess that wasn't what they were here for."

"Who?"

"Mr. Stanhunt and whoever killed him." Shand wasn't getting trapped into theorizing.

"Did you see him?"

"I saw Mr. Stanhunt."

"He registered alone?"

"Stanhunt had been here on and off for a couple of weeks, and he always registered alone. I don't hassle the guests for fun. He paid his bills."

"Yeah, he had a habit of paying his bills—maybe one bill too many. You never saw him with anyone?"

"I told you no." Shand stayed at the door with his hand on the knob, making it clear he wanted to get back to his magazine.

I sat down on the bed. "You found the body?"

"Yeah. The door was open. I looked for a minute, then

called the office. Didn't go in." He made it sound like a hand of gin rummy.

"No weapon?"

"It wasn't my job to look. If the inquisitors found a weapon, they didn't mention it to me."

I nodded. Shand just kept looking at me with those dead eyes that had seen so much that now they didn't see anything at all.

"You work here long?" I asked.

"Depends on what you call long. I've worked in places like this for a long time, but I tend to come and go."

"I guess your curiosity isn't what it used to be."

He liked that. "That's one way of putting it." He dug in his pocket and took out a little vial. I watched as he unscrewed the top, pushed his pinky in, and brought it up burdened with a little heap of white powder. He pinched one nostril closed and pushed the powder up deftly into the other, then screwed the top back down and pocketed the vial. I imagined the powder, whatever it was—Acceptol or Avoidol, probably—filling up the space behind his nightmare eyes.

The sound of a car in the lot made us both look up. He turned his back to me and said, "I guess that's it..."

"Give me a few more minutes in the room," I said.

He turned to give me one more harrowing look, then shrugged. I was being judged not worth the bother. "I'll come back and lock up," he said, and went out in the direction of the office.

There wasn't anything specific I wanted to look at in the room. I wanted to look at the room itself, to try to see it through Stanhunt's eyes. Needless to say, it wasn't pretty. I imagined Stanhunt looking at this room the way he had looked at me, which is to say, down. Everything Maynard Stanhunt said and did was a repudiation of this motel room and the kind of life that was lived in rooms like it. But something brought him here, and brought him here more than once. Something made it worthwhile or necessary for him to lower his standards and spend part of his life in this room, and eventually made it necessary for him to spend his death here too.

My job was to find out what that something was. I suspected it would be a simple thing, when I found it. But at the moment I didn't have a clue—literally.

Footsteps in the hallway interrupted my reverie. I looked up, expecting Shand, but it wasn't Shand. Standing in the doorway was the evolved kangaroo I'd seen in the bar of the Vistamont. He was wearing a canvas jacket and plastic pants with a tight elastic waistband, and his paws were tucked into his pockets. He stepped into the room. I got up off the edge of the bed.

"You're in too deep, flathead," he said. He spoke in a clipped, recitative way, in a voice that was a bit too high to sound as tough as he wanted.

"I see," I replied.

"I hope so, for your sake. I'd hate to have to cut your fucking balls off."

"That makes two of us, Joey." I tried to brush past him but he moved sideways into my path, and our shoulders met.

"Not so fast, flathead. We gotta talk. Let's find your car."

I didn't say anything. He reached into his jacket and a little black gun appeared in his paw. He held it casually, the way you hold a candy bar or a cake of soap. Only this gun wasn't going to make anyone clean.

He filled the passenger seat of my car pretty awkwardly. I

closed my door, and the overhead light went out, reducing his form to a shaggy silhouette. I couldn't see the gun in his paw anymore, but I knew it was there.

"Listen up and listen good," he said. His voice quavered, and I got the impression he'd been practicing his strong-arm style on his little brother, if at all. I'm no judge of age in kangaroos, at least not without getting a good look at their teeth, but it was obvious that Joey was a little wet behind the ears.

"You're making some people unhappy," he said. "You don't know how unhealthy that could be. Angwine's bad company; you shouldn't be seen with him so often. You should lay off and go home. We'll send some divorce business your way."

"Who's we?"

"You shouldn't ask me questions, flathead. I'm not here to answer your pee-wee amateur eye questions."

"Don't play human with me, Joey. I've got the same privilege with you as anybody has with a kangaroo. Who sent you?"

In case I forgot about the gun, he stuck it in my gut. Like so many of the evolved, he didn't like being reminded of his lineage. "I work for Phoneblum, if that means anything to you."

I played a hunch. "Danny Phoneblum?"

He prodded at my rib cage with the gun. "That's right. You might wish you never heard the name, though. Danny got sick of you from a distance, see, and I'd feel real sorry for you if he got a look close up."

His jabbing must have loosened the anti-grav pen in my shirt pocket, because now it drifted out and floated up into the space between us. The kangaroo looked confused for a moment, then reached up and batted it down to the floor at his feet.

"So you and Danny are real cozy, right?"

"That's right." He shifted in his seat, adjusting his big tail, keeping the muzzle of the gun pressed against my solar plexus. It must have been uncomfortable for him.

"So you can get a message back to him?"

"Yeah."

"Tell him next time he wants to talk to me, don't send a marsupial."

He lifted the gun from my gut, and in the darkness I didn't see where he was going with it. Then it hit my mouth hard enough to knock me back against the headrest. I tasted blood right away, but the high level of make in my system kept me from feeling much pain.

There was a moment of unnatural quiet. He was probably as surprised as I was by the actuality of the violence. Violence isn't part of the Ping-Pong game of wisecrack and snappy comeback; it puts an awkward end to all that and leaves you wishing you'd stayed in or under the bed that morning.

"Okay," I said through the spit and blood welling in my mouth. "You're a tough boy."

"You think you can bluff your way through, flathead, but you're wrong. Not this one. You gotta call it quits."

I put my hands on the wheel so I wouldn't try to put them around his thick neck. "Message received. Hop along, Cassidy."

He opened the door and the overhead light came back on. His kangaroo mouth twisted into a ragged black smile, and above it his shiny nose twitched. "You got it right the first time, flathead. The name is Joey Castle."

"I'll keep it in mind."

He backed out of his seat, keeping the gun leveled at my

craw, then slammed the door shut and disappeared into the darkness. I took the keys out of my pocket and started the engine, thinking of trailing him, but I was still in too much of a daze to drive.

So I sat in the car with the motor running and the lights off. I didn't rub my mouth because I didn't feel like getting blood on my hand. When I heard a motor kick into action, I turned around, just in time to see the reflective plates of a motorcycle vanish down the ramp of the parking lot.

I sat there for another five or ten or twenty minutes, in a dark mood. I fingered the ripped hundred in my pocket, but I couldn't bring myself to get back out of the car and face Shand with blood on my mouth.

I thought about the kangaroo, about what a punk he was. So green he couldn't help boasting, telling me his and Phoneblum's names, and admitting to the connection between them. I'd gotten a return on my mouthful of gun.

Fair enough. I started the car and drove back down to the highway along the bay. It was the long way, but there was something about the water at night that I needed to have a look at.

CHAPTER 9

I ONLY SET MY ALARM WHEN I'M ON A CASE. THAT MORN-
ing I'd been dreaming a pleasant dream of normal, genitally
reoriented sex with an idealized composite blonde—no resemblance to Celeste Stanhunt—when the alarm went off
and it projected the wake-up dream into my head instead.
The image this morning was of a series of cartoon sheep
jumping over a cartoon wooden fence against a background
of ambient white. The last sheep caught its back legs against
the top of the fence and came tumbling down in a clatter of
splintered wood and bleating. Then a giant hand reached out
of the clouds and picked up the sheep, dusted it off, and patted it on the rump to send it scurrying along after the rest of
the flock. The hand turned to reveal a watch face on its wrist,
and the watch face grew closer and closer and the ticking
grew louder and louder until I finally woke up.

I sat with a pad and pencil over coffee and tried to piece
together my next move, but the coffee stung the fresh cuts in
my gums and I ended up having to concentrate instead on
drinking through only one side of my mouth. After wrestling
down a second cup, I went back to the pad and wrote the
name *Danny Phoneblum* just to have a look at it. Underneath

it I wrote *Pansy Greenleaf,* then *Grover Testafer* and *Celeste Stanhunt.* I drew a few circles and triangles on the pad, then tore the sheet off and threw it into the wastebasket.

After breakfast I made a call and requested an address and phone number for Testafer, which I got, and the phone number for the house on Cranberry Street, which wasn't available, even after I offered up my privilege access code. Either my code had been suspended or Celeste Stanhunt's privacy rated higher than my privilege.

Either way, the result was the same: I'd have to drop in on the house if I wanted a word with Celeste, or with Pansy Greenleaf. And I did want a word—hell, maybe even a whole bunch of them strung together. But the day was young, for once. I had plenty of time. First I'd take a drive up into the El Cerrito hills and have a look at Dr. Testafer's fancy address. I was in the mood for scenery.

The doctor's house was on Daymont Court, which was a public road but just barely. It terminated in a pair of driveways, each barred with a gate to stop traffic. The mailbox on the left said TESTAFER. I parked to one side of the clearing and set out on foot past the barrier, walking with loud crunching steps in the gravel so I wouldn't be mistaken for surreptitious.

The house was a botched American replica of a French country cottage, marred by aluminum storm windows and a satellite dish mounted on the shingles of the low roof. There wasn't any car in front of the house, but I went up to the front door and pushed the buzzer anyway.

A meekly feminine voice emanated from an unseen intercom: "Dr. Testafer isn't here right now."

"My name is Conrad Metcalf," I said, not knowing if there was a microphone to pick it up. "I'm a private inquisitor. I was hoping to have a word with you." Whoever you are, I didn't add.

There was an interval of silence. I examined the doorway and failed to find the intercom.

"I—I'll be right there," said the voice.

I waited on the doorstep, but the sound, when it came, was on my right, and I turned to see a smaller door opening in the lower wing of the house. The voice turned out to belong to a black-eared ewe wearing a housecoat and slippers. She stood in the doorway with one hand on the sash of her robe, blinking her big watery eyes in the sunlight.

I went over to her little door. "I'm Conrad Metcalf," I said again. The ewe came up to about the middle of my chest, and I took a step back again so I wouldn't seem to tower over her.

"My name is Dulcie." The margin between her lip and her black nose trembled as she spoke. "Please—come inside."

I nodded.

"It's a little low," she said. "I don't have the keys to the main house." She turned and tiptoed inside, leaving the door open. I stooped to enter.

The apartment was as wide and deep as it should have been, but about half as tall. I stood just inside the doorway, bent over uncomfortably, until my eyes adjusted to the dimness; then I made my way to the couch by the farthest wall of the room and sat down. I could almost have reached up and touched the ceiling from a sitting position. Testafer had had the entire wing remodeled to fit the ewe or someone else her size. The colors in the apartment were all childish pinks and blues, and pretty much everything short of the doorknobs and faucets was carpeted. The curtains were drawn against the morning sun; the room was lit instead by a pair of big floor lamps which had to crook their necks to fit. I felt a kinship with them, real-life visitors in the dollhouse.

The ewe performed a nervous little dance before choosing the easy chair across from me and sitting down. I leaned forward with my elbows on my knees and said: "Has Dr. Testafer told you what happened to Dr. Stanhunt?"

"Well, yes," said the sheep. "He was very upset."

"We all are," I said. "Especially my client. He's about to take a trip to the freezer, and I personally don't think he killed the doctor. Did you know Stanhunt very well?"

The ewe flinched, but it could have meant anything: I was no Doolittle. "I met him once," she said.

"He came up here?"

"Yes."

"Do you ever come down off the hill, Dulcie?"

She wrenched up her mouth. "Not very often."

"Must be kind of lonely," I suggested.

"I'm not going to say anything against Grover, if that's what you have in mind. I'm quite happy here, and if I wasn't I'd leave."

"Yes, I'm sure you would. Does the name Danny Phoneblum mean anything to you? Dr. Testafer seemed uncomfortable talking about the subject, and I thought you might clear it up for me."

"I'm afraid not."

"That's funny," I said. "That's exactly what Dr. Testafer said. I mention Phoneblum, and everyone is afraid not. What are you afraid of, Dulcie?"

Her eyes widened and a funny sound emerged from her throat, a sort of strangled bleat. "I—I shouldn't be talking to you. Grover will be angry with me."

"You ever meet a strong-arm kangaroo named Joey Castle? He works for Phoneblum, or at least he did last night."

"No." She said it firmly. She seemed relieved to be able to deliver an answer.

"All right. Let's try another tack. Testafer was worried about some papers that had gotten lost, something from the office files. What can you tell me about that?"

"Nothing." She kicked the slipper off her right hoof and scratched at her left flank in an unnaturally repetitive way, as if she were being bitten by a flea under her wool.

"Okay," I said. "You're afraid of somebody and you don't want to talk. That's fine. I'm a patient guy, believe it or not. This carpet's big, but it's not all tacked down as neatly as you and Testafer. We'll find out what's been swept underneath." I congratulated myself on the metaphor and started to think about where to go next. I wasn't as confident as I sounded, and I'm not really patient—not even a little.

"Grover is under a lot of pressure," said the ewe suddenly, surprising me. "You've got to understand. It's not his fault. Danny Phoneblum is—"

"That's enough," came a voice from the doorway. It was Grover Testafer, and he had a gun pointed in my direction. It was an electronic dart gun, and he held it like he might know how to use it.

"Hello, Doctor," I said. The sheep just trembled in her chair.

Testafer stepped inside and shut the door behind him without looking away from me for a second. He'd learned the trick of bending at the knees to fit in the apartment, and he duckwalked over to a position beside one of the stoop-shouldered floor lamps. His florid face was lit up from underneath like a demonic mask. "Get up," he said.

"Right," I replied wearily.

"Outside."

I gave Dulcie a smile and then I walked hunchbacked to the door.

"Go." He turned to the sheep. "You stay here." His voice was brittle.

I put my hand on the knob. "Here's a tip, Grover. You're supposed to go first—"

"Shut up."

Well, I'd tried to warn him. I opened the door and stepped to the left and pressed myself flat against the shingles. Testafer said "Shit," and I didn't say anything back. He nearly had to bend double to get through the little door, and when his gun hand appeared, I kicked it as hard as I could, which was hard. Then I reared back and hit him with a solid right from the waist, and almost broke my hand on his jaw. His fat body sagged in the doorway, but I grabbed him by the collar before he fell back inside. I pushed him up against the side of the house and reached down for the gun, but my right hand wouldn't close enough to pick it up. So I kicked it a few feet away, and it vanished in the unmowed grass.

Testafer was pressed up against the house as if I were still holding him there, his face crumbling to reveal fifty-odd years of terror and insecurity. Drool leaked from the side of his mouth where my fist had landed. I felt real sorry for him.

"Let's go inside and talk," I said, except it came out a pant. He nodded silently and walked shakily to the big front door. Dulcie was following instructions, I guess; there wasn't a peep from the little house.

Testafer's quarters were a little more tasteful, and a lot more spacious. The living room was light and airy, at least by comparison. One wall was entirely taken up with shelves displaying old magazines in glossy plastic covers. I could see through to a kitchen tiled in white and blue and, beyond that, a covered porch on the back of the house. Testafer walked straight through and rinsed his mouth in the sink, swirling a mouthful of water like fancy wine before spitting it out. I didn't see blood, but my hand hurt and I didn't see blood on that either.

When he was done, he came back into the room and stood in front of me. He'd put his composure together again somewhere in the interval. "Have a seat," he said, and I did.

The table between us was a big cross-section slice of a tree trunk polished to a mirrored sheen. It was empty except for a little silver box at one corner, and I wasn't too surprised when Testafer opened the box and spilled some make onto the table. "You're very persistent, Mr. Metcalf," he said, and as the words came out, I could hear him working his jaw to find out what hurt and what didn't.

I decided to get right to business. I was tired of feeling people out and getting nowhere. "I need to talk to Phone-blum," I said, and tried to sound like I knew what it meant to be saying it.

"I guess I could help you with that," he said carefully. "You do things differently than the Office."

"I try to, yes."

"I should warn you that you're out of your jurisdiction on this."

"One of the pleasures of my job is deciding for myself where my jurisdiction lies," I said. "Who is Phoneblum that he commands such respect?"

Testafer leaned forward and began chopping at the make with a little ivory-handled blade from the box. He looked up at me from under his eyebrows and then down again at the make on the shiny surface. The sun threw a beam into the room that crossed the table, and as Testafer chopped, I could see little motes floating away in the light.

"I spent most of my adult life working to achieve this," he said, gesturing with his hand. "I'm not comfortable in the city. I don't *like* people. I like cooking, and music." He put the knife back into the box. "We all make our compromises. In an ideal world there wouldn't be a Danny Phoneblum."

I nodded to keep him going.

"I met him through Maynard, and I tolerated him only to the extent that I understood their relationship to be necessary to Maynard, though I never knew why. He's a dirty gangster, you understand. But he owned a piece of Maynard, and I found that out too late."

"Does he own a piece of you?"

"No—no." Testafer worked his jaw again. "Phoneblum has ways of manipulating events and karma to suit his needs—he could make my life uncomfortable, and he hasn't. But he doesn't own me. Not a bit." He took a straw out of the box and leaned over the table.

"You call him a gangster—what's his racket?"

Testafer stopped snorting, but he stayed bent over with his face in the make. "I wouldn't know."

"Who would?"

Testafer sat back up and neatened his shirt at the sleeves and waist with careful, pinching fingers. His face was still red but it looked more composed now. "Phoneblum, I guess."

"I don't know—my impression was your sheep would have told me in another minute. Since you don't know, why don't we go and ask her?"

He didn't want to talk about the ewe. His fingers whitened on his knee, the way they had back in his office downtown the first time we tangled. "Dulcie doesn't talk to strangers often," he said with effort. "She's very…impressionable." He looked closely at my face and then stood up abruptly, as if someone were jerking his strings.

"You're a young man," he said.

"I'm older than I look." The line was stolen, but I'd said it often enough to make it my own.

"You don't remember before the Inquisition."

"No," I admitted.

He stepped over to the shelves and pulled down one of the old magazines. "These are television guides," he said. "There used to be such a variety of programming that you needed a guide to decide what to watch."

"It's probably illegal to own those," I said.

"I don't care. I collect them. It's one of my hobbies. Here, look." He handed me the magazine. It was wrapped in transparent plastic. The cover featured an ensemble of performers—maybe jugglers or magicians, I couldn't tell—and the name of their show.

"Abstract television isn't an improvement," he said. "There's something missing that used to be commonplace. An art form that's completely vanished."

I wasn't impressed. "You're only remembering, through those magazines, what a lot of people know, even though they aren't supposed to. It has nothing to do with television. What's missing that used to be commonplace is a sense of connectedness in people's lives. In my line of work that's old news. The shows you're talking about were only a reflection of that."

"You don't understand. What I'm talking about is a lost art form—"

"I've never seen old television," I said. "But I'm sure television was the same then as it is now. Art mirrors the culture.

The abstract stuff they have now just shows how bad it's gotten. You think you're pining for some old program, but what you're really missing is a kind of human contact, a kind that's not possible anymore." I was making it up off the top of my head.

He took the magazine away from me. "You'd feel differently if you could remember."

"That's possible. Listen, Doctor—not that I don't find this stuff interesting, but I came here to talk about Phoneblum. I need to see him."

He put the magazine carefully into its place on the shelf and then turned back to me. His smile was enigmatic. "I've no doubt that you'll eventually accomplish that," he said. "Though I can't recommend it as an experience. But I'm powerless to put you in touch with him. Phoneblum comes and goes according to his own schedule."

"You know so much more than you're telling that it's leaking out of the sides of your eyes, Doctor. What's got you scared?"

His smile evaporated. "You really don't understand. If you could see yourself the way I see you—as far as I'm concerned, you and Danny Phoneblum are like two peas in a pod. Remember that when you meet him. You're both dangerous, temperamental men who like to barge in and demand things from people who'd rather not have anything to do with you. You impose your violent paradigms on others. The only difference is that Danny is more assured in his evil—he doesn't cloak it in self-righteousness, as you do—and therefore he's more dangerous than you. I'll place my bets on his side of the table, thank you."

"Yeah, sure." I got up to leave. "You're headed for higher ground. It's obviously a habit with you. Only this time maybe you should build an ark. It's going to be raining awhile."

"An interesting concept."

"Yeah, interesting."

I went to the door. He just stood there. It occurred to me that I ought to make some kind of crack about him and the ewe, but I couldn't think of anything. I opened the door and looked out into the sunny garden. It was noon.

I turned and looked back into the house. "See you later, Grover."

"As you wish."

I closed the door on his idiot smile. Before I walked down the driveway to my car, I went over and found Testafer's little electric gun in the grass. I clipped the safety and put it in my inside jacket pocket.

Dulcie's little door was closed, but I could see light shining through from underneath. Once he heard my engine start, Testafer would probably go in and see her, and I wondered what they would say to each other. Would they make love? Would he hit her? Did he hit her a lot?

Sometimes it's better not to think in questions, but I can't seem to get out of the habit.

CHAPTER 10

OFTEN MIDWAY THROUGH THE MORNING I START TO KID myself that I dried out during the night and that I don't need it anymore and won't ever need it again, and then it hits me, I *really* dry out, and I start rifling through my belongings to find another packet and a straw. Towards the tail end of my conversation with Testafer the last of the addictol must have leached out of my bloodstream, and by the time I got back into my car at the bottom of his driveway, I was badly in need of a line or two of my blend.

I searched my pockets, hoping to find a little something to tide me over until I made it home. No cigar. Then I thought I remembered seeing a couple of half-empty packets in the glove compartment. It was warming up into a nice day, and the clearing there at the end of the driveway was almost like a clearing somewhere deep in the forest. I couldn't see Testafer's house from the car, and the only sounds were natural ones—birds, and the wind rustling the trees overhead. I sat with the car door open and pulled the contents of the glove compartment out into a pile on my lap.

I somehow ended up with an old packet, from a couple of years back, before I'd discovered a reliable blend of make and was still experimenting with different combinations. It was clumped up in a ball at the bottom of the packet, and I broke it into pieces with my thumb and forefinger. I guess I wasn't thinking too much about the possible effects as I crumbled the little chunks one after another into my uptilted nose, and when I looked at the packet in my hand, it was empty.

I tossed it out of the car and closed the door. Waiting for the make to take effect, I was suddenly aware of the pain in my right hand, which I'd used to hit the doctor. My sense of isolation at the end of the driveway faded, and I was turning the key in the ignition when the make hit my bloodstream.

I was eased into a state of altered consciousness by the difference between this make and my ordinary blend. I was no more capable of describing the effects of my personal blend than I would have been capable of describing consciousness itself, because the two for me had become inextricable. But this older blend was different; I detected an uncommonly heavy dose of Believol, and my customary measure of Regrettol was completely missing. I sat in the car with the motor running, the sun glinting through the windshield, and let the new sensation wash over me.

Believol is funny stuff. It would be nice to succumb, and really inhabit the comfortable, reassuring world it provides— I guess that's why so many people do. But it's not for me. My skeptical faculties overcompensate and, in effect, the ingredient backfires: I become paranoid and suspicious. More than usual, I mean. Still, out in the sun at the end of Testafer's driveway, I found myself indulging the Believol, letting it sweep me away. It was a vision of a gently reconciled existence that wasn't mine, couldn't be mine, but which I could live momentarily through the old packet of make. I'd have given a lot to be able to reach back through time to warn the young guy who'd snorted make like this about what a lousy business he was in, and how a blonde with gray eyes was going to transform him into a tired, prematurely spent old fool.

When I finally looked at my watch, it was a quarter to one. I was shamed into action by the thought of Orton Angwine holed up in some bar or cafeteria, the last hours of his current life ticking away while I sat in the sun reminiscing about the drugs I used to take as opposed to the ones I take now. I eased my foot off the brake and let the dutiframe roll backwards out of the cul-de-sac, found my way out of the maze of winding roads that laced the hills, and drove back down to the flats.

My impulse was to maximize what little momentum I might have by appearing in person at the Cranberry Street house. The cobwebs cleared as I hit the breeze on the freeway, and I went back to puzzling over the case. The make effects receded—the upfront ingredients like Acceptol and Believol and Avoidol always do—but I was left with enough in my bloodstream to keep me comfortable. Scratch the surface of any blend and underneath you found the same thing, the ingredient all make has in common: addictol. The rest is just icing on the cake.

When I pulled up in front of the house at the end of Cranberry, I didn't bother hiding my car or concealing my intention of walking up to the door and ringing the bell. There were cars on the street, but none of them were familiar, so I had no way of knowing who, if anyone, was home. That was okay. No matter who I found, I'd have something to talk about, and if no one was in, I might be able to find some way of entertaining myself.

I rang the bell and waited, but nobody came to the door, and when I tried the handle it practically opened itself. I could see through the foyer to the living room where I'd sat yesterday and chatted with the kitten and then Celeste, and it was empty. I went inside, shut the door, and looked around.

Everything downstairs was neat, too neat, more like a museum exhibit than a lived-in house. The windows were designed to maximize the sun, and they were busy doing that; the house looked painted with light. Nobody had mentioned to the windows and the sunlight that there wasn't anybody home and they could relax.

I went into the kitchen. Nobody there either. I poked through the refrigerator and pantry; they were well stocked, but I couldn't quite bring myself to eat anything. I went back into the living room and faced the picture window. After all the time I'd spent peering in, being on the inside made me feel visible. I spent a long minute looking at the view, past the monorail trestles to where the fog clung to the beach. Then my focus changed, and instead of looking through the glass I was looking at it, at the reflection of me in my shabby coat and hat standing in the fancy living room getting romantic about a view of a cold, wet beach. Who was I trying to kid? The bay was a five-minute drive from my apartment, and it was a five-minute drive I never bothered to make.

When I started up the stairs, the carpet muffled my shoes, turning me into an inadvertent sneak. Everything about the house made me feel out of place. I went into Celeste's room first, lowering the shade to make myself more comfortable. The bed was unmade, and a shirt was spread out across the pillows; otherwise the room was all tucked away and tidy like downstairs. I went to the chest of drawers and pulled the pair on top open, but it was all socks and underwear. The bottom drawers were more clothing, the middle drawer almost empty. Celeste had only been living in the room a couple of weeks, and it showed. It was a guest room, and she was just passing through, and if she had secrets, she still kept them in some other place. The clothes smelled nice, and I let myself linger over them, but only for a minute, then I turned out the light and went back out into the hall.

There were three other rooms on the upper floor. I looked quickly into a messy room that must have belonged to the babyhead, and a neat one that must have belonged to the kitten, both empty. By this time I was pretty certain I was alone in the house, and I wasn't taking any particular pains to keep quiet.

When I opened the door to Pansy Greenleaf's room, it took a minute for my eyes to adjust to the gloom and make out the faded figure lying on the bed. She was bundled in bedclothes, asleep or unconscious, and her black hair, splayed out against the pillows, was the only way I could tell she was something more than an arrangement of laundry on the bed. I went inside without turning on the light.

The table by the bed was littered with piles of make, plus the equipment necessary to prepare it for intravenous injection. The needle was beside her on the bed. It was all very competently laid out, suggesting this was not the first time she'd taken it in the arm. I was reaching for her neck to feel for a pulse, when her eyes rolled mechanically open. She blinked a couple of times, and then she closed her mouth and worked up enough spit to talk.

"You're the inquisitor," she said. She didn't move a muscle. The voice was strained up from some small reservoir of life inside an otherwise dead husk.

I told her she was right.

"I knew you would come," she said. "My card is on the dresser."

"I'm not going to take any karma off your card," I said. "I'm not that kind of inquisitor."

Her eyes closed again. She was like a part of the room, gray and dim, flickering only accidentally into persona and then receding again into the grayness and pallor. I took the needle off the bed and put it on the table with the make so she wouldn't roll into it.

She was obviously an experienced mainliner, but it was equally obvious she wasn't in very good shape right now. I didn't like the idea of her dying while I was in the house. I went over to the dresser where her card was and experimented with making a lot of noise opening the drawers, but she didn't respond.

The drawers were full of papers. I started leafing through them, without any particular goal in mind. It was all bills and receipts and direct mail, until I came across a folder full of architectural diagrams and a written proposal. I glanced at the blueprints in a perfunctory way, and I probably would have forgotten about them if I hadn't noticed that the proposal was for an additional structure on the Cranberry Street lot. That sent me back for another look.

I wasn't much for reading blueprints, but the diagram of the upper floor was easy to read. It showed a wall of bunk beds, like a barracks-style sleeping quarters for an army of evolved animals. I looked closer. The beds were stacked in pairs to fit eight against the northern wall, if I was holding the diagram right. The measurement for the north wall was only twenty feet total, an allotment of less than three feet per bed. It was a funny idea, all those animals bunked up like soldiers, and it was even funnier to think of it in the backyard of the Cranberry Street house. I noted the architectural firm and slid the papers back into the drawer.

"That's my stuff," she said, while my back was still turned.

"I'm looking for a birth certificate," I said.

"For Barry…" There was a note of panic in her voice. "You won't find one."

"I don't care about Barry. I was thinking of you."

"I don't understand."

"I'm a friend of your brother's, Ms. Greenleaf. I was just wondering what happened to the name Angwine. Who was Mr. Greenleaf, and where is he now?"

She gripped the sides of the bed and turned her head towards me. "There isn't one." Her voice was a whisper.

"I see. Pansy Angwine? That's a little discordant."

"Patricia."

"Never married?"

"No."

I shut the open drawers of the bureau and went back to the side of the bed. Pansy just watched me, hollow-eyed and quiet, as I ran my fingers through the make on the table and held them up to my nose to sniff.

"Whose kid is Barry?" I asked.

I guess she thought I was going to ask her something about the drugs, because she looked at the paraphernalia on the table and up at me a couple of times, as if there was a connection. The truth was I didn't have anything better to do with my hands.

"That's my business," she said. Her eyes wanted to sag shut again, but she was fighting the nod with everything she had. I was making her nervous. If I could keep her talking as she shook herself into life, I might learn something.

"You worked for Stanhunt," I reminded her. "What did you do for him?"

A sneeze erupted from the depths of her tortured little

frame, and she covered her face with both hands and held them there the way a wounded soldier holds in his guts in a bad war movie. I folded a hundred-dollar bill into the shape of a little envelope, scooped up a sample of her make with the open side of it, and got it into my pocket before she recovered control of her face.

"Do you want a glass of water?" I asked. She nodded. I went to the bathroom adjoining the hallway, filled a glass, and brought it back. She took it in both hands and drained it quietly and steadily.

"You were going to tell me about working for Stanhunt," I said.

"Stanhunt—" She faltered and stopped.

"He bought you this house."

She looked up, almost sharply. "No. I bought it myself."

"With what money?"

She would have lied, but nothing convenient came to mind, so she just stared at me. For people who have managed to stay out of trouble for a long time the process of answering direct questions is a bit awkward. They never seem to work it all through in advance the way experienced liars do. It's as though they think questions don't need to be answered so much as swatted away, like flies.

"Your brother thinks that Barry is Stanhunt's son, and that the house is a kind of thank you for keeping the whole affair and pregnancy under wraps."

"You think that too."

"I'd be willing to hear another version. Your brother didn't do his homework. If you were Stanhunt's mistress, why would Celeste run here when she needed a hidey-hole?" Sometimes if you do your thinking out loud, people feel the urge to chip in and help you get it right.

"Dr. Stanhunt and I were never lovers."

"I believe you. Maynard Stanhunt had his hands full with Celeste. And Celeste is a handful. I guess you're finding that out now."

"Celeste is my friend," she said, straightening herself in the bed. She gave me a look that said that question-and-answer time was almost up. "I offered her the extra room. I don't regret it."

"Somehow I think it's more complicated than that."

The bell downstairs rang, and we both flinched. I'd been expecting Celeste for some time now, based on how rarely I'd seen her out of this house. But Celeste wouldn't ring the doorbell.

"I'll get it," I said. I figured if it was the Office, I might as well get it over with. My car was parked in front, and if they wanted to talk to me, they'd be crawling all over it.

Pansy put the empty glass down on the bedside table, and the condensation on it picked up a white coating of make. "Okay," she said. She was still fighting her way through a fog.

I went downstairs, took a deep breath, and opened the door. A neatly dressed woman in her late twenties or early thirties stood in the doorway, and behind her a young guy in a suit and tie was walking up the steps. "Hello," she said.

I said hello back.

"We're students of psychology. If you're not too busy, we'd like to read you a few selections from Freud's *Civilization and Its Discontents*."

It took a minute for me to blink away my confusion. This kind of thing didn't happen in my neighborhood. "No," I said. "But thanks no. I'm not a believer myself."

She took it all right, wished me a nice day. I could see the guy in the suit already sizing up the next house down the street as I closed the door on them.

By the time I got back upstairs, Pansy Greenleaf—or should I say Patricia Angwine?—was sitting on the edge of the bed, her nightdress smoothed back down and her brown eyes considerably more animated and lucid. The table beside the bed was all cleaned up.

"I don't know your name," she said.

I told her my name, and waited while she sorted things out.

"You must know where my brother is…"

"Your brother is in a lot of trouble. I let him spend the night in my office. What happens next might have a lot to do with you."

"You mean setting up maintenance for his body—"

"I mean telling me what you know about the murder so I can knock apart the frame. He's not a body yet, Pansy. He's a scared kid. He made a mistake when he tangled with Stanhunt, but I don't think he killed him. Do you?"

"I don't know."

I could only smile. "Tell me something. What happens next? Do you get to keep the house?"

"Dr. Stanhunt's death has nothing to do with that."

"I forgot. Stanhunt's death doesn't affect you in any way. But what about the babyhead?"

"You can ask him yourself," she said. She was pulling herself together, which meant she was getting a little indignant at the inquisition. "I don't think he'll show much interest."

"I guess I might do that," I said. "Where does he stay? I mean, when he's not here." I added that bit to be polite. He was never at the Cranberry Street house for longer than to grab a sandwich.

"He spends his time at the babybar on Telegraph. I guess they have someplace to sleep."

"He's getting away from you, isn't he?"

A flicker of anger appeared on her face and then vanished. "He's no different from the rest of them. It's the growth treatments. He's not the same as he was before."

"What about Celeste?" I said. "What's next for her?"

"I guess you should ask her about that."

"I guess I will. Where is she now?"

"I don't know. When I got up this morning, she was gone."

"When will she be back?"

"That's her business."

"Are you expecting her for dinner, say?"

"With Celeste I've learned not to expect anything."

The conversation had taken on all the charm of a one-sided game of table tennis. I didn't know my next move, but I could see that this one was all played out.

"I'm leaving," I said. "Are there any last words you want to convey to your brother?"

She turned away from me on the bed. She looked pretty composed, but I didn't imagine she felt too good on the inside. Ten minutes before, she'd been too far gone to move the needle from the bed to the table. "Get out of here," she said finally. I could see her hardening herself as she spoke.

I went to the door.

"You shouldn't assume that my life revolves around my brother," she said. "I haven't seen him for years. I don't know him anymore, and he certainly doesn't know me. I have my own life. If he made a mistake, then I guess he has to pay for it."

"His mistake was looking you up, apparently."

She crossed her arms over her thin chest and looked at me and through me with one poisonous, icy glance. "Get out. Stay away from me and stay away from this house. If you ever come into my room when I'm sleeping again, I'll kill you with my bare hands. I swear to God." She just sat on the edge of the bed and delivered it like it was the weather, but I could see her skinny body trembling.

I didn't bother reminding her that what she was doing when I came in wasn't exactly sleeping. I just went out to my car. I looked up and down the street, but the Freud nuts had given up and gone home. The sky was murky; the clouds were gnarled over the sun. A damp wind swept over the hills behind the house, chilling my neck. It was going to rain. I rolled up the windows of my car and drove back downtown.

CHAPTER 11

THEY WEREN'T EXPECTING ME TO COME STROLLING IN THE front lobby at the Office. They never are. When I told them my name at the front desk, the guy they sent out to meet me wasn't Morgenlander, or Kornfeld, or anyone else connected with the Stanhunt case. It wasn't a guy at all. It was a dame, a dish, a bird—I never know what to call them when I want to be other than rude. Because I'm always rude. But she made me want to be other, made me want to be someone I wasn't.

I got up from the seat I was in, and she stepped towards me, and suddenly we were closer than we should have been. I liked it, but it was too close. She couldn't even put her hand up for a shake. I backed off a bit. I may have been wrong, but I came away with an impression of the warmth of her body against me, as if she'd left a kind of heat-print on the front of my jacket and pants.

"My name is Catherine Teleprompter," she said. "What brings you in, Mr. Metcalf?"

The question told me her full name was Inquisitor Teleprompter. I'd met a couple this young, but none this pretty. I straightened out the lewd expression on my face and said: "Let's talk in your office."

She led me down a couple of hallways and around a couple of corners to her office, which was a room about the size of a shot glass. I guess she was new. She went behind her desk and I sat down on a chair in what little space remained.

She leaned back in her chair, and the black curtain of her hair swept over her shoulder, revealing a throat I could have spent an hour on. An hour a day, or maybe an hour every five minutes. We had a hard time getting the conversation started because of it. I was looking at her and she was looking at me looking, and she knew it and I knew she knew it and the whole thing again, squared. She broke the spell by turning to her console, the purplish light illuminating her face as she squinted at the screen. I had a feeling she needed glasses but didn't want to put them on in front of me.

"Conrad Metcalf," she said.

"That's right."

"Private inquisitor. License up for renewal in May. Our last entry is signed by Inquisitor Morgenlander. He says he had to kick you off a case."

"I don't know why they call this place a bureaucracy. That was yesterday. Congratulations."

"So I suppose you want to talk to Morgenlander."

"I did until you came along."

"What should I say it's concerning?" she asked curtly.

"You can say I need a jump start and I was wondering if he had a set of cables."

She opened her desk drawer. "Pass me your card, Mr. Metcalf."

I dug in my pocket. "You see—"

"Your card," she interrupted. I passed it over.

I waited while she ran it through a decoder.

"You don't have the karma of a man who wants to be

barging in here giving dopey jokes as answers to my questions, Mr. Metcalf." She put my card down on the desk in front of her.

"It's about this case," I said. "I'm supposed to lay off, only the case keeps rubbing up against my ankles and purring. I need to let Morgenlander know I tried to follow his instructions." I offered one of my better smiles, and she took it, but slowly.

"I'll see if he's in the building," she said.

"No, don't. Let me ask you a couple of questions first." I reached across the desk for my card, but she put her hand over it. I almost put my hand on top of hers but thought better of it at the last minute.

"About Morgenlander," I said, trying to keep my mind on the case. I was functionally non-male, and the sight of a pretty inquisitor shouldn't make me forget it. The limb I was going out on here was one I didn't possess. "Who's pulling his strings on this case, and why? He's an outsider, from another district; why bring him in at all if you aren't going to let him work?"

She looked at me hard. "You shouldn't ask questions like that without knowing who you're asking them of. You might get more than answers."

"I'm not sure I'd mind that." I couldn't stop myself.

"I'm sure you would, if you knew what I was talking about. Here." She slid my card to where it was within my reach. "I'm getting you out of my office. I can't afford to be having this conversation."

She pushed a button on her console and asked for Morgenlander. When he came on the line, she said my name and asked him to have me seen out, then broke off the connection.

"Too bad," I said. "We could have made beautiful dialogue together."

"You used to work for the Office, didn't you?"

"Yes."

"Inquisitor."

"That's the only way to get licensed as a P.I."

She looked me over as if for the first time. "What happened?"

"Either it'll happen to you or you wouldn't understand the answer to your question," I said. "I'm not going to try to explain it."

There was a knock at the door, or rather a scraping of knuckles against wood. Inquisitor Teleprompter nudged a button on her desk and the door slid open, revealing Inquisitor Kornfeld, the quiet one who'd glowered around in my doorway while Morgenlander talked. Apparently he and Morgenlander were still working together, despite the tension I'd sensed between them then. He nodded his head knowingly at Catherine Teleprompter, as if I were nothing more than some kind of unwieldy parcel that needed delivering, and then jerked his thumb at me and the door, in that order.

I took my card and slipped it into my jacket pocket, where I found a few dog-eared business cards. I drew one out and put it on the desk where my karma had been sitting. "Give it a call," I said, and then I couldn't think of a reason in the world why she ever would, so I just nodded and smiled and left it at that.

Kornfeld didn't look too impressed. He held the door open so as to make it clear I shouldn't linger over farewells. Inquisitor Teleprompter looked at me without blinking and said: "Don't wait underwater." But her nostrils were flared when she said it, and I had a feeling her legs were crossed under the desk. I'd gotten under her skin in return, at least a little.

Kornfeld almost closed the door on my heels. I was expecting the bum's rush, so it came as a surprise when he took my arm and turned towards the bank of elevators, away from the front entrance. I experienced a surge of paranoia as I realized I was being ushered into the dark heart of the Office, without knowing why. Not that the place had changed any since the days I walked the halls. It was precisely that pervasive sameness that made me want to pull my arm loose and run for the nearest exit.

We got inside the elevator. Kornfeld leaned against the wall and pushed at the buttons, and I stood against the back, thinking, my mind elsewhere. When the door closed, he turned to me and his eyes lit up for a second, and he came towards me with a fist coiled up at his waist, and smashed me right in the middle of my stomach.

It was the closest thing to language that had passed between us. I guess I should have been grateful to the guy for opening himself up to me like that. I doubled up completely, more out of breath than in pain, though there was plenty of pain. Kornfeld leaned back against the side of the elevator car, apparently finished. The guy was laconic even in his violence.

The elevator opened, and he took me by the arm again and led me down the hallway as I was, bent over and gasping for air. By the time we were at Morgenlander's door, I had managed to pull myself together, although standing upright made my face flush hot. Kornfeld opened the door and shoved me into the room.

Morgenlander was visiting brass, and he rated a nice layout, with carpeting, and a little refrigerator under the window for snacks and beer. The chair I fell into was leather or a deceptively real copy. Morgenlander didn't look any more shaven or less disheveled than when he'd come through my place. His hands were spread out on a pile of papers, and there was a pencil behind his ear. "Thanks," he said, looking up at Kornfeld. "Why don't you leave me alone with him, okay?"

There was an appreciable pause, and then Kornfeld said: "No. I can't do that." Morgenlander just nodded, and Kornfeld went over and sat in a chair against the wall. I had had Kornfeld figured for a rookie tagging along after the big man; I realized now I might not have the intricacies of their professional relationship worked out exactly right.

But Morgenlander recovered. "Funny you walking in here," he said to me. "You always seem to pick funny ways to do stuff. It's very funny." He leaned over the desk and cracked a knuckle for punctuation.

"I'm a comedian," I said. "Either of you guys want to play straight man, the part is still open."

"Funny," smiled Morgenlander, and he showed me his worn-out tongue again. "It's a good thing you're a comedian, because as a P.I. you're a pain in the ass. You complicate things. You know Angwine spent the night in your office?"

"I gave him the key."

Morgenlander smiled more, his eyes crinkling around the edges like a department-store Santa who gets a funny feeling when the girls sit in his lap. "Why are you here, Metcalf?"

"You took me off the case, but a lead came my way." I was fishing for a response, and willing to bait the hook. "I wanted to throw it to you. Don't ice Angwine until you get a handle on somebody named Danny Phoneblum."

Morgenlander didn't show any response to the name. He looked over at Kornfeld, and then back at me. "Who's Phoneblum?"

"You know as much as I do now. He's just a name that won't stop cropping up. Don't say I never did you any favors."

"Get him out of here," said Morgenlander. He leaned back in his chair and ran his fingers through his hair. Kornfeld got up and put his hand on my shoulder. "In my district we don't license people like you, Metcalf. You'd be lucky to stay out of the ice wagon, where I come from." He looked at Kornfeld. "Bill him twenty-five points and put him on the street."

Kornfeld took me back down in the elevator, and this time I kept my hands folded over my stomach. He walked me through the corridors and back past the front desk and out onto the street. The rain was starting to fall, in fat oblong drops that dampened the tops of my knees and the back of my neck. Kornfeld took out his magnet and aimed it at the karma in my pocket.

"I'm down to sixty-five," I said.

He just stood there.

"Forty's too low," I said. "You know that."

The wind took the rain and threw it sideways into my face. An Office vehicle pulled into the lot behind us, and a couple of inquisitors jogged past us up the steps of the Office, collars raised against the wind and rain. Kornfeld and I just stood there getting wet. He flicked his thumb, and I saw the little red indicator on the back of the magnet light up. "You shouldn't have mentioned Phoneblum," he said, with something resembling sadness in his voice.

"Thanks a lot, pal," I said. My fingers curled instinctively around the card in my pocket. "I'll remember this."

"You stupid shit," he said, and turned to go back into the building. "You stupid little shit."

CHAPTER 12

I GOT BACK IN THE CAR. I FELT PRETTY LOW, THANKS TO the unmagical combination of a punch in the stomach, twenty-five points missing from my card, and two or three lines of make missing from my bloodstream. What's more, there was rain in my collar and I needed a sandwich. The clouds were still bunched up in the sky like a gang on a street corner, and it looked to me like they had the sun pretty effectively intimidated. I didn't have a clear next move lined up, and I wasn't really getting paid enough to eat lunch in the car. So I drove home. I almost ran down some pedestrians coming around a corner, and when I leaned on my horn, the guy closest to my car took a big horn out of his coat and honked it right back at me. I'll admit it was a first.

I parked as close to the building as I could, but that wasn't particularly close. The rain was falling in heavy, languorous sheets, and it ran in dirty streams along the waste-clogged gutters. With my shoulders up over my ears I sprinted to the doorway of my building and stepped into the darkness under the crumbling archway, and stood there for a minute, watching the rain run off the sill over my head and splash a few inches from my shoes. I was playing out a hunch.

The hunch was right. It took about a minute for the kangaroo to catch up with me, and he must have been pretty sure I hadn't seen him, because he strolled up to the front of the building without taking any pains to conceal himself. He was wearing a drab rain slicker and a sort of wrapped-up turban for a hat, his ears pressed down against the sides of his head by the knotted cloth. I was well hidden in the darkness of the doorway, and I got more of a look at him than he did at me before our eyes met. The second they did, I laid into him with everything I had.

My edge was surprise. I probably had intelligence and experience on him too, but in a fight with a kangaroo I'll take surprise, thanks. I made the most of it by jumping into a clinch with him, wrapping my arms around his neck, and thrusting my knee into his gut as hard as I could and as many times as I could. I'm no athlete, but I do all right. The force of it moved us out into the rain and halfway across the pavement in front of the building.

I knew I had him, but I wasn't finished making my point. I pushed him the rest of the way across the sidewalk and backed him against a car parked at the curb, pinning him against the passenger door with my hip. My face was buried in the wet fur of his neck, and the reek of it was strong in my nostrils, but I knew that stepping away would give him room to operate with his big legs and feet, and that I couldn't afford. I brought my hands up and joined them under his chin, then smashed his head backwards against the roof of the car. The cloth around his head unfurled and fell across my arms like some pathetic flag of surrender. I smashed his head back again, straining against the muscles in his neck, and then I felt his grip around my shoulders slacken and fall away.

That was the end of it. The mindlessly capable muscles of

his lower body kept him standing upright, but the rest of him wasn't working too well. I put an arm around his shoulders and guided him into the lobby and pushed him against the wall, then fished in his pouch for the gun. The front door eased shut on its hydraulic hinges, sealing us off from the roar of the rain. The only sound was the throb of pulse in my temples. I found the gun, put it in my jacket, pushed the kangaroo off me, and slumped back against the banister. I'd won the thing, but you couldn't tell it from the way we were both slumped in the corridor, depleted and quiet. The puddles of rain at our feet crept across the lobby floor until they ran together into one.

I watched Joey's eyelids flicker open. "Motherfucker," he said. He reached up and felt the back of his head, and his paw came back wet with more than rain.

I took the gun out of my pocket. "Get in the elevator."

We went upstairs. The kangaroo looked pretty funny sprawled across my couch, his awkward legs crossed and his useless tail pushing up a corner of his raincoat like some kind of tumor or erection. I kept the gun trained on him, switching hands as I shook out of my jacket and locked the door. The dirty white cloth had somehow made it upstairs, and the kangaroo rewrapped it around his head, a bandage now instead of a turban. I wiped my face clean with a paper towel from the kitchen and sat down across from the kangaroo, the coffee table between us.

I emptied my jacket, putting Testafer's electric gun on the shelf behind me and the envelope full of Pansy Greenleaf's make into my shirt pocket. Then I set the gun down on the table and slid my mirror onto my lap.

The make in the packet on the mirror was my last. I shook it out and pushed it into sloppy lines with a matchbook cover, and the kangaroo watched dazedly while I snorted them up. The familiar blend took over, and reality became standardized and comfortable again. I wiped at my nose with the back of my hand, picked up the gun, and leaned back in my chair.

"I want you to take me to Phoneblum," I said.

"You're making a mistake."

"It's my mistake to make." I pushed the telephone across the table. "Call him."

He took the telephone and punched in a local number, and his red eyes worked nervously around the room as he waited for an answer. It came after what must have been the third or fourth ring.

"Yeah," he said. "This is Castle. I need to talk to Danny. It's important. Tell him I'm with the pee-eye. No, just tell him."

He moved the receiver away from his mouth and said: "You're in luck, if you want to call it luck." I smiled, and he handed me the phone. I kept the gun pointed at his heart— assuming I had the location right.

"Hello," came a voice on the line.

"Hello," I said. "My name is Metcalf. You wanted to talk to me, I guess."

There was a moment of silence. "I sent someone to have a word with you, if that's what you mean. I would have thought my message was clear."

"You sent a kangaroo to do a man's work," I said. "I don't scare as easily as Dr. Testafer."

The voice laughed. "Dr. Testafer has a stronger stomach than he's letting on, Mr. Metcalf. You surprise me. I would have thought a man in your line of work would know when he should abandon his investigations. We had another private in-quisitor on this case who had to be helped to understand—"

"You would have thought a lot of things, apparently. When and where can we meet to set you straight?"

There was another silence. "I'm not sure I understand what the purpose of such a meeting would be."

"It's like this. I've got a client who's headed for the freezer, and if I can't stop it, I at least propose to find out why it's him who has to take the fall and who it is he's taking it for. You can't buy me off, and if Joey here is your arm, you can't bully me off either. Meet me or he goes over to Morgenlander. I don't think your kangaroo is ready to stand up to the Office screws, Phoneblum. If you think different, call my bluff."

"Morgenlander is a problem," said the voice thoughtfully, as though confiding in a friend. "You've got pretty much everything else dead wrong, but Morgenlander is a problem. Come and see me. We'll find out who sets who straight." He chuckled, then gave me an address in Piedmont. I set the gun down on my side of the table and wrote the address on the empty make envelope. He said seven o'clock and I said okay. Then I put the kangaroo back on the phone and started emptying the shells out of the gun.

The kangaroo said yes a few times and then hung up. "I have to go now," he said. "Give me the gun."

I pocketed the shells and tossed it to him, and he caught it against his chest. "You're a good boy," I said. "Phoneblum must be very pleased with your work. Just don't come around here anymore, okay?"

"Fuck you," he said, his eyes glaring from under the dirty white cloth. I pointed at the door.

He was on his way out when I said: "Phoneblum didn't seem overly concerned about you, Joey. Don't be surprised to find the rug pulled out from under you, if what's swept underneath it doesn't stay that way." I didn't really know anything; I was just flexing my muscles while I had the chance.

Joey screwed up his mouth, flared his nostrils, and slammed the door. I went to the window and watched him splash through the puddles back to wherever he'd hidden his scooter. When he turned the corner, I let out my breath and tried to relax, but my chest was all tight and there was a ringing sound in my ears. I closed my eyes and tried to breathe evenly for a couple of minutes, before giving it up and going into the kitchen for a drink.

I stood by the window and sipped on a glass of scotch and watched the sky darken as the sun fell behind its veil of clouds at the edge of the bay. The rain had stopped, but the sun was beaten, and it was crawling away. It had my blessings; I wanted to go with it, to some other part of the earth. I looked at the clock on the wall. It was five-thirty, an hour and a half before my meeting with Phoneblum. Then I looked at the refrigerator. I didn't have to open it to know there was nothing inside.

I had the pizzeria on the line when there was a knock at the door. "Come in," I said, figuring that anyone who wanted in would achieve it one way or another.

It was Angwine, only he looked more like a projection of Angwine than the real thing. His face was white and his voice came out a whisper. I had to calm him down to get a straight answer out of him.

"I took a cab up to see Testafer. There wasn't anybody there that I could see, but the door to the little house was standing open. I went over to it, and there was blood on the doorknob. I may have gotten my fingerprints in it, I don't know."

I told the pizzeria I'd call them back. "What did you see?" I asked him.

"Just blood, everywhere," he said. "I didn't want to get caught there."

"What did you want from Testafer?"

Angwine looked at the floor. "I couldn't sit still. I wanted to find out what he knew about Stanhunt and my sister. I wasn't followed up there, I'm sure. They were tailing me, but I shook them."

"You're stupid," I said. I put my drink on the shelf next to Testafer's electric gun.

Angwine went and sat on my couch where just minutes ago the kangaroo had been sitting. I opened the drawer in my desk, put the pocketful of bullets and Testafer's gun inside, then locked it. "You stay here," I said. "I'll go and have a look."

"I had to do something. It was driving me crazy."

"Shut up, okay? I understand."

He looked up at me as I went out the door, and I thought he might be about to start crying. I couldn't think of anything nice to say, so I left without saying anything.

CHAPTER 13

WHEN I GOT TO THE TOP OF THE HILL, I STOPPED THE CAR for a minute and watched the last traces of sunset dissipate into the night. It wasn't the best I'd ever seen, but it looked better than I felt. I got back into the car and drove into the lacing of streets that led to Daymont Court, where Testafer's home was waiting, mysteriously bloodied, for someone to blunder into. I figured it might as well be me. I parked a block away this time and walked through the puddles, down to the padlocked chain at the driveway. There weren't any other cars visible, no signs of the inquisitors. I was alone, if only for the moment.

In the dark the driveway seemed longer. The trees knit together over my head, and the reflections in the puddles were like a net stretched out between the clearing and the house. When I got to the end of the drive, I stopped, but there wasn't anything to see or hear. When I stepped into the moonlight in front of the house, I could see that the door to the sheep's apartment was open.

There was blood on the doorknob, all right. Thinking of Angwine, I wiped at it with my sleeve, but it had dried. The light was off in the apartment, so when I entered the little doorway, I had to grope around for the knob on one of the floor lamps. The first thing I saw was my hand; it was smeared with red just from touching the lamp. When I looked away from my hand, I almost knocked over a chair getting farther away from the thing I was standing practically on top of.

Someone had messed that sheep up bad. Someone had pretty much turned that sheep inside out. She was lying splayed on the blood-drenched carpet, and there were little pieces of her spread out nearly to the four corners of the room. A stomach-curdling stench rising from the carcass told me the lower intestine had been opened. My hand went re-flexively to my forehead before I thought of the blood on it, and I printed my brow with sticky red. I backed away to lean against something and hit my head against the ceiling.

I looked at the corpse again, forcing myself to try to find something meaningful in the way the killing had been done, but I couldn't concentrate. The dug-out cavity was like a maze that led my eyes against their will again and again to the mu-tilated black-red heart. I didn't have what it took to search that maze for clues, so I turned off the light and went outside.

I went over to the main house and tried the handle, but the door was locked. Suddenly spooked, I put my hands in my pockets and jogged down the driveway back towards Daymont. I made it to my car without being seen, and drove out of the hills and down into Berkeley.

I must not have been paying much attention to where I was going, because I cruised right into a checkpoint cordon on Alcatraz Avenue. Before I knew what was happening the inquisitors had the whole block cut off from the flow of traf-fic. Blinding light shone into my car. I could hear a dog bay-ing somewhere, frightened by the sirens of the inquisition.

There was a knock on the window of my car. I kneaded the blood off my forehead with my thumb and rolled the window down to see two helmeted inquisitors brandishing riot wands and flashlights. The one closest to my car leaned down and said: "Hand me your card and your job license."

I dug the two chits out of my pocket and handed them over without saying anything. The inquisitor gave them to his partner and put his face farther into my car. I slumped back in my seat, but he was still too close.

"Where are you going?"

"Home," I said.

"Where are you coming from?"

"Just driving around."

"He's a private dick," said the other one. "Conrad Metcalf."

"Just driving around, eh? You on a case?"

I must have been trembling. The image of the slaughtered sheep kept replaying itself before my eyes, and for an irrational minute I imagined they knew, and that the cordon had been set up expressly to bring me in. "Nope," I said.

"Forty points," said the other one. "That's pretty low."

"That's what I said to the guy who left me that way," I said.

"What did you do?"

"Nothing."

"If we called your name into the Office, what would we find out?"

"Try it and see."

"I think I will," he said. "Pull over to the side and turn off your motor."

I did what he said, and sat in my car watching the checkpoint proceed while I waited for the guy to access my file. The boys worked the cars over pretty carefully, opening a few up, rifling through trunks and glove compartments. They ran a lot of karma through the decoder and shook their heads reproachfully before handing back the cards. At one point a bunch of them got together and strip-searched a brunette in the back of her car. It was a fairly standard operation. I'd seen more than a few in my time that were worse.

After a while the two guys came back to my car and gave me my card and license. The first one was smiling cryptically. "Your file's up for review," he said. "Unavailable."

"What do you mean?"

"Good luck, pal. Nice knowing you. Move along."

"Unavailable?"

"I said move along."

They opened up the barricade and I drove through.

CHAPTER 14

I HAD AN AWFUL SENSE OF FOREBODING GOING UP IN THE elevator, but when I got to my apartment, everything was the same, almost eerily so. Angwine had fallen asleep on the couch in the same spot he'd been in when I left. The lights were on and there was tinny music drifting out of the radio. I reached over and shut it off, and took my drink from the shelf and brought it with me into the kitchen. The ice had melted, but I didn't care.

I thought over my options. My fingerprints were all over the Testafer house, and I'd been cordoned coming out of the hills by the checkpoint boys. Assuming Testafer hadn't done the killing himself, he'd be coming home and raising quite a fuss any minute now. It was probably in my best interests to get hold of the Office and tell them what I knew before they came asking. If Angwine had really shaken his tail, I might pick up some much-needed points of karma by putting them onto him. It certainly couldn't hurt. It was time to cash in a few chips just to keep this game running smoothly—hell, just to keep it running at all.

I stood in the doorway and watched Angwine snore. I felt sorry for him but I didn't feel guilty. There was nothing more

I could do than what I was doing. He was the type of guy who once upon a time would have slipped between the chinks, back when the world still had chinks to slip through. The way it was now, his type didn't stand a chance. In fact, it didn't look too good for my type either. But I didn't have any regrets. I turned off the lights on Angwine and brought my drink into the bedroom.

I sat on the edge of the bed and called the Office and asked for Morgenlander. The girl at the other end said he wasn't in the building. I asked for Catherine Teleprompter and got the same answer. When I told her I wanted to report a murder, she informed me that she would be tracing the call. I said I was surprised she hadn't already, and she didn't say anything at all, just switched me to another line. The voice on duty was a male inquisitor voice with a weary, skeptical air.

"You want to report a murder," he intoned.

"That's right. An evolved sheep was killed. I found the body."

"That's not a murder," he said. "What's your name?"

"Private Inquisitor Metcalf. I'm working on the Stanhunt killing, and I think the two are probably connected."

"Where did this happen?"

"In a private house in El Cerrito." I recited the address.

"Where are you now?"

"At home."

There was a minute while the inquisitor played with his monitor. I could hear his fingers tapping.

"Conrad Metcalf," he said.

"That's right."

"You'd better come in, Metcalf. No, sit tight, and I'll send a man over. Don't leave your apartment. We'll come to you."

"Sounds nice, but I've got other plans. Thanks anyway."

"I'm suspending your license," he said. "Stay in your apartment."

"Sorry. We'll have to make it some other time. Tell Morgenlander he can leave a message on my home number."

I put the squawking receiver back on the hook and finished my drink. I was playing it existential, and maybe a bit stupid, but it was the only way I knew how to play it. The Office was about to throw a blanket over the case, and I had to have that conversation with Phoneblum before they did.

Phoneblum had to be the key. He had his leash on Pansy Greenleaf, Dr. Testafer, the kangaroo, and both of the Stanhunts, including the deceased. It looked like he might have one on Inquisitor Kornfeld as well. He'd flinched when I mentioned Morgenlander—the rogue brass that had Kornfeld and Teleprompter and probably the rest of the Office all jumpy.

I wished I knew more. How the sheep's murder fit in, or the blueprints for animal barracks on Cranberry Street. What Maynard Stanhunt had been doing in that fleabag motel. And what the high and mighty Stanhunts had to do anyway with the pale little junkie Pansy Greenleaf. I would have liked to believe Orton Angwine's theory, that Dr. Stanhunt had been having an affair with Pansy, but I couldn't do it.

No, I couldn't afford to wait around here for the inquisitors to arrive. I had business elsewhere, even if I didn't really know what that business was. There was only one problem: what to do with Angwine. If I left him sleeping in the apartment, the only thing missing would be wrapping paper and a bow.

I put my glass in the sink. Angwine was still snoring in the dark. I went over and nudged his leg with my shoe. His eyes flickered open. "I'm going out," I said. "The door locks by itself. I wouldn't stay here if I were you."

I took a hat from the closet, put my jacket back on, and unlocked the drawer with the gun in it. I didn't want to complicate things for the boys when they went through the apartment. As I went out the door, Angwine was sitting up on the couch with an astonished look on his face, as if he'd been interrupted in the middle of a nice, believable dream.

I'd crossed the street to my car when the Office van pulled up in front of the building. I ducked behind my car and watched through the windows as they got out and marched up into the foyer, all clustered together like a school of predatory fish. When they were safely inside, I got into my car and started the engine, my hand shaking on the safety brake. I couldn't afford to wait around and see what happened. It was pretty predictable, anyway. I drove around the block and pulled over until the shaking stopped.

In a way my work would be easier with Angwine out of my hair. I'd been overextending myself to protect him, losing my objectivity. Now I could operate as a free agent, protecting nothing but my own interests. It suited me better. If I could untwist the truth from the untruth in the process, then maybe Angwine would get his money's worth. If not—well, I would have tried, and besides, it wasn't really his money in the first place. I felt okay.

I felt like an absolute bastard.

CHAPTER 15

It was six-thirty. I drove into Oakland, parked on a quiet side street, and walked down to the avenue. The makery was the only storefront open on the street, and its neon lights were reflected in the puddles of rain and on the windows of the closed shops. There was a stiff wind rushing off the bay towards a collision with the hills, and it bit at my ears and nose as I went up the steps to the makery entrance. An electronic bell sounded as I opened the door. I lowered my collar and walked up to the counter.

"I'll be right with you," said the maker, squinting into his monitor, his lined face and wire-rimmed glasses bathed in green. He was maybe forty-five, but his hairline had backed away to leave him a high, wrinkled forehead, and the hair at his ears was as white as the powder lying in careful little piles on his lab table. He copied a chemical formula onto a pad at his left without looking away from the screen, then punched up another set of names and recipes and muttered to himself about what he saw. I just stood and watched.

"Name," he said, turning to me. His eyes, magnified in the lenses, worked over me quickly and indifferently while he waited.

"Conrad Metcalf," I said, and then surprised him with my blend code. I had it stuck in my head. I don't know why.

He turned back to the keyboard and punched it in. "Acceptol," he said.

"Mostly."

"Don't see many blends without Forgettol nowadays," he said.

"Never liked it—"

"One man's—"

"Right. Listen…if I gave you a couple of names, could you dial up the recipes for their blends on that screen?"

He stopped what he was doing at the keyboard and turned to stare at me blankly. "That was a question you just asked me, mister."

I put my license on the counter and waited while he looked at it. He held his glasses with one hand and kept the other hand in the air, as if touching the thing would bring him bad luck. When he looked up again, I slipped it back into my coat pocket.

"What about it?"

"You know I can't do that," he said in a pinched, reproving voice. He squinted at me painfully. From my jacket I brought out one of Angwine's hundreds and tore it in half up the middle, and put it where my license had been. The maker looked at it a little more favorably than he had the license. He adjusted his glasses with a little push at the nosepiece, and then looked up at me with his hand still in the middle of his face.

"I'd want one like that for each name," he said quietly.

I smiled and took out another hundred and ripped it and put the same half out on the counter. The other two halves went in my pocket. "Grover Testafer," I said.

He turned nervously to his keyboard and punched it in. "It'll take a minute," he said. "I have to search the code. He uses another makery." His fingers moved indecipherably fast on the keys, his brow furrowing into the green light, as if he were some kind of subterranean creature worshiping a phosphorescent god. A recipe appeared on the screen. "Standard," he announced. "Forgettol, Avoidol, addictol. Nothing special. Lots of Avoidol."

"Tell me about Avoidol. I don't use it."

He liked shoptalk. It relaxed him. "Accelerates repression, basically. And equivocation. I'll add it to your blend if you want to try it out."

"No thanks."

There was a sound at the door that made us both turn and look. I went quickly over and pulled. The guy on the other side had his hand on the knob, and I yanked it out of his hand.

"Excuse me," he said.

I took out my license and flashed it too fast for him to read. His mouth opened and worked for a second, but nothing came out.

"We'll be closed for a few minutes," I said. "Sorry for the inconvenience."

The guy saw I wasn't moving. He went away mumbling, and I closed the door and went back to the counter. The two ripped halves of the hundreds had disappeared from view; in their place was a fresh vial of my blend, labeled with the makery sticker and my recipe code. I slipped it into my coat pocket and said: "Okay. Forget Testafer. Try Maynard Stanhunt."

If he recognized the name from the radio murder report yesterday, it didn't show. "This is a little more interesting," he said after the formula flashed up on his monitor. I looked over his shoulder, but the symbols didn't mean anything to me.

"The blend is almost straight Forgettol," he said. He looked more closely. "What's funny is the stuff he's taking as a modifier." He rolled the formula off the top of the screen and studied the rest of Stanhunt's file.

"What do you mean?"

"I've heard this was on the way," he said, "but this is the first I've seen. He's using a time-release ingredient. It's a way of linking up doses so you don't ever come clean. Very clever, if you can handle it."

"What if you can't?"

He snickered. "You'd forget what you do for a living, what street you live on, your name—that sort of thing."

"What are the advantages?"

He looked at me quizzically. He'd caught himself running on and suddenly thought better of it. I was afraid he'd clam up completely, but he said: "I don't know what it is I'm getting myself into."

"You're not getting yourself into anything. I'll walk out of here and you'll be two bills richer. What are the advantages of the modifier?"

He rubbed at his forehead with pinched fingers, and I could see him swallow hard. "Your man is a doctor, or he's got a doctor helping him out. Or he's very stupid. Anytime you try to regulate Forgettol, it's a delicate balancing act. Someday they'll work it out, but they haven't yet." He smiled a funny smile. "If he's doing it right, he can eradicate whole portions of his experience with the make, then sew up the gap for a sense of continuity. That would be the point: to be busy at things you don't want ever to think about. No return of what's repressed. That's if he's doing it right, which he isn't. Because it can't be controlled like that." He looked at me angrily. "If that's all…"

"Not quite." I dug in my hip pocket and came up with the folded hundred-dollar bill full of make scooped off Pansy Greenleaf's night table. It was a payoff and a container all in one. "Take a look at this," I said, sliding it across the counter.

His goggle eyes darted from my face to the packet a couple of times, and then his curiosity or greed got the better of him, and he took it to the microscope. I leaned across the counter and watched. He glared up at me from the eyepiece of the microscope and then started flipping through a reference volume that was open on the table. He went from viewer to book to monitor, then scooped the make into a manila envelope and put it back on the counter. The hundred had vanished.

"I wouldn't go showing that around if I were you," he said carefully.

"What is it?"

"Blanketrol. A controlled ingredient. Put it away."

"What does it do?"

The lines on his forehead doubled. "I'll tell you about Blanketrol," he said, "and then I want you to take it and go. I'll pretend I don't think you know all about it already."

"Whatever makes you happy."

"Blanketrol is very crude stuff," he said. "It was the original prototype for Forgettol. They withdrew it when they found out it was completely hollowing out the inner life of the test subjects. The users went on functioning, but just by rote." He pinched at the nose of his glasses again. "Think of it as the opposite of déjà vu—nothing reminds you of anything, not even of itself."

"Lovely."

"I'm glad you think so. Now put it away, give me my money, and get out before I call the Office."

I looked up into his magnified eyes, and they blinked away from the contact. I took the packet and put it in my pocket. The makery sickened me suddenly, and nothing seemed lower or dirtier than this owl-eyed little germ of a maker sententiously deeming one ingredient more legitimate than another. I reached across the counter and got him by the collar before either one of us had any idea what I was doing.

I improvised. "Keep your half of the money," I said. "And I'll keep mine. I'll need your help again before too long. If you want to call the Office, go ahead. I think we both understand why that wouldn't be such a bright idea. See you in a day or two." I pushed him away from the counter, then buttoned up my coat and went outside without giving him a chance to say anything back.

When I got into my car, I rolled down the window and sat there for a minute, the wind whistling through the grille and pushing a series of brittle leaves over the hood and away up into the hills. My mood was sour. I wasn't sure I liked the idea of a case where the only thing I had to go on was the different drugs the principals took. Reminded me too much of my life.

I felt in my pocket for the new vial of make, just to be sure it was there. It was—and so was the packet of Blanketrol. I thought for a long, bleak minute about using it, and then I took it out and opened the car door and scattered it into the gutter.

CHAPTER 16

THE ADDRESS PHONEBLUM HAD GIVEN ME TURNED OUT TO be a house in the hills, and this house in particular had one hill all to itself. It was pretty impressive. But as I walked up to it in the darkness, I saw the luminous glow of holographic projectors on both sides of the pathway, and when I crossed the beam, the house dissipated into the night, to reveal a tin-roofed stairwell jutting out of the ground like a subway entrance. I turned the handle and opened the door. The steps were carpeted with orange Astro Turf, and there was illegible graffiti scrawled and then rubbed out on the walls. Phoneblum disappointed fast. I might have stopped and scrawled something myself, but I was already late for my appointment, and besides, I couldn't think of anything to write. Maybe on the way out.

At the bottom of the steps was a harshly lit concrete floor. I could make out a shadow crossing back and forth in front of what must have been an unshaded bulb, nothing more. I went halfway down the steps, and a pair of feet came into view, peeking out from underneath some kind of table or desk. They tapped out a lackadaisical rhythm on the concrete. I went the rest of the way down the steps.

The guy behind the desk couldn't have been more than fifty, but his face was all blossomed with red, as if his veins were working their way out of his skin in some sort of escape bid. Once I caught a whiff of his breath, I didn't blame them. The smell infiltrated my nose and started tugging on my nostril hairs. If this was Phoneblum, our conversation wasn't going to last very long, and if it wasn't, I understood why the guy had been retired to an underground desk. He wouldn't have been much use in the field: the breath was an unmistakable tattoo, the ultimate fingerprint. The guy smiled to let more of it out of the corners of his mouth, and I almost fainted. He looked pleased to see me, and when the gun muzzle bumped into my spine, I understood his confidence.

The gun turned out to be attached to the kangaroo. He kept the nose of it pressed into my back while he worked over my pockets with his front paw. I lifted my arms and waited for him to finish. When he came to the pocket with the vial of make, he reached in and drew it out. I watched over my shoulder as he tried to read the label, his furry brow knit in concentration, his throat bobbing as he worked out the syllables subvocally. I grabbed it and slipped it back in my pocket to put him out of his misery.

He pushed me forward with a thump on the shoulder and said: "He's clean." I think he was disappointed at not finding an excuse to kick me in the stomach.

"Good," said the man at the desk, smiling again. "Take him down."

The kangaroo put his hand on the back of my neck and guided me down the hallway and through a couple of doors and into a waiting elevator. We got in and turned around to face the door, ignoring each other like real passengers in a normal elevator—except for the gun in his hand. After his humiliation at the front of my apartment building, the kangaroo was pretending he didn't know me. It suited me fine.

We sank slowly past a couple of levels and hit bottom with a grinding of gears and a rattle of chains. The door opened, and the kangaroo pushed me out into the living room of what had to be Phoneblum's hideaway.

The place was mocked up to suggest the house that must once upon a time have existed on top, where now there was only the hologram. Antique furniture was arranged in a broad circle around an authentic-looking fireplace, and there were even logs piled to one side, so maybe it wasn't just for show. The ceiling was scrolled with ornate plasterwork, but I couldn't avoid the feeling that this was just an attentive detail on an old-time movie set. It was more thorough than most fakes, that's all. There were curtains, but I could see there weren't any windows behind them. If there had been windows, they would have opened onto dirt and earthworms, like a science-class diorama. It would have been interesting, but I guess it wasn't quite the effect they were after.

"Put the gun away, Joey." Phoneblum—this time I was sure it was Phoneblum—entered the room through the bedroom doorway and stubbed out a cigar in an ashtray on the desk. When it was out, he held it to his nose and sniffed at it, then put it carefully alongside the ashtray. His fingers were fat but graceful—I reserved judgment on the rest of him. There must have been the skeleton of a colossus under that flesh, but if there was a bone or a sharp edge of any kind in him, I couldn't find it. He was wearing a shirt and pants but, stretched over that much bulk, they looked like a tarpaulin or sailcloth. There was an enormous sweater over that, and then a matching scarf around his neck to pin his white beard against his expansive chest. His forehead was high, but a plentiful thatch of hair rose up above it to sweep back over his skull, and his eyebrows were cocked intelligently above eyes that were nearly buried in flesh. Despite all this he carried himself with a kind of grace or vanity that contained within it a memory of something that once was: the suggestion of a young, thin man entombed inside this old, enormously fat one. "Go upstairs," he said to Joey, and the kangaroo went obediently back to the elevator. I stood staring. The fat man turned to me and smiled without malice. "Have a seat, Mr. Metcalf."

I sat down in a chair and left the couch for Phoneblum. He'd need it. When the elevator closed on the kangaroo, the fat man moved to a position behind the couch and gripped the back of it with both hands, then tilted his bulk over it. His scarf tumbled loose across the cushions. "You say we have something to talk about," he said. His voice was deep and theatrical, with a quality of burnished wood, but the tone was neutral.

"I keep turning corners and bumping into your kangaroo," I said. "That'll do for starters."

"You are an inquisitor."

"That's right."

"Do questions make you uncomfortable? I prefer to relax the conventional strictures."

"Fine with me. Questions are my bread and butter."

The fleshy pie of a face laughed. "Very good. And I'll help you to understand which side your questions are buttered on, and who it is that does the buttering. You see, I'm old enough, Mr. Metcalf, to remember a time when—ah, but you'll grow impatient if I allow myself to reminisce. Permit me to offer you a drink…"

I nodded. He pushed his bulk away from the couch with

surprisingly little effort, and opened a cabinet full of amber bottles and matching beveled glass tumblers. Without asking he poured me a glassful of what turned out to be scotch, and I took it without saying thank you. I sucked down about half of it while he settled himself into the couch.

"Joey has an egotistical streak," he said, almost apologetically. "He doesn't mean any harm. He tries to please, and he's quite intelligent. I have to help him learn to curb his enthusiasm."

"Where I come from, you don't teach puppets. You just pull their strings."

"Oh! That's not fair to either of us, Mr. Metcalf. Joey's far more than a puppet, and I prefer to think of myself as something more subtle than a puppeteer. A catalyst, perhaps."

He was a talker, in an age where talkers were few and far between. I was a talker myself, but I was a jaded professional. Phoneblum looked to have a hobbyist's passion for it.

"I'm not really that interested in your opinion of yourself," I said. "You sent Joey to muscle me off the case. I've got a chipped tooth to show for it."

"I would think that sort of thing was a part of your chosen profession."

"It doesn't mean I have to like it. You want me off this case. Why?"

"I don't care one way or another about the case. You were upsetting people I care for, and I asked you to stop."

"People you care for. Who would that be?"

"Dr. Testafer, Celeste Stanhunt, and the children at Cranberry Street."

"There's only one child now at Cranberry Street, Phoneblum, and that's the kitten. The people you say you care for—it's the same bunch that turns white at the mention of your name."

That slowed him down. His eyebrows knit together and then rose skeptically across the broad canvas of his forehead—they seemed to have developed compensatory powers of expression as the rest of his body grew blunt. He raised his drink and took a sip, drawing it out until he could think of a reply.

"My life is complicated," he intoned. "The inquisition has taken my most cherished possessions from me. I live at cross-purposes to society. I do my best to maintain the fragile connections between what was and what is, but as often as not, the thread is broken…" He squeezed his eyes shut in pain.

He was a ham. I was a method actor, but he was a ham. "Dr. Testafer called you a gangster," I said. "He's not so young—"

"Dr. Testafer may not appreciate my benevolence," he interrupted angrily, "but rest assured, he lives his life out according to my good graces."

I threw a curve ball. "I was up there tonight. Somebody butchered his sheep."

Phoneblum looked momentarily startled. He stretched out and put his glass on the wooden arm of the couch.

"Don't worry," I said. "They'll pin it on Angwine. It's made to order."

"You lose a client," he said.

"That's right. You may live at cross-purposes to the Office, but from where I stand you both look to benefit from Angwine's frame."

"I've never even met Angwine."

"You'll never get a chance to now. His time is up. You and the Office went to dinner and he's footing the bill."

"Then what, if I might ask, is the purpose of continuing your inquisition?"

"I'm restless. I think the frame is jerry-rigged. If I find the right nail to pry out, the whole thing'll come crashing down around your shoulders."

"A beautiful image. I wish you luck. You don't seriously think the Office will entertain your suspicions for long, once they've closed the case themselves, do you? How good is your karma?"

"My karma is none of your business. It'll hold out long enough."

"Oh my." He picked up his drink again, and sighed philosophically—he was the kind who could do it. "You remind me of myself, once upon a time. We're not really that different even now. We chafe at our bits—but you're stubborn, inflexible. Stupid, finally. I've learned to compromise. In negotiation lies power, viability. Your inflexibility has rendered you marginal."

"It isn't me who lives underground, Phoneblum."

"That's it. Growl and nip. It's very frightening."

"I didn't need to growl to frighten Celeste Stanhunt," I said. I wanted to bring it back to the facts of the case, the clues, if they could be called that. "She was scared because she got me confused with one of your goons. What've you got on her?"

"You misunderstand our relationship. I introduced Maynard Stanhunt to his future bride. You might say they were my creation. Celeste is very forgetful, but she owes me a great deal, and in her more lucid moments she'll acknowledge it."

"Towards the end your creation wasn't doing so well.

Stanhunt hired me to keep tabs on Celeste when she ran away to Cranberry Street."

"Yes," he said darkly. "She is like that. We were always 'keeping tabs' on Celeste."

"Is Pansy Greenleaf Celeste's girlfriend?"

His eyebrows almost managed to tie themselves in a knot. "No, no. Nothing like that. A friend of the family."

"Another one who lives her life out according to your good graces?"

"As you wish."

"Well, your graces aren't so good for our little friend Pansy. I found her nodding out on illegal make, taking it in the arm. Something called Blanketrol, for people who aren't satisfied just to forget. According to a maker I talked to, Pansy is scooping out the insides of her head like a Halloween pumpkin."

"Her brother committed a murder. I understand why she might want—"

"Yeah," I said, cutting him off. "Who supplied her with the stuff?"

"Are you accusing me of something?"

"As you wish."

He smiled and took another sip from his drink. I took the opportunity to lean back and breathe slowly. I needed it. I wasn't accustomed to the questions going in both directions. Plus I felt a little hemmed in here, in Phoneblum's underground house. I thought about the kangaroo and the man with the breath waiting in their brightly lit concrete bunker, and I wondered if it would be as easy getting out of this hole as it had been getting in.

"I don't even use make," said Phoneblum after swallowing the gulp of scotch. "Let alone distribute it. I've known about Pansy's indiscretions for years, and it's very distressing to hear she's taken up the needle, but I've learned I'm power-less to stop it. Are you a user? I've never understood it, myself."

"I've got a blend for when I need it." I cursed myself silently for the defensive way it came out.

"The Office and the makery—they're one and the same to me," he said. "Make is a tool for controlling great masses of people. It homogenizes their response to repression, don't you think? You consider yourself an outsider, a seeker of truth amidst lies, yet you've bought into the biggest lie that can be told. You snort that lie through your nose and let it run in your bloodstream."

"Fuck you."

"Woof."

"Let's get back to specifics," I said. Control of the con-versation kept reeling away from me. Phoneblum had actu-ally reminded me that I could use a line or two of my blend, but I didn't see anywhere handy to spread it out. "You've known Pansy for a couple of years. Who fathered the kid?"

"I have no idea," he said.

"Who paid for the house? That's a pretty nice neighborhood."

He sighed again. "You're forcing me into some uncom-fortable revelations, Mr. Metcalf. Pansy Greenleaf worked for me once. I helped her acquire the Cranberry Street property two and a half years ago."

"Two and a half years ago. The same time Celeste mar-ried Stanhunt."

"Is that true? How interesting."

"Yeah. Interesting. Were Celeste and Pansy friends back then?"

"I recommended Pansy for a job in Maynard's office," Phoneblum explained. It started to smack of improvisation, but his verbal skills were bridging the gaps in logic. "It didn't work out, but the women remained friends."

"A few years ago that wasn't Maynard Stanhunt's office," I reminded him. "It belonged to Dr. Testafer. I guess you helped with the transition."

"Indeed."

"Why your interest in the practice? What was in it for you?"

"I have need of doctors," he said. I waited for him to continue but he didn't.

I finished my drink and put the empty glass on the floor between my feet and his. "You mentioned another detective who warned off better than I did."

"After you refused Maynard your services, he turned to me to arrange for someone to 'keep tabs,' as you said, on Celeste. I hired another man to pick up where you left off. Maynard left it to me—after his bad experience with you he didn't want to meet the new fellow, and I obliged him in that."

"What's his name?"

"I have a feeling you want to go and bother the man."

"That's right."

"He didn't last long, you know. He was fired six days before the murder."

"Great. What's his name?"

The big man chuckled. "What would be my motive for telling you that?"

"Simple. I'll find out one way or another. Either you tell me or I bother your loved ones about it."

"Very well. There's something I like about letting you go

on thinking your threats are effective with me. I suppose I admire your bluster. His name is Walter Surface. But you'll find he knows nothing."

"I'm still interested. Who watched Celeste after Surface?"

"After two failures I was able to convince Maynard of the futility of outside surveillance. He requested that my staff keep an eye on Celeste, and I agreed. That was the end of it."

"Was anyone shadowing her at the time of the murder?"

Phoneblum's face clouded. I'd stumbled onto something, but I didn't know what. He puffed up his cheeks and then let them slacken like a rubber bellows. His free hand stroked his beard while his forehead enacted its ritual dance. "Unfortunately, no," he said softly. "We have no record of her whereabouts."

Had Celeste done the killing, after all? And was Phoneblum trying to cover for her?

It seemed wrong, but I didn't know what seemed righter. "What was Stanhunt doing in the Bayview Motel?" I asked.

"If only I knew."

"Were you ever questioned by the Office? You're in this up to your neck."

"The Office doesn't question me," he said in a flat tone. I guess he was just being honest. He seemed to have fallen into an introspective, distracted mood. "Besides, my hands are clean. That must be evident even to you."

"The Office doesn't seem to bother you—yet on the phone you jumped at the mention of Morgenlander. What makes him different?"

"Morgenlander is an outsider. He's a crusader, and he's unwelcome."

"You contradict yourself, Phoneblum. The Office is your friend or it isn't. You can't have it both ways."

"The Office and I have arrived at an understanding. An iconoclast like Morgenlander is a threat to stability. He pokes around at things that don't require his attention. Like you."

"Thanks. I felt an instant affinity with the guy when he smacked me in the mouth."

"You're quite a complainer, Mr. Metcalf. I should think you take such things in stride by now."

Trying to think of an answer just made me feel tired. I picked up my glass and got out of the chair.

"I'm sorry," said Phoneblum. "I should have offered you a second."

"No, but thanks no. I'm drinking on an empty stomach." I put my glass in the cabinet with the bottles and wiped the condensation from my hands on the seat of my pants. "I guess I'll stop bothering you. Thanks for your time."

"Just a minute. Why do you think I permitted you to question me?"

"You tell me."

"I like you. I believe your intentions are honorable. It pleases me to save you trouble. Drop the case now and I'll see to it that your missing karma is restored. There's no future in this inquisition, Mr. Metcalf. No future at all."

"You like to mix up your threats with your enticements, Phoneblum."

"I haven't threatened anyone. I simply want to repair the damage that's already been done."

"The damage to Angwine is on the verge of becoming unrepairable. Nobody will maintain his body. He'll get shuffled into some cut-rate ice chest and disappear forever."

Phoneblum smiled in a complicated way. It gave me the feeling I was touching on something again, but I didn't know what, and Phoneblum wasn't about to set me straight.

"You have a very cynical view of our penal system, Mr. Metcalf," he said softly. "Cynical, yet somewhat naive. What makes you think unsponsored bodies necessarily remain frozen?"

"You mean the slave camps," I said, and shuddered. I hoped it didn't show. I got the feeling that Phoneblum was subtly boasting, that he just couldn't help showing off.

"Yes."

"I've heard that rumor," I said, regaining my poise. "Personally I don't see much difference between the big freeze and crypto-life with a slavebox on your skull. But if I see Angwine again, I'll ask him which he prefers and let you know—maybe you can arrange something."

I was ready to leave, and I started leaving. I was over to the elevator before I realized there was a keyhole where the button should have been.

"It's rude of you to suggest I could arrange such a thing," said Phoneblum, ever coy. But when I turned around, I saw he wasn't smiling anymore. "But then, I'm learning to expect that of you. You're rude generally."

"Thanks."

"Now you want to leave."

"That's right."

"I'd like to hear you say you'll leave the case alone."

"I'd like to be able to say it."

Phoneblum frowned. He picked up the phone on the desk and pressed a single button. "Yes," he said immediately. "Send Joey downstairs, Mr. Rose. Our visitor is ready to leave."

He put down the phone. "Please—have another drink while you wait."

I didn't get a chance to refuse his offer. The elevator door opened behind me, and before I could turn, something dull and heavy smashed itself into the back of my neck. I had long enough to think: the kangaroo had found his chance. Then the floor peeled up in a curl to embrace the sides of my head, and the weave of the carpet spiraled up to tickle the inside of my nose. It was a very interesting sensation.

CHAPTER 17

I CAME TO IN MY CAR. I COULD THANK THEM FOR THAT. They put my keys back in the wrong pocket, so I knew they'd gone through my clothes, but otherwise it was pretty much as if I'd fallen asleep in the car on a stakeout—except for the pulse of pain in my neck and the ringing in my ears.

I was alone. I turned my head slowly, experimenting with my neck, and looked out the passenger window. The holographic house stood still and dark and peaceful, looking very much the same as when I'd first approached it. I'd learned a few of its secrets since then, but they didn't show on the house. With a little luck the world could end, and that house would still be projected onto the crest of the hill, still and dark and peaceful. It was almost comforting.

I looked at my watch. It was ten. I'd spent two hours with Phoneblum, and maybe half an hour out cold in my car. I was hungry and I needed a line of make, and after that I might need a drink—I wasn't sure yet. I needed to sort out what I'd learned from Phoneblum and figure out where it left me. The big man had his fingers all over the case, but I didn't see any clear-cut culpability for the murders, not yet.

All I knew was that I had to go back two and a half years,

to when Celeste met Maynard Stanhunt, and Pansy Greenleaf acquired her baby and her house. What happened then, whatever it was, set the stage for everything that followed.

I'd also grown more than a little curious about the exact nature of Phoneblum's racket. If he supplied Pansy with her illegal Blanketrol, it would explain one of the key lines of influence. And if he really had as much sway with the Office as he suggested, I needed to know—to protect myself.

Other, more basic questions remained unanswered. What *had* Maynard Stanhunt been doing in that motel room? I could have laughed at myself, but I wasn't in a laughing mood.

I took a minute to rub the back of my neck, then started the car and drove, aimlessly, down into the flats. I had a feeling the Office would be waiting for me when I got home, and I wasn't quite ready to face them. They would want answers I didn't have, to questions I would rather ask than be asked. I'd left them Angwine gift-wrapped, but I had a feeling it wasn't as easy as that.

There was some kind of factionalism going on between Morgenlander and Phoneblum and their separate spheres of influence, and until I understood how things had shaken out, it was best to stay out of the Office's hands. If I knew the Office machinery, they'd seize on the killing of the sheep as the last nail in Angwine's coffin—but I had to wait until the news came out tomorrow morning and made it official. A closed case would be harder to solve, but I'd step on fewer toes trying.

Everything pointed towards spending some time in my office. I could order a sandwich and lay out some lines and wait for the stakeout in my apartment to get tired and go home. If the inquisitors wanted me, they could find me—I wouldn't be hiding, just cooling my heels. I liked the place at night; cool, dark, and no dentist. Maybe I'd get some thinking done.

I guess I should learn that it's never that simple. When I left the elevator, I smelled perfume, and it got stronger as I went down the hallway to my office. There wasn't anybody in the corridor, but the door to the waiting room was unlocked, and inside, sitting cross-legged on the couch, was Celeste Stanhunt. I must have surprised her, because she quickly swung her legs off the couch and arranged her skirt down over her knees. It didn't matter. I don't possess an eidetic memory, but I had a picture of her knees—and the creamy inches of skin above them—burned into my consciousness from the brief flash as I walked in. I could draw on that for reference if I needed to.

"Metcalf," she said, and it sounded like she'd been practicing while she waited.

"How'd you get in?"

"I came earlier—"

"The dentist."

"Yes. Don't be angry."

"I'm not angry," I said, and I crossed the room and unlocked the door to my inner office. "I'm tired and hungry and my head hurts. I'm tired of talking."

She followed me in. "Pansy said you'd been to the house."

"That's right. I was working."

I sat down behind the desk and wiped at the wooden surface with my forearm, took out the vial of new make, and sprinkled a healthy portion of it onto the desktop. I guess Celeste figured out that for the moment she wasn't the primary focus of my attention. She sat quietly in the chair opposite the desk and waited while I snorted up some lines.

"You hungry?" I asked.

She shook her head as if the question frightened her. I called downstairs and ordered a pizza. I had to wheedle a bit to get them to put mushrooms on a small, but they finally came around. I put down the phone and leaned back in my chair and savored the feel of the make flushing through my system. Like looking at the world through a rose-colored bloodstream, or something. Celeste arranged herself in the seat and ended up showing knee again, which quickly refocused my attention.

"Where were you when I came by the house?" I asked.

"You ask too many questions. It makes me nervous."

"Try answering one. I hear it helps."

She blinked at me. "I—Grover Testafer called me. We met for lunch."

"What for?"

"He wanted to talk about the practice—the settlement of Maynard's share. He wanted to talk about Pansy's brother, and about you—"

"Do you stand to benefit from Maynard's death?"

She looked at me sharply, and I got a momentary glimpse of the tough girl who confronted me the first time, on Cranberry Street. Then she smoothed her feathers back down and her voice came out pretty. "Not really. I'll probably turn it over to a lawyer to handle. I don't want anything to do with it. Maynard had a substantial income but very few assets…"

"You sound like you know what you're talking about."

"I didn't until this afternoon, when Grover filled me in."

I tried to put the chronology together. Grover had been home waving an electric gun at me at eleven in the morning—and by the time I got to Cranberry Street, Pansy Greenleaf was already alone in the house nodding out on Blanketrol.

That meant Testafer could claim Celeste as an alibi for the killing of the sheep. It also meant Celeste had been out somewhere, doing something else, before her lunch date with Testafer.

My train of thought was interrupted by a knock at the door. I said it was open, and a human pizza-boy came in with the white cardboard slab and laid it on the desk. He was gangly and pimpled and kept glancing furtively at Celeste Stanhunt while I dug in my pocket for something smaller than Angwine's hundreds. I paid and tipped him, and he left. The pizza was hot, but it was the second time around for the crust, and the mushrooms weren't embedded in the cheese, just thrown on top. I took a couple of bites off the end of a slice, then fit it back into its place in the pie, unable to sustain my interest.

"What's next for you?" I asked. "The case is closed."

"I don't know how to do this," she said. "I...I want to hire you."

"In connection with what?"

"I don't think Pansy's brother killed Maynard. I'm frightened." She stretched the last word out so it included all sorts of cozy erotic promises. "I need your protection."

"Have you told the Office?"

"I don't understand."

"Angwine's been set up from just about every angle. If you told the Office you didn't think he was guilty, it might pull some weight. You're the wife."

"I'm the widow." She smiled, but it wasn't coy.

"The widow," I repeated. "And you need protection. Who from?"

"From whoever killed Maynard. You're the only one who seems interested in finding out."

"I might be losing interest. The returns are diminishing."
I was playing hard to get. I was interested in her money and
possibly more, and she knew it as well as I did.

She put the quaver back in her voice—it was obviously
available when she needed it. "If you won't help…"

"First you have to level with me, tell me everything. Answer my questions. Think of it as an audition. If you pass,
we'll talk terms."

"I've told you everything I know."

"I'll try not to laugh at that. Just answer my questions.
What did Pansy Greenleaf do to get rewarded with the house
on Cranberry Street?"

Celeste blinked at me, but I wouldn't blink back. She
swallowed hard and said: "She was working for Danny
Phoneblum. He bought the house. He likes to take care of
people."

"What did she do for him?"

"I wouldn't know."

"Does he supply her with drugs?"

"I don't mean to appear stupid, Mr. Metcalf, but I
thought drugs were free. You get them at the makery."

"Not the kind Pansy uses. Come on, Celeste. She leaves
the needles lying out."

This time she stared without blinking, and her voice was
completely lacking in affect. "He gives them to her. He'd kill
me if he knew I told you that."

"I already pretty much knew."

"With Danny it doesn't matter. Just the principle of my
telling you something—"

"Is that where his money comes from?"

"I—I don't know that much about Danny's business. It's
better not to."

I picked a mushroom off the top of the pizza and put it in my mouth. "Let's change the subject. You married Stanhunt and Phoneblum bought Pansy the house and Dr. Testafer retired from his practice all at the same time. What happened two and a half years ago?"

She thought about it. "When Maynard and I made the decision to stay and get married, Grover decided he could retire and turn over the practice—he'd wanted to for some time. Maynard wouldn't say yes or no until he settled down, with me."

"What about Pansy?"

"You're making too much of the coincidence. There's no connection." She said it straight, but she looked uncomfortable.

"What did you do before you met Maynard?"

"I...I was on the East Coast."

"What's it like there?"

"Excuse me?"

"I said what's it like there? You don't have to say if you can't think of anything."

She looked up wonderingly. I got up out of my seat and went to the door and held it open. "Go home, Celeste. You're lying through your teeth. It's a waste of my time."

She stood up, but it wasn't to leave. She applied herself to the front of my body like a full-length decal, seeking points of pressure all the way up and down, and working them until they responded. Her mouth drove into mine, and her scent filled my nostrils. She wrapped her arms around my neck and stood up on her toes to nuzzle at my face, making the most of the friction between our bodies as she rose. There were two or three layers of cloth between us, but I swear I felt her nipples grazing my ribs to rise and burn against my chest. My hands came out of my pocket and off the doorknob and went around the back of her to grip her snug buttocks and hoist her thighs even higher against my own, to bring her tongue even farther down my throat.

I felt something hard between our stomachs, like a sausage or screwdriver trapped absurdly between our bodies, and for a brief moment I thought she was carrying a gun. Then I realized it was my penis, insensate but still physically present and fully aroused. All I felt was the usual feminine tickle, like a meshing of soft, long-inactive gears. I was probably capable of making love to her if I wanted to, but I wouldn't be feeling what she would think I was feeling. The contemplation of it must have stopped me in my tracks, because she rolled her tongue back in and stepped away to look at me quizzically.

"Conrad..."

I didn't say anything. The kiss had affected me more than I wanted to admit. It had sent me spinning back to a time that was gone, when someone completely different wore my hat and coat and name. Celeste had filled me with desire, but it wasn't really Celeste I wanted. With Celeste I wouldn't recapture the thing I needed. It might be beyond recapture, or it might not, but Celeste wasn't the one.

She could only reawaken the frustrations, the anger. For Celeste, I knew as surely as our hips had ground together, danger was the intoxicant, and if there wasn't danger there would have to be something else, some other malign aphrodisiac. I wanted to hit her as much as I wanted to fuck her, and she probably wanted to be hit as much as she wanted anything.

So I hit her. I was certainly more equipped to do that than the other thing. I backhanded her across the teeth the way I'd been hit so many times, and she stumbled backwards in panic until she fell into the dusty chair in the corner. I went back to my desk and sat down and held my head in my hands.

After a minute she got up and came to the desk. I thought she was going to hit me, but she pulled out some money instead and threw it in front of me. I looked between my fingers. It was two thousand dollars, in four bills.

"That was good," she said. "I understand now. You're tough. You'll protect me, I know you will."

"I'm not tough," I said. "You don't understand."

"Take the money."

"I'm not for hire," I said. "I'm still working out the remainder of Angwine's fee. Until then I'm booked up."

She didn't say anything. I opened up my drawer and got out the cigarettes, put one in my mouth and offered her the pack. She refused. I lit mine and took a big drag. The building around us was quiet, deathly quiet, and outside my window the night was like a dark nullification of the existence of the city. But underneath night's skirts the city lived on. Disconnected creatures passed through the blackness, towards solitary destinations, lonely hotel rooms, appointments with death. Nobody ever stopped the creatures to ask them where they were going—no one wanted to know. No one but me, the creature who asked questions, the lowest creature of them all. I was stupid enough to think there was something wrong with the silence that had fallen like a gloved hand onto the bare throat of the city.

I stubbed out the butt and looked back up at Celeste. She was standing in front of the desk with a faded expression on her face, her hands pressed together over her heart like a schoolgirl making a promise. When she realized I was looking up, her eyes focused again and her lips moved together soundlessly.

"What are you afraid of?" I asked again.

She looked at me with wide eyes, and for a moment the mask fell and she was naked and honest, and for all of that moment I wanted to hold her and kiss her again, but then it was gone, vanished, replaced by the version that was hard and cynical.

"I'm not afraid of anything," she sneered.

"I see."

She scooped the money off the desk and curled it back into her pocket. "I don't know why I came here," she said.

"I guess that makes two of us."

"We'll never be two of anything." She knew it was a good enough line to leave on, and she turned to the door. I didn't see any reason to stop her. She shut the door firmly behind her, and I listened as her footsteps trickled to silence in the corridor.

I went back to my pizza, but the cheese had clotted. I picked off a few more mushrooms, turned off the light, and went down to my car.

CHAPTER 18

INQUISITORS KORNFELD AND TELEPROMPTER WERE WAITing for me at my apartment. I looked around for Morgenlander but he wasn't there. The apartment looked okay—if they'd gone through things, they'd done it gently—and Angwine was gone, all trace of him removed. The inquisitors had left depressions in the couch where they'd been sitting, but when I opened the door, they were on their feet. The depressions weren't so close together that I had to feel left out of something; if Kornfeld and Teleprompter tussled, they didn't do it on company time, or at least not on a stakeout. I would have preferred to think Catherine Teleprompter kept clear of the Office clowns, but it really wasn't any of my business.

"Out late," said Kornfeld, too jauntily. "On a case?"

"Not really," I said. I was tired, despite the fresh infusion of make, and I wasn't in the bantering mood. I wouldn't have minded talking to Catherine, but Kornfeld seemed to want to express himself verbally for a change.

"You must have been somewhere," he said. "We've been waiting since eight."

"Thanks, it makes the place feel lived in. I really appreciate it."

"You've been warned off this case. More than once."

"I've been warned off this case even more than you think. It's getting pretty dull."

The door was still open. Kornfeld went around me and closed it. "We don't really want to talk about the case. The case is closed. We wanted to let you know that Orton Angwine is karmically defunct. As far as we're concerned, that's the end of it."

"Great." I turned away from Kornfeld and faced Catherine Teleprompter. She seemed smaller and less formidable out of the Office, which didn't stop me from wanting to grab hold of her—it just made it seem more possible. She had her black waterfall of hair pinned back with a clasp this time, and it gave me a nice view of her throat. I watched it bob as our eyes locked, but she didn't say anything.

"There's just one more piece of business," said Kornfeld from behind me. "I need your card."

"Who gets credit for the nab?" I asked as I dug in my pocket for my card. "Morgenlander?"

"Morgenlander was transferred off the case this afternoon," said Kornfeld. "He wasn't familiar enough with the beat. It was a mistake bringing him in."

I handed him my card. Kornfeld took it and switched on his magnet. I assumed this was the part where they built me back up to an acceptable level as closure to the case. Sort of a payoff for swallowing their interpretation of events without gagging too loudly. The red light on Kornfeld's magnet blinked, and he ran it across my card, then handed the card back.

"How'd I do?" I asked.

"You're down to twenty-five points, Metcalf. Your file is up for review. Don't ask me any more questions or I'll be forced to cave your face in."

I was stunned. I put my card in my pocket and sat down on the couch, oblivious to Catherine Teleprompter, the case forgotten. My karma hadn't been this low since I first dropped out of the Office. It made me feel nauseous. I could tell myself it was just a scare tactic, that karma didn't really mean anything anyway, that all I cared about was having the minimum so I could walk the streets—I could think all those things, but it still made me sick to my stomach to have it get so low. I could feel the moisture on my tongue evaporating.

Catherine stepped past me like I was some kind of car wreck and went to join Kornfeld at the door. I barely had the heart it took to look back up. Kornfeld's paw was on the doorknob, but he wasn't going anywhere yet, just watching me suffer on the couch, and when our eyes met, he smiled.

I'd underestimated him. I assumed anyone who started out gut-punching you in an elevator couldn't have all that much else in his arsenal. For instance, I had no idea he could smile, let alone at such an inappropriate time.

"You're a big man, Kornfeld," I said. "But not too big to fit in Phoneblum's pocket. He really knows how to pick 'em. You and the kangaroo."

"You're talking off the top of your head," said Kornfeld.

"And you're talking through a buttonhole on your shirt collar. The whole thing stinks of Phoneblum's last-minute patch-up. Only the plaster won't hold over a gap this big." The first thing that goes is my sense of metaphor. "You brought Morgenlander in for show and even he knew it wasn't clean. What you did to my card just shows how bad you're scared."

"What I did to your card came from the top," said Kornfeld evenly. "I don't make karma decisions. You ought to know that."

"Don't make me laugh. You're the inquisitor on the case. Morgenlander is out—you said it yourself."

"The order came from higher up. It's not my problem if you forgot how to play the game, Metcalf. The rules haven't changed."

I looked at Catherine. She didn't want to look away, but that meant she ended up blinking to break the tension. "You heard him," I said to her. "It's a game. You don't have to feel bad about it. I forgot how to play."

She still didn't say anything.

"How'd you end up riding around with Kornfeld anyway?" I asked her. "Didn't you work the day shift?"

"I expressed interest in the case," she said.

I couldn't help smiling. She looked like she wanted to say something but couldn't in front of Kornfeld—or maybe that was just wishful thinking on my part. There was half a minute of awkward silence and then she opened the door and went out into the hall. Kornfeld closed it again and said: "I didn't take away your license."

"Gee, thanks."

"No," he said. "I mean I meant to. Hand it over."

I gave him the license. He folded it into his jacket pocket along with his magnet, and straightened his coat on his shoulders with a tug at the collar. He looked at me with a deadpan expression for what I guess he thought was the last time, then shrugged and reached for the door.

I almost let him leave, I swear to God. But something took over in me and I came out of the couch and converged on him, grabbing his collar where he'd just adjusted it and pinning him against the door with my elbows. His face turned red and his mouth opened to speak, but he didn't move except to squirm, and nothing came out of his mouth. I could feel the pulse of his neck against the base of my thumb. It felt nice and soft. "I'll cost you everything you cost me and more," I said. "I'll break you wide open. That's a promise."

Roughing him up could cost me the rest of my karma, but I didn't think he had what it took to rub it off my card right here and now. That wasn't Office style, and Kornfeld was Office all up and down the line. I'd get a night to sleep on it, and there would be a knock on the door in the morning.

Besides, as much as he hated my guts, I didn't think Kornfeld really wanted to see me go down on karma. I didn't think he could afford it. The result would be an inquiry, into a thing he was obviously eager to wrap up before anyone got too close a look at it. Grabbing his collar was a calculated risk, only at the time I did it, I hadn't yet calculated. I just went ahead and did it.

"You're a fool," he panted.

"No kidding," I said, and tightened my grip on his neck as I said it. "You think I need you to tell me that?"

"Let me go."

"Give me the license." I pushed with my thumbs on the part of his neck where it mattered most. "They can take it," I said, "but they'll have to send a bigger man than you to do the job."

He brought it out of his jacket pocket, and I let go of him and took it from his hands. He rubbed his neck and patted down his hair, his eyes full of incredulous fear. "Enjoy it while you can, Metcalf," he said. "I wouldn't count on it lasting too long."

"Fuck you."

Kornfeld opened the door and went out. I heard him speak in muffled tones to Catherine Teleprompter and then I heard their paired footsteps tramping down the stairs, and then I heard the whine of the air hinge on the front door of the lobby. I looked down at my hands. My fingers were clenched as if I still had hold of Kornfeld's throat. I un-clenched them.

And then I made a vow. Nobody was going to end this case but me. I'd answer all my questions, the old ones and the new ones, and I'd live to see Orton Angwine walk out of the freezer. Not because I liked the guy so well. It wasn't that. At that moment I hated Kornfeld more than I liked Angwine, but it wasn't my hatred that would carry the vow either.

If I was doing it for anyone, I was doing it for Catherine Teleprompter, oddly enough: I wanted to answer her ques-tion about why I'd left the Office. I wanted to show her what my job meant, and what it looked like afterwards when I got it right. How different it was from the Office version.

But I wasn't doing it for her either, finally. It always came back to me, me and my old-fashioned sense of outrage. I could only laugh, even as I was making the vow. Either I or the entire rest of the world needed fixing, bad. Probably both.

The rest of the evening I passed one way or another. From the empty ice trays in the sink the next day I suspect it had something to do with a connect-the-dot series of drinks, but to tell you the truth I don't remember a damn thing.

CHAPTER 19

I GOT UP THE NEXT MORNING WITH A HEAD THAT FELT like the change you get back from a five-spot when you spent it on a $4.98 bottle of wine. Determined nonetheless to act like an inquisitor on a case, I reamed out the insides of my skull with toothpaste, mouthwash, eyedrops, and aspirin, and at the same time drew up a mental list of places to go and people to talk to. First on the list was the architectural firm of Copperminer and Bayzwaite. That was the name I'd read off the blueprints in Pansy Greenleaf's dresser, and it seemed like as good a place to start as any.

The musical interpretation of the news that morning was superficial and blithe, and it didn't go too well with my headache, so I turned it off. The information I wanted wouldn't be on the musical news anyway. I made myself a cup of coffee so strong it snarled, and chased it with a piece of dry toast and a couple of bites of a moldering apple. By the time I got out of my apartment, the sun was bright and high in the air and my watch said eleven.

I drove up University to the parking lot in the Albernathy Overmall, where Copperminer and Bayzwaite kept their offices. The Overmall was all glass and chrome, and blinding to look at coming up from the bay. When I drove into the shade underneath it, I was plunged into a darkness so complete that I almost caromed my car off a concrete embankment. I gratefully turned my car over to the bulldog running the lot and took the elevator up into the Overmall.

Architectural offices are always a good argument against architects, and Copperminer and Bayzwaite was no exception. The outer room served just about any purpose imaginable except those of walking in, talking to the receptionist, and sitting down to wait. I enacted these procedures anyhow, only I skipped sitting after taking a look at what passed for chairs. The room had been shaped from molten glass, pierced through with beams of burnished aluminum, and although several of these met in a confluence meant to suggest a seat, it didn't look like something I'd be able to get back out of, so I let it pass.

After a few minutes a door opened in the back and one of the architects came out to see me, his hand extending for a shake from halfway across the oversized room. He was well groomed and looked alert, with a lick of hair sticking up in the back to create an impression of boyishness. I stuck up my hand to intersect with his—if I hadn't, he might have charged right past me or jammed his hand into my stomach in his enthusiasm. I guess he thought I was a client.

"Cole Bayzwaite," he said.

"Conrad Metcalf," I answered, trying to slow him down by drawing the syllables out.

"Let's go into my office." He stepped to one side and pointed the way, then bent over neatly at the waist and whispered something to his secretary. I went inside and picked out the most user-friendly chair and sat down. Cole Bayzwaite closed the door and went around to his reclining leather chair. I took out my license and put it on his desk.

His face fell, as if it had been supported only by his billowing optimism. The corners of his mouth tightened in an expression of distrust.

"You must think I can help you in some way," he said.

"That's right. I found your name mixed up in a case, and I was wondering if you would answer a few questions."

"I guess that would be all right."

"Your firm drew up a set of blueprints for a sort of bunkhouse, to be built adjacent to an existing property. Do you remember the design I'm describing?"

"We draw up proposals on blueprint all the time," he said. "I'd need a name."

"Maynard Stanhunt."

He tapped it into the keyboard on his desk and squinted at the monitor. "No. He's not on our client list."

"Try Pansy Greenleaf. That's whose room I found it in."

He looked at me oddly for a minute and then entered the name. "No. Sorry. You must have the wrong firm."

"Nothing under Stanhunt? His wife's name is Celeste—"

"Nothing at all. I'm sorry."

I was coming up empty, but I didn't want to let it go. I had to find some way to justify myself to Bayzwaite, and buy some time. "All right," I said. "Let's start over. Let me tap your intelligence. Let me describe a room to you: eight bunk beds crammed against a wall, with less than three feet allowed for each bed. This room is upstairs in a kind of clubhouse that's a stone's throw from a big, well-equipped modern house, in a fancy neighborhood. What would a thing like that be for?"

"I—I really couldn't say."

"Animals," I said. "That's what I think. Evolved animals. Some kind of servant's quarters, maybe."

"We have a sheep," he said. "Built her a room on the back of the house. But she likes to sleep curled up."

"Who has a sheep?"

"My family. I'm just saying I think animals, evolved ones even, probably don't sleep all lined up in bunk beds."

I'd managed to get Bayzwaite interested, but it only made me wonder if the whole architectural angle wasn't a waste of time. Maybe whoever drew up the diagrams, assuming the diagrams meant anything at all, stole the paper with the logo from Copperminer and Bayzwaite's office supply. Maybe I should have been questioning the secretary.

"Okay," I said. "Good point. But then what are the beds for? Sixteen beds, remember. That's a lot of people in the same room."

"Sounds like kids," he said.

"Kids."

"Right."

"What kids? There are no kids. There's babyheads. About how tall is a babyhead?"

"Tall enough for those beds of yours," said Bayzwaite.

"Jesus Christ."

"Excuse me."

"I said Jesus Christ, Cole. I'm just feeling a little bit stupid. There's babyheads in this case, at least one, so I should have made the connection earlier. You've been a great help."

Bayzwaite was all smiles. He'd helped a private inquisitor on a case, and it made him feel good inside. He'd have a story to tell his pals. It was worth my not being a new client. I shook his hand again and got out of my seat. And that was that.

Almost. Maybe I just don't like happy endings, but something made me feel not right as I was reaching for the door. I turned around, and Bayzwaite's smile plastered itself back into position, but not before an appreciable interval. In that interval I spotted what the smile replaced, and it wasn't pretty.

I put up a smile to match Bayzwaite's but I let go of the door handle.

"Just occurred to me," I said. "Would you mind trying one more name on that client list of yours?"

"Shoot," he said, and made a gun out of his thumb and forefinger and pulled the imaginary trigger.

"Danny Phoneblum."

The name was magic. It stiffened up conversation wherever it was used. Bayzwaite's face had fallen when he saw my license; now it froze into a mask of tension, but not without retaining the all-important smile. He put his hand on the keyboard and tapped in the name.

"Nope."

I moved around to where I could see the monitor. "You spelled it wrong," I said. "Pee-aitch, not eff."

I watched his hands this time, and he knew it, and spelled it right. The name blinked into existence, along with the address of the place in the hills. I'd almost walked out of the office without making the connection, but the name was just sitting there waiting for me to find it.

"What a coincidence," I said. "He must have been the one who ordered those blueprints. I guess he didn't go ahead with the project and you forgot all about it. But the name stayed in your files. I guess—what, do you keep a mailing list? Invite people to brunches and stuff?"

"We just keep the names," he said stiffly.

"Lucky for me. So, let's see—you must have the designs filed away somewhere too, right?"

At that moment I became aware of a subtle shift. We'd been bodiless, even as the banter got hostile. Now we suddenly came into our bodies and sized one another up. I wasn't any taller, but I probably had a few pounds on him. Not that we were about to pounce on each other, but the physical element was suddenly tangible.

"I'm not sure," he said carefully.

"Let's have a look." I stepped up to his desk and put my hands on the keyboard, and I had to nudge him aside to do it. "Index." I spoke aloud as I tapped out the commands. "Client, file. Phoneblum." The set of diagrams blinked into existence.

I stepped back. "So. You thought a design like that was meant for babyheads. That look like what I described?"

"Yes."

"You draw this up?"

"We draw up thousands of proposals—"

"Right, right. You remember Phoneblum?"

"No." Too fast, too firm.

"What if I told you those blueprints were found curled up in the fist of a dead man?"

Bayzwaite swallowed hard. "I guess I'd say that I wanted to contact the Office before I said anything further. I'm not so good at this game of questions and answers."

"Well they weren't, so relax." I laughed. "Nobody's good at questions and answers anymore, so don't worry about that either." I realized I wasn't learning anything. I'd already seen the designs, and I'd more than confirmed the connection. Twisting Bayzwaite's arm wasn't going to get me any more. If I was hard up for arms to twist, I could come back later. He wasn't going anywhere.

I took my business card out of my pocket. "Call this before you call the Office. I'm working on keeping a guy out of the freezer, and I'll take any help I can get. If you or your partner remember anything..." I put the card on his desk and picked up my license. Bayzwaite took the card and put it in the drawer of his desk. His face was blank.

I went outside, nodded at the receptionist, and passed through the cavern of poured glass to the exit doors. Coming this way, I almost liked the effect of the early afternoon sun on the distorted walls of the office, all blurry and chiaroscuro, like some kind of underwater dream. I went into the corridor and pressed the button for the elevator.

The attendant handed over my car, and I drove out into the sun and parked on a side street behind the Overmall. I pulled out the mirror in my glove compartment and snorted up a couple of lines of the new batch of make, the first I'd used today. It had the effect of flashing my memory back over the events of the past two days: the kangaroo in the rain, Morgenlander in my office, and, most of all, Angwine in the bar of the Vistamont. The drug should have provided the sense of remove I craved; instead it served to focus and intensify my disquiet.

This case was like some kind of invasive malignancy. It filled whatever space it was given, and worse, blended itself into the healthy tissue so you didn't know where to make the cut. It had blended itself into my life. I'd already lost most of my karma to it, and my client was already frozen and shipped. I thought about Celeste Stanhunt and Catherine Teleprompter and decided it was also fair to say I'd lost my sense of objectivity.

With that cheery thought I put away the mirror, closed up the glove compartment, and started the car. It was time to find the babyheads. One in particular.

CHAPTER 20

TELEGRAPH AVENUE IN OAKLAND WAS A DUMP, AND IF there was an exception to that rule, the babybar on 23rd Street wasn't it. The bar took up the bottom floor of an abandoned transient hotel, and the facade of the building was brownstone eroding into dust, like some kind of urban archaeological dig. The windows above the storefront were boarded up or sealed with sheets of tin, and the long narrow window of the bar itself was crammed full of dusty cardboard Santas and wreaths of archaic tinsel. The babyheads were reputed to sleep upstairs in the hotel when they didn't feel like going home to their parents—and judging from what I'd seen at Cranberry Street, they didn't go home to their parents very often. I was hoping to find Barry Greenleaf at the bar, and I was hoping he wouldn't be too soused to talk. If Barry was like the other babyheads I'd met in my work, he was drinking himself to death trying to counteract the unpleasant side effects of the evolution therapy he'd undergone, and in a babybar the drinking started early.

There weren't any signs of life beyond the glimmer of lights in the window and the creaky strains of music seeping out to where I stood in the street, but compared to the surrounding neighborhood it seemed almost inviting. I stepped into the shadow of the entrance and tried the door. It was locked. I rattled the handle, and the door opened a crack and a babyhead looked up at me from behind it, his distended bald head gleaming with reflections from the barroom behind him. He was dressed in a toddler's red jumper with a little embroidered yellow fish on the chest, and he had a cigarette tucked behind his ear. "Let's see some ID," he said gruffly, in a high-pitched voice.

"What?"

"ID, pal. You look over-age to me."

I showed my license. He took it and shut the door, and I heard the bolt slide back into place.

After a couple of minutes it occurred to me that I'd just given away the same piece of paper that last night I roughed up an inquisitor to keep. I knocked a few times with my knuckles, then slapped at the door with the flat of my hand, and then I started kicking it.

I was getting ready to bust it down with my shoulder when the door opened again. A different babyhead appeared in the space and said: "You ought to cut that out."

I grabbed the edge of the door and forced myself past him, into the gloom of the babybar.

A row of shiny heads at the bar turned as I stumbled in, and clusters of them bobbed at the table. The place was lousy with babyheads, more than I'd ever seen in one place at a time, more than I really wanted to believe existed. The interior of the bar, like the window, was draped with dusty, out-of-date holiday decorations, obviously leftovers from the bar's previous life: a red-faced Irishman guzzling a mug of draft which never emptied, a winking, leering Santa with an unhappy reindeer in tow, and a New Year's banner that read 2008! LOVE IT OR DRINK AT AL'S. The fluorescent fixtures were carpeted with dust, and the one behind the bar flickered lazily, scattering flashes of light and shadow across the ceiling like an ambulance parked in a narrow alley. Music oozed out of the back room.

I scanned the place for the babyhead who'd made off with my license, but he wasn't in the room, or if he was, I couldn't pick him out of the crowd. The kid I'd bowled over coming in was back on his feet, and he scooted around me from behind like I was a pylon in the middle of the road, and disappeared into the back room. I went and sat down at the bar. Conversation in the room hadn't been impressive; now it stopped completely.

"Whiskey and soda," I said.

The babyhead behind the bar was elevated to my level by a crudely constructed ramp, and he moved over to where I was sitting and put his face in front of mine.

"You've got no business here," he said sneeringly, his smooth, elongated brow wrinkling in exaggerated disgust.

"If I didn't before, I do now," I said. "One of you kids took my license. I need it back."

"What type of license?"

"Private inquisitor."

By now the whole room was listening. I could hear the stirring of little feet behind me. I considered the possibility of a physical confrontation with a roomful of babyheads all clinging to my legs and climbing on my back, and decided I wanted to avoid it. The image of piranhas kept coming up.

"A question asker," said the bartender. "That's delicious. We don't need your license, Mr. Inquisitor. Take it somewhere else. We don't need a license to ask questions. We ask questions any time and any place we like." The kid smirked, and his eyes bugged under the hood of his forehead.

"Congratulations," I said. "Big fucking deal."

There wasn't any answer. I took another one of Angwine's hundred-dollar bills out of my pocket and tore it in half on the counter, then put half back in my shirt pocket, but slow, making sure everybody got a good look. Then I wiped my brow with my sleeve and crossed my legs, to draw the moment out. "That's for three things," I said. "I want my license back, and I want to talk to a kid named Barry Greenleaf." I paused. "And I ordered a whiskey and soda. Then you'll see the other half."

I must have made an impression. The bartender turned and began fixing me a drink. A couple of the babyheads behind me scuttled nervously into the back room. I guess the babyheads were short on cash this week. I heard a couple of quietly muttered conversations resume under the music.

A drink appeared on the counter in front of me, and I tilted it back and poured some past my teeth. It wasn't bad but it wasn't good. The whiskey was real, but what should have been soda was more like effervescent dishwater. I drank about half, then set the glass on the bar. The bartender came over and plucked away the ripped half hundred. I felt in my pocket to make sure the other half was still there, and then I knocked back the rest of the whiskey, doing my best to keep my tongue to one side as it passed through my mouth.

Another babyhead came out of the back and waddled purposefully to where I was sitting. He was dressed in a sheet pinned up like a Roman toga, high-top sneakers without any socks, and a plastic digital wristwatch. He vaulted in one motion onto the seat beside me and put his hands on the bar, fingers spread, as if he were feeling for vibrations in a Ouija board. After a minute like this he turned to me and reached under the sheet, pulled out my license, and slid it to where my hand was resting on the bar, running it through a pool of spilled drink in the process. I took it and put it in my pocket without saying anything.

"Barry's upstairs," the babyhead said. "You mean to take him away?" His voice was high and inquisitive—almost like a child's, come to think of it. I could smell the liquor on his breath. Despite that, and despite the way he was dressed—or maybe because of it—I had the feeling I was in the presence of the baby-boss.

"No," I said. "I just want to ask him a few questions."

"He doesn't want to come downstairs."

"I'll go up."

"What do you want?"

An idea occurred to me. "I'm working for an inheritance lawyer. Barry may be due to come into some karma, plus a house and cash. If he's not interested, he can sign a waiver and it'll go to his little sister. She's a cat."

"Let me see."

"Don't waste my time. If Barry isn't here—"

"He's upstairs. Give me the money."

"Take me upstairs."

The bartender came over and showed the babyhead in the toga the ripped half of the hundred. "Take him upstairs," he said. "Let Barry decide."

The babyhead looked down at his wristwatch and then back up at me and nodded, as if the time was a factor in his decision. Maybe it was. "Okay," he said. "Come on." He hopped off the stool, gathered his skirts up around his ankles, and scuttled quickly into the back. I followed.

The babyheads had the back room converted into a dark, musty-smelling conversation pit, and a group of them were seated there in a circle, passing an enormous fuming pipe back and forth across a low wooden table with peeling veneer and a cinder block in place of one of the legs. A radio hung from a nail on the wall behind them, and music came out of it shrouded in static. I almost gagged on the sweet, humid smell of the smoke from the pipe.

"I've got a full house: three questions and two answers," one of them was saying.

"A dunce cap is just an ornamented cone," came the reply.

As we passed through the room, the talk halted, and they looked me over with jaded, indifferent eyes. I couldn't make sense of the conversation from that one little snippet, but I didn't let it bother me. I probably couldn't have made sense of the stuff from a big fat dictionary full of it. The babyhead in the toga led me through a service door in the back of the room, and as he closed it, I heard the conversation pick up again.

We emerged into the moldering lobby of the hotel. The windows were boarded up, but enough light leaked through for me to tell that what felt like moss under my feet was actually rotting chunks of old carpet, and what felt like rain on my shoulders was spiderwebs. I was a decade or so early—rain and moss would make their appearance here, just not yet. I paused at the elevators, but the babyhead went on, to the stairwell, and started waddling up the steps. Either the elevators didn't work anymore, or the babyheads weren't tall enough to reach the buttons.

I followed him through the hotel to a room on the second floor. There were four of them inside, including the kid with the fish on his jumper who'd taken my license, and a couple that looked like girls. I went in. The one lying stretched out on the bed picked up his head and stared at me, and I recognized him immediately from my days of peeking in the window at Cranberry Street.

For a second I thought he had a full head of hair, but then I saw it was a woman's blond wig cut so short that it stood out like a ragged, overgrown crew cut. It didn't fool me long. I don't even think it was meant to. Underneath it Barry Greenleaf was as bald as the rest of them.

No one said anything. I tried my best to find a resemblance in his features to Pansy Greenleaf, Maynard Stanhunt, or just about any of the other principals in the case, but I came up empty. The distortion of the evolution therapy had warped any resemblance beyond recognition.

The other babyheads were sitting in a loose circle by Barry's bed, and they scuttled away on their haunches to make a space for me in the middle of the room. Barry propped himself up on one side, his head braced against his arm, and the matted blond wig slid sideways, covering his ear. There wasn't anywhere for me to sit except the floor, and after taking a good look at that, I opted to stay on my feet.

"Hello, Barry," I said. "My name is Conrad Metcalf. I'm working for your uncle Orton."

"Uncle who? I don't think I know who you mean." His voice was soft but it dripped contempt.

"Orton Angwine, Pansy's brother—"

"Okay, okay. What do you want?"

"I'm working on your family tree, only there's a couple of missing branches. Who's your father, Barry?"

"I don't have a father."

"Is it Maynard Stanhunt?"

"My father's Dr. Theodore Twostrand. That's the inventor of evolution therapy. He's everybody's father." He turned to his little audience. "Who's your father?" he asked.

"Dr. Twostrand," echoed one of the other babyheads obligingly.

Barry looked back at me. "He's everybody's father."

"I was visiting an architect this morning," I said. "He'd drawn up plans for a babyhead quarters for the backyard at Cranberry Street. Somebody paid him to do it, and I don't think it was Dr. Twostrand."

"Go ahead," said Barry. "Make your point."

"Somebody cares about you, Barry. Somebody thinks you'll come back home and is willing to spend a lot of money making sure you'll want to stay when you do. I knew Maynard Stanhunt. He had plenty of money, but it doesn't fit. I don't see him spending it all on you."

Barry pretended to yawn.

"Who's your father, Barry?"

"The architect, probably. What's your theory?"

"The closer I look, the more connection I see between Danny Phoneblum and the Cranberry Street property. His name was on the blueprints, not Stanhunt's. Pansy is supposed to have worked for him, but nobody will say what she did. Maybe carry the big man's baby, that's my guess. She bore him a son and got paid off with a house and a lifetime supply of illegal make and needles."

It was only a theory before I said it, but once it was out, it sounded good. Good enough to work with, anyway. I probably couldn't get confirmation from the kid, though. The more relevant question was whether he even knew.

"You've got all the answers," said Barry. "What do you need me for?"

"You're a member of a family, Barry. It may not be much of a family, and you may want nothing to do with it, but that doesn't change anything. You're right at the heart of this case. You don't have to do anything, you don't have to make a move, but you're still a player. When I find out more, I'll be back. In the meantime, here's my number." I handed him one of my business cards. He took it without looking at it and tucked it under the bare mattress.

I turned to leave. I wasn't disappointed. I'd found Barry, and now I had an angle I could work from. I was eager to get to it. But when I reached for the door handle, Barry said: "Wait a minute. I want to ask you a couple of questions."

I turned. "Yeah?"

"Who's paying you?"

I thought about it. "No one, anymore."

"What happened to my uncle what's-his-name?"

"The Office took him away."

"You don't like the Office much, do you?"

"I don't like the Office," I said. "But maybe I don't like it in a different way than you don't like it."

He chewed on that for a minute, then let it go. "Is Pansy very unhappy?"

"You should ask her yourself."

"Maybe I will." He looked down from the bed at his balloon-headed compatriots. "What about it? Anybody want to go for a picnic in the fancylands?"

"If that's it, I'll leave," I said.

"One more question," said Barry. His eyes lit up, as if they were opening for the first time, and I had a glimpse of some demonic intelligence at least glancingly in residence there.

"Yeah?" I said.

"How's it feel to be a worthless jumbo diddly-ass puppetool?"

CHAPTER 21

BARRY'S FASCINATING QUESTION TURNING ITSELF OVER IN my brain, I went downstairs, passing back through the dark back room and the dilapidated bar—where I forked over the other half of Angwine's hundred—and out into the afternoon sun on Telegraph Avenue. It was time for me to go find Walter Surface, the detective who'd stepped into my shoes in the Stanhunt case—the first Stanhunt case. He might turn out to be Phoneblum's stooge, and he might not, but either way he was sure to supply some interesting answers, provided I could come up with the right questions—and get my foot in the door long enough to ask them.

His address and phone number were listed in the public directory I kept in my car trunk, but when I pulled up alongside a phone booth, my search for change on the floor of my car turned up nothing but some empty packets of my blend and the anti-grav pen the kangaroo had slapped out of my shirt. I considered stopping at one of the storefronts on Telegraph for change and then decided not to bother. If a private inquisitor couldn't drop in on another private inquisitor without calling ahead, who could?

Surface's office was on the top floor of a seven-story

building on the edge of the warehouse district. It was the kind of neighborhood where you give your car a little involuntary glance back over your shoulder after you park it, and if you have any doubt whether you locked it, any doubt at all, you walk all the way back just to check. From the look of the neighborhood, Phoneblum had managed to dig up the one P.I. in the book in worse need of a buck than me. It made sense. Desperation was a quality Phoneblum obviously prized when he found it—and cultivated when he didn't.

The voice that called me in from the hallway was female, and I figured it for a secretary, which was a happy surprise in my otherwise low estimation of Surface's setup. But there wasn't anything behind the door beyond a single office, and the woman had her feet up across the only desk. The office was a little smaller than mine, a little uglier, a little dirtier. That was the way it went in my head. I compared his office with mine, and I knew that when I met Surface, I'd search his features for clues to the face I saw when I looked in the mirror.

"I'm looking for Walter Surface," I said.

"I'm taking messages," said the woman. She was either looking good for fifty or bad for thirty-five, and the latter seemed the safer bet. She turned to face me and her feet came off the desk, which left a scuff in the otherwise perfect coat of dust that covered it.

"I need to see him," I said. "And I'm in a hurry." I put my photostat on the desk.

"He's not here," she said.

"Can you call him?" I pointed at the telephone. The dust over it was just as thick as the dust on the desk.

"I don't want to get him out of bed," she said. "I'll take a message. You should have come sooner. He could have used you a week ago."

"What happened?"

"You didn't see the blood in the lobby, I guess. Walter got hit. He can't see visitors now. I think you understand."

"Who are you?" I asked her. She didn't seem to notice the questions. I guess she'd spent a lot of time around inquisitors.

"I just used to help Walter out with things," she said. "I guess I will again if he gets up out of that bed." As she spoke, her eyes detached from mine, without seeming to focus on any new object, and her voice grew dimmer and dimmer.

"You and Walter are close," I suggested.

She said yes, but it was mostly just a sigh. I realized that she was like the desk or the phone; what happened a week ago had put the three of them out of business, and they'd been gathering dust ever since.

"I really need to see him," I said. "Why don't you take me there yourself, make sure he's all right. You don't need to stay here."

Her eyes brightened somewhat. "No one ever calls," she said. "It's like they already know."

"Yeah," I said.

"I might as well be with him," she said, but she was talking to herself. Then she looked up at me. "He's not good."

"I understand." I let things get quiet for a minute, waited while she blinked away her tears, and then I said: "Listen. Walter was doing a very important job when he got hit, trying to help someone who really needed it. Still does. If I can talk to him—just for a few minutes—maybe I can pick up where he left off." It sounded nice, but it was a little inaccurate. Angwine was already frozen, and it was stretching the truth to imply that Surface's involvement, as I understood it, anyway, had been doing anyone the least bit of good. But it was certainly what his girlfriend seemed to want to hear.

I went and got her coat off a hook on the wall, then took a step towards the door. "I'll follow you in my car," I said.

"It's just a few blocks," she said softly, and got up from behind the desk. She was careful not to brush up against me as she slid her arms into the coat. I got my license off the desk and wiped the dust on my pants leg, then we went down in the elevator together.

I parked half a block behind her, and watched as she went up the porch of a shabby green clapboard house. She turned and looked back at me from the steps, and I waved her in. When the door shut behind her, I got the mirror from the glove compartment and tapped out a line of make and sniffed it up.

I finished the make, put away the mirror, and went up the steps to the door. Surface's girlfriend hurried over when I came in—I guess she would have put my coat on a hanger if I'd taken it off. Instead she just sort of hovered. When my eyes adjusted to the gloom, I wished they hadn't: the place was a sty. There wasn't any comparable delay for my nose, which had begun picking out the acrid components of the smell the moment I inhaled. Surface or his girl kept an animal of some kind, and they hadn't done too good a job of cleaning up after it the last week or so. The house badly needed an airing. I could forgive them, but my nose couldn't. It was all opened up from the fresh make, and I was afraid I wouldn't be able to carry on a conversation with Surface without making faces. So I got out my cigarettes. The woman saw what I was doing and dug a blackened ashtray out from under a pile of soggy newspapers and handed it to me.

"Thanks. Where's Surface?"

"In there." She pointed. "He was asleep again." She didn't say anything else, but she didn't have to.

I went in. It was a big room full of a chair and a dresser and a big double bed. The only light was the television. It was tuned to the Muzak station, where aquamarine triangles did an endless soporific dance against a translucent, watery background. The white blue light of the tube glowed over the dark form stretched out in the middle of the bed.

I stepped up closer. The body in the bed seemed awfully small. When he turned his dark face up from the pillow, I realized Walter Surface and I didn't have as much in common as I'd hoped, or feared. The animal in the house was Surface. He was an evolved ape. The surprise of it took my voice away for a second, but at the same time I didn't doubt for a minute that this was the guy I was looking for. His face was human enough to look weary with trouble, creased with the contemplation of things most humans, let alone most apes, never see. If he were a man, I'd have said he was a tired fifty years old. For an ape I couldn't or didn't want to figure it out.

"You're Surface," I said when I located my voice.

"Right." His thin lips barely moved, but the voice purred out of him surprisingly loud.

"My name's Metcalf. I'm working in connection with the Stanhunt case." I didn't extend my hand because I didn't really want to hold his, even for the duration of a handshake. The smell was coming from him. I could tell when he rustled the bed sheets. I guess his girlfriend was used to his stench the way she was used to questions. Love is sometimes more than just blind.

Surface closed his eyes. "Nancy let you in."

I said yes.

"She said you wanted to ask me some questions." He pursed his mouth and blew air through his nose. "You got to understand, Mr. Metcalf. I don't know you. I don't know what you want." The television flickered out, and we were thrust into darkness. I thought he'd accidentally dropped the remote control, but when the light came back on, he had a gun in his hand. It was a nifty stunt.

"Move and I'll make you breathe funny," he said, his leathery mouth all stretched out at the corners. The gun looked pretty comfortable in his little black paw. "I'd be pleased to teach you how to blow red bubbles out of your shirt," he went on. "It's a little trick I learned last week. I can dish it out as well as take it."

"And you ought to," I said. "Only I'm the wrong guy. I didn't dish it out, and I don't want to take it. Lay off the heat."

"Sit down, put your hands in your lap, and shut up. I heard enough to tell me I don't want to hear no more. I've got the gun and I'll ask the questions. I've got a license for both."

I sat down, set the ashtray on the arm of the chair, and put my hands in my lap like he said.

"Where's the kangaroo? He's the one I want to plug."

"That makes two of us, Surface. I wouldn't be seen walking around with the kangaroo unless somebody cut his hide into a nice pair of shoes."

His ape face squinted into some kind of bitter smile. His teeth were yellow. I thought about apes killing kangaroos, and maybe kangaroos killing sheep. Dr. Twostrand's evolution therapy was a real hit. He'd really lifted the animals out of the jungle.

"All right," said the ape. "What can you say to make me think you don't work for Phoneblum?"

"Probably nothing," I said. "Let's forget it." The door behind me opened. It was Nancy, carrying a couple of glasses, playing hostess. She'd put herself back together while she was away, but when she saw the gun in Surface's hand, she got teary again.

"Jesus, Walter."

"I don't trust him." The ape pushed himself up in the bed, the covers bunching at his waist. He had a big patch on his ribs, white cotton stained yellow with Mercurochrome. Nancy just stood there with the glasses in her hands.

"I want him out," said the ape. "You're too fucking trusting, Nancy."

"He could have come in with a gun at my head," she said.

"Listen to her, Walter. I'm on your side."

"Oh, fuck." Surface let the gun drop to the bed. "Gimme that." Nancy brought him the drink, and he tossed half of it back in a gulp. She gave me the other one and then leaned against the wall and crossed her arms.

It was a big glassful of gin, just barely haunted by the specter of tonic. I didn't mind. My cigarette had gone out in my mouth; I laid it in the ashtray and took a big drink of the gin. It was another way to deaden the endings in my nose.

"Phoneblum's boys want me dead, they'll find a way," said Surface, working his logic out loud, reminding me of myself again. "You wouldn't come walking in here and let me pull a gun on you."

I didn't say anything, just sipped my drink.

"What's your racket?" he said. He scratched gingerly at his bandage with the nail of his thumb.

"Same as you," I said. "I was the guy you were hired to replace. I balked at the job I was asked to do and was shown the door, same as you, maybe. Only I didn't end up with a bloody lobby."

"Lucky fucking you."

I took another sip, slowly. "I'd like to bring Phoneblum down, Surface. Maybe you can help me."

"And maybe you can help me get killed. No thanks."

"Nobody knows I'm here. Besides, you said it yourself. They want you, they got you. Why not talk shop with me for a few minutes? Get it off your chest."

Surface's intelligent eyes glistened in their worn, pouchy sockets. He ran them back and forth across my face for most of a minute.

He sighed, looked down at the gun and the drink in his hand.

"Shoot," he said finally.

I could see Nancy relax her posture against the wall. She obviously liked to see the ape sitting up and talking.

"Phoneblum said he hired you to watch Celeste," I said. "You ever have contact with her husband?"

"Dr. Stanhunt?"

"Yes," I said. "Maynard Stanhunt."

"Never laid eyes on him. Seemed like that was the point."

"With me it was the reverse. I was hired by the doctor, and never met Phoneblum. I guess Maynard didn't enjoy working with me and asked Phoneblum to take over the arrangements."

"I guess." Surface put the gun down on the windowsill beside the bed and poked at the curtain. A beam of sunlight flicked across the bed, disappeared.

"How long did you tail her?"

"A week."

"Learn anything?"

"Only what Phoneblum obviously already knew."

"What was that?"

Surface made an impatient face. "The boyfriend." Then he saw the look of nonrecognition on mine. "You knew about the boyfriend, right?"

"No."

Surface squinted into my eyes.

"That's what Dr. Stanhunt was looking for," I said, "but I never saw a thing. Are you sure?"

He wrinkled his brow, skeptically. "Of course I'm sure."

"Where?"

"That motel. The Bayview. The place Stanhunt got bumped off at."

I was baffled. "Tell me more."

"She went up there twice or three times, spent a long time in a room, came out with a mussed-up hairdo. Standard stuff." He looked at me like I was crazy, and I felt crazy. Either he was lying or I'd missed it completely.

"You see the guy?" I asked.

"Once. I couldn't pick him out now."

I thought about it a little. Suddenly there was a gaping hole in my picture of things, a hole shaped like a third party in a love triangle, a hole shaped like a prime suspect in the murder inquisition that should have been. It didn't completely rule out Angwine, except that the image of Angwine and Celeste as lovers was laughable. She'd eat him alive.

I tried to think of who that left, and couldn't come up with anyone.

"How'd you get in so bad with Phoneblum?" I asked.

Surface emitted a short, shrill laugh. "He wanted somebody to play the tough guy, which I sometimes do. Only this time it looked more like fall guy than tough guy, and I said no. He didn't like that." He grimaced, and it reminded me I was talking to an ape. Then he put his hand over his bandages. "We tossed some threats around. I guess he made good on his."

"I guess. They wanted you to hurt Celeste?"

Surface gave me that sour look again. "That what Phoneblum told you he wanted from me?"

"Phoneblum didn't say. But I took my orders from Stanhunt, and he asked me to poke Celeste a couple of times and send her home."

"That's nice." Surface's voice was grim. He looked over at Nancy. "You hear that?"

Nancy didn't say anything.

"I might have considered that," he said, turning back to me. "Hell, I probably would have done it. Only in my case it was a little different."

"Different how?"

He sighed. "When Phoneblum told Stanhunt about loverboy, the doctor had an attack of jealousy," he said. "Phoneblum got back to me with an offer of five thousand dollars to take the boyfriend permanently out of the picture."

"A killing."

"That's right. Only I said no."

"And Phoneblum panicked. He thought you knew too much."

"I guess so."

The Muzak on the television changed colors, and the room went from pale blue and green to white and gold. Surface switched on the lamp on the windowsill and turned off the television with the remote. Nancy took away my glass and left the room.

I was used to Surface's smell by now, and I guess he must

have gotten used to whatever it was that most grated on him about me. He put away the gun and slid back down into the big bed. When he spoke again, his voice was softer.

"What did you learn about Celeste?"

"Not that much, really," I said. "I spent a lot of time up on Cranberry Street learning she doesn't close the blinds when she changes clothes."

"I could have told you that."

"I was first, smart guy."

I'd made the ape smile, almost laugh, but as soon as he opened his mouth, he grimaced from the stress on his ribs. I watched while he swallowed the pain away.

"I'll tell you what I've got," I said. "You fill in the gaps."

He nodded.

"She's a hard one, or she was once. Knew Phoneblum in a business way. About two and a half years ago she has a change of heart, and leaves town for a while—or maybe she's asked to leave. At which point she has her past customized, slimmed down, and her prospects lifted and firmed up. When she marries the rich doctor, the job is apparently complete. Except Phoneblum still has his strings on her. He won't let go."

"That sounds about right," said the ape.

"Tell me what you know about Phoneblum."

He narrowed his eyes. "Tell me what you don't know."

"Just about everything. What's his racket?"

"Racket? Sex. Drugs. Karma. What isn't his racket?"

"I get your point," I said.

"You know the club called the Fickle Muse? That's his place. Get into the back room and ask for a guy named Overholt."

I repeated the name.

"What he sells is what Phoneblum's got," said Surface. "Meaning anything you want."

"Phoneblum must have the Office in his pocket."

Surface smiled again, closed his eyes. "Yeah. I think so."

I got out of my chair. It was almost five o'clock, and the light outside was fading. I wanted to go see Pansy, and Celeste if she was home. It sounded like I might want to visit the Fickle Muse too.

I moved a little closer to the bed. Surface's eyeballs were trembling under their dusky lids. His skin, where it showed in all the hair, was fine, like an old woman's.

I stepped back again. "Thanks, Walter," I said. "You've been a big help. Someday I'll return the favor."

He spoke without opening his eyes. "No problem."

"Thank Nancy for me."

"Yeah."

He was the battered professional to the last, and I felt more than a little admiration for him. I might have offered him some of Angwine's money if I didn't think he'd throw it right back in my face.

I laid my business card on the dresser and went out into the dying minutes of the day.

CHAPTER 22

I WAS TIRED OF THE HOUSE ON CRANBERRY STREET. I drove up there in time to see the sunset reflected brilliantly across the bay windows, but the sunset didn't do the trick. I knew too much about the house and the people in it to like it very much. Yet for all of that I still didn't know enough. I was back banging on the door.

Pansy Greenleaf answered it. She stood there for a moment, wide-eyed and tentative, and it was like we'd somehow started over with each other. As if we forgot that the last time I was here she'd risen out of a drug-induced torpor to swear an end to my life if I ever came back. The moment went on long enough that I began to wonder if she *did* remember that last encounter. Then the soft flesh of her cheeks tightened, and her eyes narrowed, and her fist clenched on the edge of the door.

"Hello, Patricia."

She didn't say anything.

"You look better," I said. "That's nice to see. We have to talk."

"I'm busy."

"Somebody here?" I stood on tiptoe to look past her into the house. "Celeste? I need to talk to Celeste too."

"No. No one's here."

"I see. You're busy like yesterday, you mean. That's bad stuff, Pansy. I had somebody look at that stuff under a microscope. It eats you alive."

"That's my business."

"That's Danny Phoneblum's business, princess. You're just the customer." I went into the house, and had to shoulder her aside to do it.

When I turned the corner into the living room, I was greeted by the sight of three babyheads lined up in a neat row on the couch. They didn't go with the house, to put it simply. Their existence seemed absurdly literal, like the punch line of a joke someone misunderstood and took seriously. Sasha the kitten—who was nowhere to be seen—belonged in this house more than the babyheads ever would. She was more human.

Barry sat at one end, a little apart from the other two, his loud yellow wig still jutting at an idiotically jaunty angle on his head. The babyhead in the toga who'd taken me upstairs in the hotel sat at the other end, twisting his sheet into a dirty gray rope around his fingers. Between them sat another one I didn't recognize, wearing a little red Spiderman outfit, dark glasses, and a baseball cap on his oversized bald head.

"Barry," I said. "Long time no see."

"Mr. Asshole," said Barry. "Have a seat."

Pansy came in behind me. I turned and smiled at her, and caught an eyeful of daggers.

"My apologies," I said. "You've got visitors. Go ahead with what you were saying. I'll be quiet as a mouse."

Pansy didn't say anything. Barry wrinkled his forehead and said: "Quiet as a mouth." The other babyheads snickered.

Pansy retreated behind an empty chair. "A man named Kornfeld was here looking for you," she said. "He told me I should call him if you bothered me again."

"Office boy," I said. "No big deal. He owes me some karma, probably wants to pay up."

"You're in trouble," she said. "I don't have to hate your guts. I get to feel sorry for you."

"Thanks, Pansy. Think of me next time you roll off the bed onto your needle."

"Why don't you get lost, big man," said Barry. "You're butting in."

"Butting in is my life," I said, turning to face the baby-heads. "Indulge me."

The babyhead with the dark glasses had taken them off and clipped them onto his collar. He and the one in the sheet stared up at me together, hollow-eyed and vaguely bemused despite the eddies of emotional turbulence stirring the air in the room. The two faces created a kind of stereophonic effect, the woofer and tweeter of eeriness.

I turned back to Pansy. "I'm looking for Celeste," I said. "Have you seen her?"

"You're too late," she said. "She was here this morning, but she left."

"Did she say anything about where she was going?"

"She was upset. She said you refused to help her. She wanted to call Inquisitor Morgenlander and tell him Orton was innocent."

"What did you say?"

Pansy's hand gripped the back of the chair, and her eyes sought the floor. Then she looked up at me resentfully. "I said

it was stupid. That it was obvious Orton had done it." Her cheeks turned red, but she didn't look away.

"That was brave." I sort of meant it.

"Go to hell," she said, and turned and walked out of the room. I listened and could just make out her footfalls on the carpeted stairs. Then the squeak of a bedspring, upstairs.

Barry looked smug, as though he'd choreographed Pansy's actions and was pleased to see them performed so precisely. Woofer and Tweeter just rolled their eyes like spectators at a tennis match.

"Why'd you come back?" I asked.

"I haven't been here in weeks," said Barry. "From what you said, it sounded like it was getting interesting."

"What do you think?"

"I was right. It is interesting."

"Do you love your mother, Barry?"

"I don't *love* anything." He spoke the word as if he knew what it meant and I didn't.

"Then what I'm about to tell you won't matter."

"Nothing you've said has yet."

I took a deep breath. It mattered to me. "Celeste Stanhunt's your mother, not Pansy Greenleaf. It took a while, but it all came clear. Pansy works for Danny Phoneblum, but no one will say what she does. She's a *nanny*, Barry. Or she was until you left the nest."

Barry just smiled. "You can't imagine how little this interests me."

"I don't believe you."

"My motives are beyond your comprehension."

"I guess." I went behind the kitchen counter, found a drinking glass on the sideboard, and filled it with water at the tap.

"You never answered my question," said Barry.

"What's that?"

"How it felt to be what you are."

"The question wasn't quite that simple, when you asked it," I said. "You used some words I didn't understand."

"You're an asshole," said Barry. "The worst kind. You think you represent Truth and Justice, or something."

I took a big drink of water before I answered. I was getting a little steamed, even if he was just three years old. "Truth and Justice," I said. "I wonder if you really know what the hell it is you're talking about, or whether words just keep pouring out because of the thing they did to your brain. Truth and Justice. Nice, easy words."

I caught myself. The speech was wasted on babyheads—maybe wasted on anybody.

Then I made the mistake of deciding to give them something to think about. "What if I told you I thought Truth and Justice were two completely different things?"

Woofer liked that a lot. He turned to Tweeter and said: "What if I told you I thought Truth and Justice were four different things?"

Tweeter chimed in right on cue. "What if I told *you* Love and Money were six different things?"

"Some other time," I said. "I'm not in the mood." I put the glass of water back on the counter and went to the door.

"What if I told you I thought Time and Mood were twelve different things?" said Barry behind me.

CHAPTER 23

I'D BEEN TO THE FICKLE MUSE ONCE OR TWICE AS A CUS-
tomer, to take advantage of the late hours they kept, and a
couple of other times to track someone who burned the
bottle at both ends and didn't mind sitting in a dirty little
hole of a bar to do it. I'd even heard about the back room, but
I'd never been in it. The name Overholt was new to me. I got
into my car and drove there now, though I wasn't sure the
place would be open this early.

It was. In fact, stepping into the Fickle Muse from the
parking lot was like stepping through a miniature time machine that took you from six o'clock to sometime long after
midnight. The guys at the bar looked like they'd already made
the rounds and ended here only by default, and the floor already had a night's worth of cigarette butts marinating in
puddles of whiskey and melted ice. The jukebox was playing
that kind of lugubrious one-last-drink song, where everybody at the bar mumbles along with the chorus, only you
knew at the Fickle Muse there was no last drink. Or if there
was, it wasn't one, it was several.

I went and sat down as close as I could get to the door to
the back. The barkeep was a big hulk of a guy who probably

did his own bouncing, the few times the sight of him didn't keep bouncing from having to be done. It took him a while to get around to taking my order, and another little while for him to bring me the drink. I didn't mind. I should have felt worried, and pressed for time, but here in the Fickle Muse I felt enclosed in a pocket of timelessness and anonymity. Who needed karma, anyway? I drained the glass and slipped fifty dollars more than it cost under the coaster.

When the barkeep looked at the money, his eyebrows moved, but just a little. He probably would have kept the extra without even asking if I hadn't crooked my finger and hissed at him.

He put his head near mine.

"I want to talk to Overholt," I said.

"Maybe Overholt ain't here yet." He said it so fast and smooth it was like a pilotfish riding on the back of what I said. He was almost finished before I was.

I took out one of the ripped hundreds that now littered my pockets. He mistook it for the whole thing until he got it in his hand. His eyebrows moved again.

"I'll fix it after I see Overholt," I said. "I'll make it good as new."

"I don't care about new," he said. "Just good." His eyes flickered over to the door on the back wall.

"Thanks," I said.

"Don't thank me," he said. He picked up my glass and took it to the row of bottles against the mirror, then brought it back full. "You don't owe me no thanks. You like to pay big for your drinks, that's all." He went back to his regulars.

I took the drink and went through the door. The back room was nothing more than a pool table with walls around it, so close on three sides you could tell it ruined shots. A dark

hallway extended off the rear wall. The one light dangled down from the ceiling to hover a foot above the balls—a bad hop, and you could break the bulb. There was a big guy and a small guy, both leaning on cues while they studied the table. I shut the door behind me and set my glass on the felt.

When the big guy looked up at me, I knew the small one was Overholt. Some people have things written all over their faces; the big guy had a couple of words misspelled in crayon on his.

But he had grace. He stepped over and took my glass off the table and put it back in my hand. Then he made his shot. It was good, and Overholt and I stood in silence while he ran a series of balls. He only butted his cue into the wall a couple of times, and it never threw him. He just angled the end of the cue upwards and made the shot anyway.

When he missed one, he just grunted. The cue went end down on the floor again, and he went back to leaning on it. For a minute I thought I was going to have to wait the game out. Then Overholt spoke.

"This isn't the way to the bathroom," he said.

"I'm looking for a guy named Overholt," I said back.

Overholt smiled a little. His lips were cracked, like he licked them too often. He ran his hand over his hair and then put it back on the cue. "I'm him," he said.

"Good," I said. "I heard you could get me some things nobody else could get me." I didn't know exactly what I was talking about.

"It's been known to happen," he said. It was like an admission of a habit he couldn't break.

"I'll pay to have it happen now," I said.

"Maybe." He looked me over. "I need to know your name, and how you got mine. I need to see your card."

There was no bluffing. I could only hope he didn't know my name from Phoneblum. I tossed my card out under the light, careful not to displace the balls. "I met a guy named Phoneblum," I said. "He recommended your services." Overholt leaned over and read my name. "Big fat man," I continued, nervous. "No offense."

Overholt smiled grimly and put my card in his pocket. I got ready to bolt. I could leave without my card if it meant preserving my neck. The card only had twenty-five points on it anyhow.

"He's a big fat man, all right," said Overholt. "Doesn't get out much."

There was a moment of silence. I watched Overholt as carefully as I could without looking like I was doing it.

He patted the pocket with my card in it. "Don't worry," he said. "You'll get it back. Security."

I realized I was holding my breath. I let it out slowly. "He said you could help me get hold of some Blanketrol."

He looked over at the big guy. I looked too, but there wasn't anything to see. Then he looked back at me, and met my eyes for the first time. "Sometimes," he said.

"I want it."

"You don't want to use that stuff. That's bad stuff." The concern sounded almost genuine.

"That's my business. I want it."

He sighed. "I'll need five hundred dollars."

I laughed to myself. I had one like that left from the envelope Angwine had given me in the bar at the Vistamont. There was something funny about spending it on drugs I'd so recently dumped into the mud by the side of the road. It didn't make sense that it should cost so much, and I wondered if I was buying more than just the drugs. I couldn't answer that question without spending the money, though.

And what would I do with the new packet of Blanketrol? Maybe I was ready to use it.

"No problem," I heard myself say.

"Okay," he said. "Let's go upstairs. I'll make a call."

He handed the cue to the big guy, who looked only a little peeved. He'd been winning, but there were obviously plenty of rounds of pool in his past, and plenty more in his future. Business came first.

"Follow me," said Overholt. He went into the dark of the hallway behind the table. I followed, and he led me up a short flight of stairs to a little smoking room with a television and a phone and a couple of chairs. He told me to have a seat, and I had one.

"Money," he said. I got it out. He looked it over and said: "Good."

I felt stupider and stupider. I wasn't learning anything. I tried to think of a way to eke out a little more for my five hundred dollars, but nothing came to mind. I'd followed the lead like some kind of automaton and confirmed theories that didn't matter in the first place. I was wasting time.

I was about to make a scene and get my money and my card back when Overholt spoke again. "She's in through there," he said, pointing. "If you like it, there's more."

I didn't want Overholt to register my confusion, but I guess it must have shown.

"Danny told you—"

"Yes," I assured him. "Danny told me." I got up and went through the door.

It was a bedroom. The light was dim, but not so dim that I couldn't see the way the walls were rotting at the baseboard. The place smelled of mold, and I figured a pipe somewhere was leaking into the walls. The girl was already undressed. She was lying on the bed, and when I came into the room, she turned and smiled at me and beckoned with her white arms. She was beautiful to look at, but there was something clumsy in her movements. I had a bad feeling right away. I closed the door behind me and went over to the bed and let her put her arms around me.

I took her head in my hands and held it close to mine so I could look into her eyes. She was smiling with her mouth, but the eyes were blank. They were pointed at me but focused somewhere in the middle distance, about where I'd been standing when I first entered the room. I waited, but she didn't make the adjustment. She was looking right through me. When I moved my hand up the back of her scalp, I understood why.

The slavebox was buried in her hair, a little cluster of wire implants soldered together with a glob of plastic. It didn't seem to hurt her when I touched it, but her arms fell away from me to rest on the bed when she realized I wasn't paying any attention to her body. Things got through to her, to some operative fraction of her consciousness, but it took a while. Given the way she was spending her time, and the place she was spending it in, it was probably just as well.

I pushed her back on the bed. All I meant to do was get away from her, but I guess I pushed a little harder than was necessary, and she giggled. It stirred up an old memory in me, something bitter, and involuntary, something I'd have thought was completely gone by now. I guess the act of pushing a naked woman back on a bed is always going to contain a sexual element—whether playful, hostile, or both—no matter how long it's been.

I got up from the bed. Through my haze of disgust some things were finally making sense. Phoneblum's allusions to the slave camps fit in nicely now, and I understood why he needed to maintain a relationship with the Office. He needed to be tipped off when a nice-looking body was getting iced. The girl on the bed was all I needed to picture how it worked. And I could think of dozens of unpleasant reasons why Phoneblum might need the part-time services of a doctor or two.

I opened the door and went back out to where Overholt was waiting. He looked at me questioningly, almost sympathetically. "Something went wrong," he said.

"No," I said. "It's okay."

"We got all kinds, you know. Men, women, groups. Any age you like. Don't be shy."

"Right."

"We're always here." He furrowed his brow, truly concerned. I was touched.

"Okay," he said, after a minute. "Here." He handed me an envelope, too flat to hold drugs. "Take this to the makery on Telegraph and 59th. They'll give you what you want."

I stuffed it into my jacket pocket.

"We don't handle the drugs out here," he said. He wouldn't stop talking now. "Too dangerous. It's just a sideline, anyhow."

"I understand."

"Okay." He went behind the little table with the phone. He seemed disappointed I wasn't more interested in the girl or the talk.

He held my card out to me. "We ran this through our decoder," he said. "Twenty-five is real low. I can help you with that..."

"No," I said. "But thanks no. It wouldn't work. The Office is watching me close right now. They'd catch on."

He smiled broadly, like a pitchman who'd been fed a line by his shill. "You don't get it, Mr. Metcalf. The karma we sell is good. The Office can't touch it. I've got an inside line." He paused. "And frankly, you have a bit of leftover credit with us here."

The sick irrational part of me that was still trembling in fear at how low my karma had gotten made me stop and think it over. But it didn't take a lot of thinking to realize it really wouldn't make any difference. Overholt didn't know who I was, or he wouldn't be offering.

"Thanks, really," I said, trying to put some heart in my voice so he wouldn't feel too bad. "It just wouldn't work in my case."

"Okay." He threw his hands open in a gesture of resignation. I took my card back.

I left him there sitting behind the phone, and went out alone. When I was out of his sight on the stairs, I stopped and leaned back against the wall and caught my breath. The thing with the girl had shaken me. It was easier for me to think of all the people, dozens, maybe hundreds, Phoneblum had taken out of the deep freeze than it was for me to think of this one girl smiling blankly, holding her arms up in a cold damp room, with a clump of wire and plastic in her hair. I couldn't banish the image, so I let it sit there for a while and tried to get used to it.

After a couple of minutes I went the rest of the way down the steps, and passed back through the room where the big guy was lurching between the pool table and the wall. He was setting up shots now, moving the balls around, holding three of them easily in one of his big flat hands. I looked at him and he smiled. I guess I'd been upstairs long enough for him to think I'd had a quick one off with the girl. I tried to feel angry, but I couldn't muster it up. I smiled back and went into the bar.

Things had progressed as usual in the Fickle Muse, which is to say the air was thick with the unique perfume of men sweating out alcohol and breathing out cigar smoke. The music was louder but it wasn't any more lively. I wanted a drink, but the room was full enough that I couldn't get to the bar without pushing and shoving for a place. It wasn't worth it. A line of make in the car would do fine.

As I shouldered through the crowd, making my way to the exit, I heard the voice of the big barkeep, the one with the half hundred in his pocket. I didn't turn around to look. I just somehow wasn't in the right mood to pay up. I figured he'd have as much trouble getting through the crowd as I had, and if there was one thing I'd gotten good at in this life, it was starting a car in a hurry.

I went to the exit and put my weight behind it, but it turned out I didn't have to. Somebody pulled the door from outside, and I almost stumbled into his lap. I started to mutter and curse at the guy, then saw who it was. Standing in my way like a cowardly, red-faced linebacker was Grover Testafer. It wasn't funny, but I wanted to laugh. A second later, when the kangaroo stepped up behind him like the punch line of the joke, I did.

CHAPTER 24

THEY MADE A PRETTY HUMOROUS PAIR. TESTAFER WAS nominally in charge, I guess, but when he saw me, he turned to Joey for his cue. The kangaroo just screwed up his face. I quit laughing and pushed out between them to go to my car, knowing as I did it that it wouldn't come off. And sure enough, before I got my key in the lock, I heard their footsteps behind me, and a shadow passed between the moon and its reflection in my window.

"Hello, Grover," I said as I turned around, but it was the kangaroo who stood closest to me, and he had the little black gun in his paw again.

"Hello, Metcalf," said Testafer, a little weakly. He just wasn't used to this much action, I could tell. He stepped up closer but kept behind the kangaroo and the gun.

"Why don't you call Joey off, and we'll talk," I said.

"Fuck you, flathead," said Joey. "Nobody calls me off. I call myself on or off. Nobody else."

"Okay," I said. "Just put the gun away."

"I think the gun is a good idea, Metcalf," said Testafer. "You're a violent man."

"Product of my times," I said. "You know how it is."

I rested against my car, and put my keys back in my pocket. If we were going to talk awhile, I wanted to be comfortable. It was cool out, and the air was dry. There wasn't any fog, at least not yet. I was recovering from my jolt upstairs. I wanted a line of make, but otherwise I felt okay.

"We're looking for Celeste," said Testafer. "You'd better tell us if you know where she is."

"She's not in there," I said, nodding at the Fickle Muse.

Testafer was feeling his oats now, hiding behind the kangaroo's gun. "Maybe you should tell us if you've seen her today," he said. "And maybe you should explain what you were doing in there." He'd figured out a trick for asking questions without offending his own delicate sensibilities, and I guess it gave him an exhilarating sense of freedom.

"Maybe you should tell me what you want her for," I said. "That's what I think maybe you should do."

"She's running her mouth off," interjected the kangaroo. "She's causing trouble."

"That doesn't sound so bad," I said. "Let her run it off. Why should that bother you?"

The kangaroo scowled and pushed the gun out at me, like he thought that his having it meant I didn't get to ask questions.

But he was wrong. "What are you afraid of?" I said. "Or is it Phoneblum who's afraid, and he's just got you out on the streets doing his worrying for him?"

Just then the barkeep came out of the front door of the Fickle Muse. He had a pal along, the big pool player from the back room, to make him look small. Only he wasn't small. The two of them looked around the lot and then started towards where I stood talking to Testafer and the kangaroo. They moved well together. I had a feeling it wasn't the first time they'd fallen into formation.

The situation was entertaining. Here Joey and Grover and I were leaning against the car having a nice quiet talk, while the two toughs from the Fickle Muse crossed the gravel, obviously gearing up to take on the lot of us. The moon was out, but Joey's gun was black and he held it low. In reality, it was four against one, but the four all thought it was two against three, and the one wasn't about to set them straight.

Testafer looked unhappy. He didn't know whether to hide behind the kangaroo and his gun, which looked smaller and smaller all the time, or bolt for his car. He opted for the first. The barkeep brushed past him and the kangaroo both and took me by the collar. I was already conveniently pressed up against the car, so he just held me as if he'd put me there himself. The other guy hovered behind him like an extra pair of shoulders.

"Hundred bucks is big news around here," I said. "How many ways you gonna split it?"

The barkeep turned to his companion. "Check out tough boy here with his questions."

"I'm inquisition," I said. I left out the part about the private license. "Ask Dr. Testafer here. He was just answering some questions about the little room upstairs. How Overholt keeps the bodies from rotting when they stub their toes."

The barkeep turned and stared at Testafer. I put my hands over his and helped him let go of my collar. He was too busy looking and thinking about Testafer to notice.

"I've seen you," he said. "You go around with the fat man."

Testafer just about swallowed his tongue. He was looking even smaller than the kangaroo's gun. I'd seen the guy in his

element—up on the hill, surrounded by upholstery and antique magazines and a little filigree box full of make—and
this was definitely not his element. I don't know how Phoneblum convinced him to go out with the kangaroo and play
errand boy, but it wasn't a happy arrangement.

The kangaroo wasn't so far out of his milieu, but he
seemed a little disconcerted anyway. He stumbled backwards
in the gravel, waving his gun, not knowing where to point it.
The big guy from the poolroom was squaring off against him,
instinct telling him to go up against the one carrying the gun.

It occurred to me that I was witnessing a conflict between people who all essentially worked for Phoneblum.
The fact that they didn't know each other suggested that
Phoneblum's position was less secure than he'd pretended,
that he couldn't afford to let his cronies here at the Fickle
Muse know about the trouble he was having with Celeste,
and the Office, and me.

The speculation was entertaining, but I couldn't afford to
wait and see if the misunderstanding continued. I got my
keys out again and began working on unlocking the car door
behind my back.

Testafer definitely didn't like the situation. He looked at
the kangaroo, desperation in his eyes. "This is pointless," he
said. "She's not here. Let's go."

The kangaroo agreed. "Call these goons off, Testafer. It's
you they know." He thrust the gun out, but the big guys
didn't look frightened.

"We could break thumper's head," the pool player
suggested.

"Forget the kangaroo," said the barkeep. "He's not important. Give me his gun. Then go get Overholt. I wanna
consult."

Cue Ball laughed. He and the barkeep were too big even considered separately, but together they were like halves of something you didn't want to think about. He stepped over and twisted the gun out of the kangaroo's hand. Poor Joey. He didn't know the rules. He'd brandished the gun without using it for so long that now he didn't count as having one. He looked with animal stupidity down at his empty hand, as if blaming it for failing to shoot. Cue Ball gave the gun to the barkeep, then turned back to the kangaroo. He took Joey roughly by the shoulders, if you could call them shoulders, and shoved him down onto the gravel. Then he headed back to the bar.

Joey got up and dusted himself off. I got out one of the half hundreds in my pocket and handed it to the barkeep. "Here you go," I said. "Don't spend it all in two places." I opened the door to my car.

Now it was the barkeep's turn to wave the gun. "Stay out of there," he said. "All three of you, get against the car."

The kangaroo was in a trance. He and Testafer crossed between me and the barkeep, trying to obey orders, and I decided to make some trouble. I took them each by the neck and pushed them into the barkeep's gun hand, and when the dust cleared, the kangaroo and the barkeep came up wrestling for the gun. Testafer crawled away to cower behind a car. I couldn't figure out who I wanted to see win the prize, so I just leaned back against my car to watch.

The barkeep knocked the gun to the ground, but it only seemed like a good idea, because that gave Joey the chance to get his big foot up in position between them. At this point I almost wanted to look the other way, because I knew what was about to happen, and from the look on the barkeep's face he knew it too. Time seemed to stand still as he groped for the gun—he might as well have been rubbing two wet sticks together to get the jump on a guy with a flamethrower. Before the gun was off the ground, the kangaroo delivered a series of short, fast, and devastating blows to the center of the barkeep's body. The barkeep doubled over, clutching at the kangaroo's leg for support, and collapsed when it was pulled away. He almost looked small curled up on the ground. The night covered him up like it was done with him.

It was a pretty impressive vindication of Joey's animal lineage. I didn't want to stick around for the second act. I got into my car and put the keys in the ignition. Unfortunately Joey wasn't finished. He picked up the gun from beside the writhing figure on the ground and let off a shot that splintered the windshield in front of me. "Get out," he said raggedly.

I took my hands off the wheel, left the motor running. "Put the gun away, Joey."

"Fuck you, flatface." He twisted his muzzle into a sneer. "I've had enough of you. Get out."

I sighed and got back out of the car. The barkeep was motionless now on the ground, and Testafer was long gone, so it was just me and the kangaroo squaring off in the dark of the parking lot. The lights and music of the Fickle Muse seemed far away now. Joey was breathing heavy, his eyes wide and crazed. The broken glass of my windshield was proof enough that he'd found his trigger finger.

"Okay, Joey," I said. "It's your show. Just keep in mind if you don't hurry, you'll have company." I nodded my chin at the lights of the bar.

I couldn't believe it. He took the bait and looked. It was the last brushstroke in the portrait of the kangaroo as rank amateur. I unclipped the anti-grav pen from my shirt pocket and lobbed it gently at his face. When he turned back and caught sight of the pen in the air between us, he made a calculation of its trajectory based on a weight it didn't have, and batted at it with his free hand at about chin level. The pen soared through the air, the proverbial rising sinker, and hit him in the eye. He squeezed off a shot in the air before I landed my right fist on the underside of his jaw.

I made contact so solid, I almost regretted it. The hand was instantly useless. I didn't have time to weep over spent knuckles, though. I put the bad hand around the back of his neck and moved in close to smash his nose with the hand that still worked. I got in about three good ones before I had to let both hands dangle, but by then Joey wasn't looking so great. A dewy string of saliva stretched between his mouth and my fingers. The gun was still in his paw, but when I jostled it with my knee, he didn't even look to see where it fell. I'd learned from the last encounter that it was a waste of time trying to get a kangaroo to fall down. I kicked the gun under a car, grabbed my pen, and left him there swaying on his big feet.

The two shots brought Cue Ball and some other guys tumbling back out of the Fickle Muse. I took this as a hint to get in my car. My hands didn't work all that well on the steering wheel, but I managed to put the car in reverse and peel out of the space just as the first guy jogged up to my window. I screwed the wheels around to face the exit to the street, and caught one last glimpse of the scene in my rearview as I drove away. The barkeep was up on one knee. Someone else was digging under a car for the gun. I could even make out Testafer's pink face hovering between two cars. They looked like a group of white dolls or puppets acting out some idiotic farce in the middle of a black night which then swallowed them whole. I pressed the gas pedal to the floor and squealed away from there before somebody got hold of the gun and started taking potshots at me again.

A few miles away I pulled over into a driveway and turned off my lights. Nobody was following me. I folded my hands together, which took some doing, and flexed them until the knuckles cracked back more or less into their original positions. The pain almost had me screaming. When I felt ready to use my fingers again, I broke up some make on the dashboard mirror. There was a bleak interval while I waited for the drug to hit my bloodstream, and then the pain went away. I waited another few minutes for my heart to stop hammering, and then drove down the hill to my office.

CHAPTER 25

I WAS THROUGH THE REVOLVING DOORS IN THE LOBBY OF my building when Catherine Teleprompter came out of the shadows and took my arm. Her hair was loose again—I mention this because it was the first thing I noticed. She pulled me into the darkness against the wall of the lobby, a finger raised to her lips. I smiled and put up a finger to match hers. My hands felt better if they were elevated, anyway. She put her mouth close to my ear and started whispering. I had trouble concentrating on anything but the heat of her breath against my face.

"They're upstairs," she was saying.

"Then they must want to see me," I whispered back.

"Kornfeld's taken your file off the computer," she said. "I don't know what it means."

I turned so she could see me smile in the dim light of the lobby. "In my day," I said, "that was the end of the line." I laughed without making any noise. "But that doesn't necessarily mean anything. My day came and went a long time ago."

She didn't say anything. She still hadn't let go of my arm. I certainly wasn't taking it away from her. I just hoped she wouldn't try to hold my hand.

"I don't want you to go upstairs," she said finally.

"Okay," I said. "But I want to talk to you. That is, if you feel you can afford to be having the conversation. Last time you weren't so sure."

The weight of the enormous scrolled ceiling of the lobby seemed to press down on us as we huddled in the corner. The building was quiet, but I could sense Kornfeld, or whoever it was, waiting in my office. In fact, I could sense them across town too, waiting in the living room of my apartment. That time had come. I would have liked to go somewhere with Catherine Teleprompter, but there wasn't much of anywhere to go.

So I suggested we sit in my car.

"Let's make it mine," she said. "I can listen to Kornfeld on the radio."

I told her it sounded okay and followed her out to her car. She sat behind the wheel and fiddled with the Office radio until it came in low and clear. The voice of the dispatcher droned on ceaselessly, spewing codes and coordinates, stirring up old memories in me of nights out cruising, alone or with a partner, listening to the voices on the radio, knowing and caring what they meant. I didn't anymore. I knew I could sit in her car for as long as I liked and not care once. Unless maybe they mentioned my name, and even then only maybe.

I kept my foot on the passenger door so the overhead light would stay on, but I didn't look at Catherine. I was a million miles away. On my drive from the hill the bullet-cracked glass of my windshield had fragmented my reflection into a thousand pieces. Now, in Catherine's car, I was one piece again—one piece stretched out in the warped Plexiglas of the Office vehicle, until I looked like the fat man at the sideshow. Or Phoneblum.

"Tell me what you think," I said softly, after a little time had passed.

"I think it could blow over in a few days," she said. "But I wouldn't be you around here until then. I'd be somewhere else or I'd be someone else. Kornfeld doesn't like you."

"I figured that out."

"There's no point in going on, you know. Angwine is gone. Morgenlander was sent away. The case is closed."

"The case is closed. It's so easy to say. The inquisitor's mantra: the case is closed, the case is closed."

She almost laughed. "How'd you last a day in the Office?"

"One of us has changed since then. Me or the Office. I haven't figured out which."

"I think it was you," she said.

I turned and looked at her. She was sitting sideways behind the steering wheel, and I could see she'd been watching me the whole time. Once I turned, I had no choice but to look into her eyes. I took my foot out of the door and let the light go off, solving the problem for the moment. I wasn't making a decision about eye contact between us, I was putting it off.

"You went around with Kornfeld," I said. "You must know a certain amount about the case."

My eyes were getting used to the darkness. Street light leaked through the windows, outlining her neck and jaw against the black backdrop of her hair. I watched her throat bob as she considered an answer, but nothing came from her mouth. Except, I imagined, the sweet, warm mist I'd felt on my ear a few minutes ago.

I sighed. "Okay, Catherine. Think of it like this, if it doesn't make you laugh too much. Think of me as the conscience of the Office, the tiny vagrant molecule of conscience that got loose and won't stop, even when the case is closed, even after it's become more than a little dangerous. I'm your big chance, Catherine. Get it off your chest. Tell me what you know about the case. Then you can forget it, even forget you told me what you knew. It'll help you sleep."

We were quiet again. I could make out the little wrinkles in her brow, and the tension around her mouth. It was a speech I'd delivered before, and maybe even believed in. Either way, it seemed my words had actually touched something in her.

When she spoke again, her voice was deeper, less breathy, like she was talking out of hypnosis, out of some truer self. "I don't mind if you ask me questions," she said. "Find out what you need to know."

I looked, but her eyes were hard. It could be I was advancing my case at the expense of what was in the air between us.

"Okay," I said. "First of all, what's the case against Angwine? What was in the letter they found?"

"I only saw the letter once. I wasn't on this case until yesterday, and I read through a lot of material to try and catch up. My impression is that Angwine wanted money, for him and his sister. He got self-righteous, accused Stanhunt of moral indiscretions. Angwine saw himself as representing the interests of his sister and her baby against Stanhunt, and when Celeste moved into the house, he took up her grievances too. He didn't approve of Stanhunt's heavy drug use, and he accused him of seeing a woman on the sly."

"I was working for Stanhunt. He wasn't having an affair. He wanted Celeste back."

"We're pretty sure he was meeting a woman in the Bayview Motel."

I shook my head. "He went there to spy on Celeste. She was having the affair. You can talk to another P.I. named Walter Surface. He even saw the boyfriend once, he says. Maynard Stanhunt took a room to keep an eye on her. A jealous confrontation—that's a better motive than anything I've heard said against Angwine."

She sighed. "Listen. All I can do is tell you our case. Your material doesn't fit."

"What's your case? I still don't get it."

"Angwine threatened in the letter that he'd follow Stanhunt. Made it clear he didn't approve of the affair, whoever the woman was. So Angwine tails Stanhunt to the Bayview and finds out that the woman in question is his sister. She's been hiding it from him. But it happened once before, which is how she got the child, and maybe the flame never went out. Angwine goes out of his head and kills Stanhunt. It accounts for everything, including Pansy's reluctance to shield her brother."

I have to admit it stopped me dead in my tracks. It was the first coherent explanation I'd heard, and that included any I'd cobbled together in my head. I would have liked to believe it, except I was getting pretty attached to my idea that Celeste, not Pansy, was the mother of the babyhead. Anyway, Angwine was innocent. He hadn't played it completely straight with me, but he hadn't done the murder. I'd stake my life on it. Hell, I already had.

"What about the sheep?" I said.

She got sarcastic. "Aside from Angwine's prints in the blood we don't have much to go on. Maybe you can clear him of that one."

"He stumbled into it, came running back to me," I said. I

realized that sounded lame. "He didn't do it, Catherine. Take my word for it. It's too easy."

"Sometimes easy means right. Jesus, Metcalf. What am I doing? I should be taking you in, or maybe letting you go— anything but sitting here giving you ammunition for this idiotic, wayward inquisition of yours." She frowned at me in the darkness. "Don't judge me, all right? You're on your track, I'm on mine. I said you could ask me questions. But that's it. Don't get me tangled up in your eccentric theories."

I turned away, chagrined, angry at myself. I was a guy with twenty-five points of karma sitting talking to an inquisitor. Definition of a fool.

"Sorry," I said. "I'll try to be a little more professional. What do you know about a guy named Phoneblum?"

"I don't recognize the name."

I thought about opening the car door again to look her in the eye, but I didn't do it. "He's in this case up to his fat neck. Kornfeld sure knew the name—it cost me twenty-five points to mention it in his presence. I got the feeling he was protecting Morgenlander from something."

"Morgenlander was a clown," she said. "He came on way too strong. He kept filing complaints with the Main Office. Nobody could say anything around him."

I put my hands on the dashboard, and remembered they hurt. "Morgenlander thought there was more to this case," I said. "He was trying to keep it open."

"I know. He was doing a good job of that until the sheep turned up."

"Too bad."

"Too bad for you, I guess."

I snickered. "Morgenlander wasn't exactly making my

life pleasant. His nickname for me was Dickface. I don't think he saw me as an asset to his inquisition."

She was quiet. I guess she was waiting for me to run out of questions.

"Where are you supposed to be, right now?" I asked. "Were you staking out my lobby?"

"I'm on my own time." It could have been encouraging except she said it so neutrally. I wanted her to be on my side in the case, and if I scratched the surface of my feelings, something I try never to do, I wanted a whole lot more. But it wasn't happening. She sensed my desire for her professional allegiance, and it made her nervous. If she sensed the other desire, she was keeping her feeling about it hidden.

Something in the drone of words coming from the radio suddenly caught my attention. I thought I heard the name Stanhunt. Catherine must have thought she heard it too, because she turned up the volume and we both got quiet and listened.

They gave the address of the sex club downtown, and said something about a murder, no suspect, or a suspect, no murder. I listened for a while, but the voice looped around to other things and then back to the excitement at the sex club without giving the name again. I looked at Catherine at the same moment she looked at me.

"Maybe we ought to go have a look," I said.

"Maybe I ought to go have a look," she said. "You should steer clear, and you know it."

I smiled. "I'd just go in my own car, which is a waste of gas. You might as well take me."

She sighed and turned the key in the ignition. We didn't say anything the whole way over. It gave me the chance to fantasize that we were just two people together, for no special reason except we liked it, and we were going for a drive, maybe to a show or a restaurant, maybe even into the country for some overnight deal. It wasn't completely implausible. I closed my eyes and let the image wash over me while she drove, but it was pretty effectively extinguished when we pulled up in front of the sex club amidst the sirens and flares of the inquisition.

CHAPTER 26

I FOLLOWED CATHERINE PAST THE BARRICADES WITHOUT anyone asking me questions I couldn't answer, and without having to flash my license even once. It took only a few words with the inquisitor watching the door of the murder room to get us inside. The club was a place where you could rent the equipment—leather stuff, chains, electronic safety devices—and a soundproof room to use it in, as well as the assurance that anything went, as long as both parties walked out more or less alive. That was what hadn't happened here, and the inquisitor at the door let us know it was Celeste Stanhunt it hadn't happened to.

I went into the room behind Catherine. But she'd only taken a step or two inside before she turned quickly, her head lowered, hand over her face, and went back out. Which left me with nothing between me and the pile that had been Celeste Stanhunt except a short stretch of floor. The blood was on my shoes before I'd had a chance to consider staying out of it.

Someone had started from the bottom on Celeste, which is sometimes okay, but they'd kept going long past where it was a good idea to stop. They'd done a real nasty job on her.

If that sounds cold, it's the only way I can put it. She wasn't wearing any clothes, but I was going to have to rely on my Peeping Tom memories to know what she was like undressed, because you couldn't figure it out from looking at her now.

I stood there looking and thinking, and not feeling anything at first, and then it hit me, and hit me hard. I didn't experience nausea the way Catherine had—that went away a long time ago and never came back—but I felt pretty much everything else. I started sobbing into my sleeve, the first time I'd cried in years. It went away fast, but it left me feeling like my face was a baby's behind that needed changing, diaper rash and all. I stopped being able to look at the corpse. I backed out of the room past the inquisitor at the door, and I went and leaned against a wall. I closed my eyes, but the picture didn't go away.

My work at putting myself back together was interrupted by a familiar, if unexpected voice.

"It's a setup," said Morgenlander. I opened my eyes. He was talking to Catherine and the inquisitor at the door. "We're meant to believe she forgot to insert her death control device," he went on. "But I for one don't buy it."

It was the same old Morgenlander, with his fat head and his black-looking teeth and tongue, and I was pretty sure he'd say something stupid when he saw me, but in a funny way I was glad to see him. He was a wretched excuse for a human being, but for an inquisitor he wasn't half bad. If Kornfeld was the robotic visage of the future of the Office, Morgenlander was a throwback. He represented the human face, for what that was worth.

"You can file a report," said the inquisitor who'd let us into the room.

"Fuck that," said Morgenlander. "I wasn't here."

"I understand," said the inquisitor.

A team of evidence guys crowded the hallway on their way into the room. I wished them luck. When they cleared out, Morgenlander caught sight of me, and screwed up his features in an expression of distaste. It wasn't a long distance for his features to go.

"I don't believe it," he said. "The fly in the ointment. How'd you get here?"

"Hello, Morgenlander." I wasn't really up to repartee.

"I'm surprised you're still on the streets, Metcalf. Didn't I bill you enough karma?"

"Plenty, thanks. I thought you were off this case."

"The case is closed. Go home, Metcalf. Don't be stupid."

"The case was closed," I said. "Angwine didn't kill Celeste Stanhunt too."

Morgenlander just stood there in his baggy, disheveled suit and stared at me, as if what I'd said was something other than obvious. He moved his big jaw like he was sanding the roof of his mouth with his tongue.

Then he shook out his sleeves the same way he did in my office the first time I met him. "Okay, Metcalf. Let's go have us a little talk. Teleprompter, bring your pal here downstairs. I'm gonna use him to bounce some ideas off of. We'll see if they knock holes in him or just leave dents."

We all went downstairs, Morgenlander at the head, pushing through the milling inquisitors, head lowered, hands in his pockets. When we got outside, it was quieter. Some of the cars were gone, and the street was opened back up for traffic. Someone still thought it was important to flash a light around, and when Morgenlander stopped on the pavement and turned to me and Catherine, his face was lit into a series of red masks which pulsed and faded, one after another. I

guess I was in pretty poor shape, because the effect hypno-
tized me. I didn't notice what the man was saying until
halfway into his saying it.

"Celeste tried to call me twice," he was saying. "Wouldn't
leave a goddamned message. The Office didn't tell me until
about an hour ago, which is about the time she was getting
cut up." He sighed. "I told them to put a trace on her. Fucking Kornfeld."

"Last night she told me she was afraid," I said. "She didn't
think Angwine was the killer. That's what she would have told
you if she found you."

Morgenlander twisted his mouth. "That wasn't what she
told me when she had the chance."

"She changed her mind a lot."

He chewed his mouth for a minute and then spat into the
gutter. "Fucking case," he said.

"The case is closed," I said. I just wanted to be the first to
say it, for once.

Morgenlander turned to Catherine. "Where's Korn-
fuck?" he asked.

"I don't know," she said.

"He know you're going around with this hobbyist?" He
pointed a finger at my chest, came just short of prodding me
with it. "Last I heard, he wanted your ass, Metcalf."

"We're sort of steering clear of him for tonight," said
Catherine.

"Good luck," said Morgenlander. "Remember the walls
have eyes. Kornfeld's eyes." He gestured past me, at the pair
of inquisitors leaning against the doorway of the club. "He's
got Eastbay in his fucking pocket. Hell, I don't know why I'm
telling you this. Odds are you're part of the problem." He
laughed his wet, ugly laugh. "It doesn't matter. I'm out of

here. Someday me or somebody else is coming back to nail your little boyfriend's butt to the wall. I just couldn't do it alone. He kept me smothered in disinformation."

I kept quiet and listened.

"You made it tough, Morgenlander," said Catherine. "Why be surprised at the backlash? You made everyone nervous. It's been played a lot cooler than you played it."

"Fuck you, Teleprompter. Angwine was going down, and he wasn't the first. I'm supposed to do something about it."

Catherine made a face. "Go back and file your report, Morgenlander. Tell yourself you understood what was going on."

Someone turned off the lights. I looked around. The cars were thinning out in the street behind us. The crew upstairs would work the body and the room over for most of the night, but everyone else was going home or back on the street to work on their quotas. You had to change a couple of hundred points of karma in a given night or you weren't doing your job.

Teleprompter and Morgenlander just stood in the darkness and glared at each other. I had a feeling the conversation was about wrapped up. I myself would have liked to go home and curl up around a line of make, but I had another feeling there was more I should get out of Morgenlander while I had the chance.

"You ever hear the name Phoneblum?" I asked. "I mean, from anyone besides me." I hoped he wouldn't balk at answering a question. "My job lately has consisted of tossing his name at people and watching them flinch—except when I get punched in the stomach."

"Which do you want this time?" said Morgenlander sourly. When I didn't answer, he said, "Aw, get out of my face." He turned and walked quickly away. For whatever reason, I looked down, and even in the darkness I could make out the bloody footprints he'd left behind on the pavement. I didn't check, but I knew I was making footprints like that myself.

Catherine and I went back to her car in silence and sat down in what were now feeling like our accustomed places. I guess we would have driven somewhere if we'd known where to go. The radio was still mumbling at us, and Catherine reached and turned it off.

When she spoke again, I could hear a tremble in her voice. The mess upstairs had unsettled her, and her neat ideas about the case were no longer looking so neat.

"Who killed her?" she asked softly. It was like she'd decided to try believing me, to see if it felt better than buying Kornfeld's version.

I almost blurted out: *Who didn't?* But it was an ugly remark and I held it back.

When I got into this business, I had the stupid idea that my job was picking the one guilty party out of a cast of innocents. The truth was it was more picking the one or two innocents worth helping out of a cast of villains. I'd failed with Orton Angwine, and now I'd failed with Celeste Stanhunt. It was tough when the way you figured out who to trust was when they turned up hacked in half in a soundproof sex club.

"Phoneblum's kangaroo was looking for her a couple of hours ago," I told Catherine. I tried to keep my mind focused on the specifics of the case, and blot out the guilt and outrage that made me want to do crazy things like confess to the murders myself. "For that matter, so was Dr. Testafer," I went on. "But that didn't look like the work of a doctor."

"It looked like the work of a maniac."

"Maybe Barry Greenleaf killed her," I said, getting silly. "I told him this afternoon I was pretty sure Celeste was his mother."

"Were you in love with her?" Her voice was still soft. I turned, but she wasn't looking at me.

"Where'd you get that idea?"

"It's in your file," she said.

"I thought my file was out of access."

"I got access."

I allowed myself a smile. I knew now that the something I felt in the air between us was more than just my wishful thinking. I didn't know what to do about it, but I had my confirmation.

"The file is a little inaccurate," I said. "We met twice. The first time I was drunk, and the second time she was lying. I guess I hit her once. That's about it."

Catherine murmured, as if she understood why Celeste might need to be hit by someone, or why I might need someone to hit.

"You and Kornfeld?" It wasn't structurally a question but I put a question mark at the end of it. "Morgenlander called him your boyfriend."

It was her turn to smile to herself. I guess she was getting the same kind of confirmation I'd gotten. "He wanted it," she said. "But no."

"Wanted it?" I said. "He gave up?"

"Wants it," she said with a sigh.

"Guess that's part of what's making my life so fucking difficult right now, isn't it?"

"Could be."

I had to laugh. If Kornfeld understood the current status of my sexuality, he'd be laughing with me. I guess it wasn't in my file. She sat and listened, and if she wondered what was funny, she kept it to herself.

Eventually I shut up, and when I did, it got quiet in the car, for a long time. We were both looking out the front window, only I was looking at the reflection of Catherine, and when I found her eyes, I could see she was looking at the reflection of me. And then we were holding hands. It was just like that; one minute we weren't and the next we were. I want to say it made me feel like a schoolboy, but I hadn't done anything like that as a schoolboy. It made me feel like someone else who had done it as a schoolboy and was being reminded of it now. It made the back of my neck flush. It made me nervous as hell.

We held hands until our palms were sweaty. I realized that maybe it was me who was supposed to make a move. She didn't know I lacked the nerve endings for what was developing, and I wasn't about to tell her.

"Let's go somewhere," I said. "Your place."

"My place isn't good," she said. "Let's go to yours."

I looked at her funny. "Isn't Kornfeld supposed to have somebody watching it?"

"Yeah," she said. "Me."

CHAPTER 27

I WENT INTO THE KITCHEN TO POUR US A COUPLE OF drinks, and while I was there I laid out a line of my blend on the table. After a moment's hesitation I snorted it up with the tap running to cover the sound. I don't know where my sudden bashfulness came from, but there it was. When I went back out, she was sitting comfortably right in the middle of the couch, so whichever side I chose to sit on, I'd be close. That was okay. She looked good in my apartment, better than I did. I guess she'd had some practice sitting in it in the past few days.

I handed her the drink.

"Sit down," she said.

I sat down. We were close, all right.

After that I kind of lost track of the time. We just drank and talked, and after a while I got tired of going into the kitchen for drinks and brought the bottle out and put it on the coffee table. It was twelve, and it was one, and it was two, and I didn't care. We talked about a lot of stupid things, which was nice, and then we talked about a lot of nice things, which was nicer. But we never talked about the case. Not once.

When the conversation finally lagged, I kissed her. It wasn't like kissing Celeste. It was the first time I'd really kissed a woman in years, because the other night with Celeste didn't count, didn't prepare me at all.

We put the drinks aside and spent a while on the couch. I tried to keep us going slow, but it wasn't easy. When her breast fell into my hand, it was like the first drop of rain hitting a piece of metal so dry and rusted and hot in the sun that the water evaporates and the metal is instantly dry again. I didn't pay any attention to the pain in my fingers. It had been a long time, and a couple of possibly broken fingers was hardly enough to stop me.

We went in and stretched out on top of my bed. I put out the light. When she took me in her hands, I closed my eyes. The sensations weren't exactly right, but it didn't matter, it finally didn't matter at all. I liked the way it felt, and if I moved my hips a little, I could detect my weight in her hand. We stayed like that for a while, and then I took myself out of her hand and leaned over and put us together. She put her arms around me, and I unfolded my legs and let my body fall slowly on hers.

It wasn't as bad as I'd feared. Maybe it was my imagination, or the seepage of old memories into the present, but I swore I could feel her around me, the way I was supposed to. I fell out a few times, and my hips kept on thrusting before I figured it out—but I wasn't such a pro that that hadn't happened before anyway. I had her convinced that I was a man and she was a woman, and once we got into the rhythm of it, I had myself half convinced too.

And then it all came back, and I almost started weeping over her shoulder, into her black hair. Everything hit me at once. I knew suddenly that what I was after wasn't something lost in the past. I swear it came to me in those exact words.

I knew all at once that I didn't care about the woman who'd left me like this, that I didn't want her back and I didn't want revenge, and I didn't want Celeste, or anybody else, only the woman moving under me right now. I wanted Catherine, I wanted her with everything I had—except I didn't have it anymore. What I had to offer, or should have had to offer, was missing, and I'm not talking about my penis. I wanted Catherine, but I wanted to take her with a different self, a self that wasn't available. The thing I wanted wasn't lost in the past at all, and it never had been. It was lost in the future. A self I should have been, but wasn't. A thread I'd let go of in myself, thinking I could live without it, not seeing what it meant.

Then the physical aspect overwhelmed introspection. I held her and I fucked her for all I was worth. My fervor probably resembled anger. Actually it was longing, and fear, in roughly equal measure. When I felt I could, I looked in her eyes, and held her head in place to make sure she looked in mine. The finish took a long time, and I didn't rush it, and I didn't let her rush it. We ended crushed in a heap together at the top of the bed, her knees up against my chest, my head in the crook of her neck.

She fell asleep, but I didn't. When I thought it wouldn't wake her, I disentangled myself and went to the bathroom, and spent a while looking in the mirror. My penis was glistening, and I didn't wipe it off. In the dark I looked okay, my form outlined in the street light coming through the pebbled glass of the bathroom window, but I knew better than to turn on the light. I'd joined the ever-growing category of things that look better when you leave the light off. I didn't need to see the veins in my eyes and the red rings around my nostrils and the bruises and welts on my hands to know they were there.

When I got tired of looking at myself, I went and peeled the covers back and had a look at Catherine, just because I was in the mood. I looked at her up close, my face a few inches from her skin, and then dropped the covers and stepped back to see her in the context of my room. She looked fine at any distance. I covered her up again, put on a robe, and went out into the living room.

Our glasses and the bottle were still on the table, and her coat was slung across my chair. Otherwise it was just my apartment, with nothing to reveal the fact of a woman asleep in my bed for the first time in years. Hell, I've been known to drink out of two glasses when I get confused. It was easy to imagine I was alone. I got the vial of make from the kitchen and spread what was left of it, which wasn't much, onto the table.

The sky outside my window was warming up at the edges, and the stars were being bleached out of the picture. It was morning. I watched the night slip away from the buildings while I sucked up the last of my make and thought about my next move.

My hope didn't lie with the Office, despite the inquisitor sleeping in my bed. Catherine didn't swing enough weight, and anyway, she wasn't necessarily all that sold on my theories. If Morgenlander was still on the scene, I might be able to cajole him past his distaste for me and my profession, but that was a long shot. I had a funny idea about going back to confront Phoneblum with what I knew, but in the unlikely event he capitulated I didn't know what to ask for. If I got him to clear up my karma trouble, I'd be yet another grub squirming under his thumb, like Pansy, and Stanhunt, and Testafer, and so many others. Including, most likely, Kornfeld.

I was sure now I could solve this case. The question was who to go to once I solved it. I'd had a client once—a couple, if I counted Celeste—but they were out of the picture. I could solve the case, but for the sake of my own neck I might be better off if I didn't.

Kornfeld entered while I was wiping up the table. He didn't knock. He looked like he'd been up all night, but then I'd been up all night too. At least the guy was fully dressed, including a gun. I was in my robe.

"Get your clothes," he said.

I did what he told me to do. He didn't look in my bedroom, and if he recognized Catherine's coat or her lipstick on my glass, he didn't say anything, just stood and watched while I fumbled with the buttons on my shirt. The sun came in the window and glinted off his gun. When I had my shoes on, he asked me for my card and my license.

I handed them over. He put my license in his pocket and ran his decoder over my card. I held out my hand to get it back but he put it in the pocket with the license, and smiled.

"That's just a souvenir," he said. "You'll get a new one when you've done your time."

I must have stared.

"Welcome to the world of the karma-defunct, Metcalf. Get your coat."

We went downstairs to his car. I'll never know for sure, of course, but I don't think Catherine so much as tossed in her sleep.

PART II

SIX YEARS LATER

CHAPTER 1

IT WAS SHORT, BUT IT WASN'T SWEET. I WOKE UP FEELING like I still needed the night's sleep I'd missed when Kornfeld took me in. They had me in a set of ugly pajamas in a room that was blank and square and white, a room a whole lot like the one I'd been in what felt only minutes ago, with the doctors who'd readied me for the freeze.

An orderly sat in a chair in the corner, looking at a magazine. I got off the table, peeved, about to squawk about the thing not even working. Then the guy noticed that I'd come around and handed me my street clothes, all clean and folded, and I realized with a jolt that I'd done my time. The funny taste in my mouth was six years old.

I got dressed, slowly. The orderly didn't rush me. After a while he asked me if I was ready, and I said yes, and we went out into the corridor and took the elevator up to ground level. Inside the elevator the orderly looked me over and smiled. I tried to smile back, but I was pretty confused. I wanted to feel intuitively that six years had passed, but the feeling wasn't there.

He led me to an office where an inquisitor sat tapping something idly into a desktop console. He kept going for a minute after we came in, then he stopped and folded the screen back into the desk and smiled. I sat in a chair and waited, and while the orderly and the inquisitor initialed some paperwork and mumbled something to each other, I looked out the window at the sun glinting off the glass of the building across the street.

It was probably just a function of my newly defrosted eyes, but I swear it looked all wrong to me, the colors too bright, the outlines blurred. Like a badly retouched photo. It occurred to me that I was about to walk out the doors of the Office into that badly retouched photo forever. This was my world now, and the rest was gone. I realized that I was still all wound up inside about the case, and I had to laugh. It was pretty goddamned funny. As if there was still something to call a case.

The orderly left, and the inquisitor opened a drawer in the desk, pulled out a little metal locker about the size of a shoe box, and put it on the desk in front of me. Inside was the stuff they'd taken out of my pockets six years ago, all carefully tagged and wrapped in plastic. It wasn't much. The keys to my car and apartment, each of which had disappeared about five years and eleven months ago, when I stopped making the payments. The keys made a reassuring lump in my back pocket— I could use them to clean under my fingernails.

The rest was the ripped halves of six different hundred-dollar bills, and the anti-grav pen. I played with the money for a minute, trying to assemble something that looked like I could pass it through a bank teller's window, or at least across a counter in a darkened bar, but apparently I'd been in the habit of pocketing the same half of each bill. Until I ran into some other guy with the opposite habit, the paper was useless. I folded it and put it into my pocket anyway.

I was pulling the tags off the keys and the pen when I noticed the inquisitor leaning across the desk and staring at me, not a little intently. I looked at him, and he grinned. He was probably in his twenties, but I got the feeling he'd already seen a lot of karmic flotsam like myself coming and going out of the freeze, and that it made him feel smug to watch me struggling with my pathetic little array of possessions.

He got up suddenly and closed the door to the hallway. "I've been waiting for you."

"Oh, good," I said, bewildered.

"I'll give you fifty dollars for that pen," he said, moving around again to behind the desk. "That's the first of its kind." He spoke the way you spoke to children, back when there had been children. "It's a collector's item," he explained.

I had to smile. "That pen saved my life," I said.

He took it for a bargaining position. "Okay," he said. "A hundred."

"It's not for sale."

He looked at me funny. "I'm trying to do you a favor, old-timer. Your money doesn't look so good."

He had a point. "Hundred fifty," I said.

He leaned back in his chair and smiled without opening his mouth, then chuckled and took out his wallet. "I could have just taken it, you know."

"No, you couldn't," I said, a little miffed. "If you could have, you would have."

He opened his wallet, and there was music in the air, a little fanfare of horns that lasted until he gave me the money and put the wallet back in his pocket. It made my skin crawl. I hoped the music was in the wallet, not in the money.

He opened up another drawer in his desk and took out a

little envelope, sealed with a plastic ripcord, and a fresh card with my name on it.

"Seventy-five points," he said. "Best of luck." He flashed me his idiot grin. My exit interview was over, apparently. When I pulled the little cord, the envelope turned out to be full of generic make. A touching gesture.

I put the stuff in my pockets. I had an urge to wipe that smile-colored stain off the lower part of his face, but I held it back. I flipped him his pen, and he made the adjustment in his calculation of its trajectory and grabbed it before it soared over his head. But only just. "So long," I said, and got up and went out.

I passed through the empty lobby and into the sun. I didn't have my next move figured out, but my feet knew enough to create some distance between myself and the Office, and they got right to it.

When I got to the corner, I felt someone come up behind me and tug on my arm. It was Surface. The ape looked small and hobbled over, but then six years had passed, and anyway I'd never seen him out of his bed before. He was wearing a dirty gray suit and a red tie with little embroidered polo ponies on it. He had a pretty nice pair of shoes, but they were buried under a couple of centuries' worth of scuff marks.

He looked up at me. The leather of his face was wrinkled like foil. His expression was surprisingly gentle. "I saw in the paper you were listed as coming out," he said. "I thought you might need somebody to buy you a drink."

I was touched. I wasn't sure I liked having someone who looked as bad as Surface feeling sorry for me, but I was still touched.

"Sure," I said. "Lead the way."

The old ape turned his rounded shoulders and walked up

the block. I went after him. I didn't know what time it was, but the sun was high, and it occurred to me that Surface must have gotten out of bed early to catch me. It made me feel like a stray picked up at the pound, and it made me wonder if he thought maybe I needed more than just a drink to get me on my feet.

We went around the back of the building into the big parking lot. There were just a couple of people on the pavement, apart from the inquisitors coming in and going out to their black cars. When I tried to meet their eyes, the people turned to look at their watches, or the sky, or the gutter. My paranoia was functioning as usual; at the drop of a hat, it told me that my time in the freeze had left some mark, some indefinable tattoo on my aura, which would trigger recognition until I found a way to conceal it. Then I laughed at myself. What I needed was a drink, and a line of make.

I tapped Surface on the shoulder. "Where do I go to get my license?"

He looked at me and winced. I didn't think a face could get any more wrinkled than his already was, but it did. The wrinkles doubled in on themselves. His face practically collapsed.

"Hold off on the questions," he said through his teeth.

CHAPTER 2

WE GOT IN HIS CAR AND HE DROVE ME TO HIS APARTMENT and poured me a drink in his kitchen. The place was even more squalid than the house I'd found him recuperating in six years ago. I also didn't see any sign of his girlfriend, and maybe one was the cause of the other, though in which direction I didn't want to guess. The world he had built up around him then seemed to be gone. Once upon a time he'd been an ape P.I., with trimmings. Now he was just an old ape.

We didn't talk for a while. It seemed to suit us both. The bottle he produced was half empty to begin with, and we didn't have to struggle to finish the job. It hit my empty stomach pretty hard, but that was fine with me. I didn't really want to see what kind of food he'd provide.

I decided to find out what make was in the envelope. It was another buffer to put between me and this new world. I was afraid that when I started asking questions, I wouldn't like the answers I got. I wanted the make to help me forget all my questions.

I dumped the whole packet out on the table. It wasn't enough to divvy into portions. It was hardly enough for now, whatever the ingredients. I crushed it with my thumb and rolled up the envelope to snort with.

"I wouldn't do that if I were you," said Surface.

"I'm way past that lecture," I said.

He gritted his teeth and pushed away his empty glass. "Slow down, Metcalf. I'm trying to tell you you don't want it."

"Not want," I said. "Need."

"That'll give you what you're looking for and then some," he said. He licked his lips and spoke carefully and slowly, the second person in an hour to treat me like a child. I didn't like it. "You haven't got any memories to wipe out yet," he said.

"I've got plenty, from the first time around," I said. "Trust me. I can spare a few."

"The make is different," he said. His voice was low and insistent. "Do me a favor and skip it."

I sighed, unrolled the envelope, and used it to scoop the make into a little pile to one side of the table. My good feeling was gone. The alcohol was already going sour in my stomach.

"Okay, Surface. I'll do you a favor." I looked as deep as I could into the black of his eyes, but he didn't blink. "And you do me a favor back. Tell me what turned you into a pussy. You had more backbone lying in bed watching Muzak." I made myself laugh to cover my fear. "If I'm about to get like you, let me know so I can put a bullet through my head while I still have the guts."

His gaze fell, finally, and he reached for his glass, but it was empty. "You'll have to make some adjustments, Metcalf. That's not my fault. You just don't walk around spouting questions anymore."

"I mean to get a license."

"There's no license anymore," he said.

222 of JONATHAN LETHEM

"There's inquisitors," I said.

"No private."

"Well, there is now," I said, feeling full of bluster. "Here I am. There's no other name for what I do."

"Your role is obsolete," he said, too firmly, his voice heavy and dead. "You were walking that line before and you knew it. It's finished now, Metcalf. Let it go."

"Look who's talking," I said, and then stopped. It was supposed to be the beginning of something snappy, but my heart wasn't in it.

His lips peeled back in a grim smile.

"I consist solely of my role," I said, half to myself. "There's nothing else. I've looked."

"Look again," he said. "The role is gone. You can't even go around talking this much. Forget questions."

"Forget questions," I repeated. "I'll keep it in mind."

I ran my finger through the pile of white powder and drew a little path of it across the table. I wanted some up my nose. "What's wrong with the make?"

"There are no individual blends anymore. Just standard issue."

"What's standard issue?"

"Time-release Forgettol, mostly. It's all the rage. Snort it if you like—just make sure you write your name and address on a matchbook cover first. In big letters."

"I think I'll pass."

"Whatever." He sighed. "I might as well clue you in, Metcalf. Don't go around talking about the past. Memory is rude. That's what this stuff is for, and everyone uses it. In Los Angeles it's illegal to know what you do for a living. If you don't use it, pretend you do. And if you see people talking into their shirtsleeves, they aren't talking to you. Don't gape."

I waited for the rest, but his lecture was finished. He got up and went to the cupboard to rummage around, presumably for another bottle. I just sat there and let what he'd told me sink in, or tried to. It kept getting jammed about halfway down.

He located another bottle, less empty than the one we'd just polished off, but not by much, and dribbled what there was evenly into our two glasses. Then he sat down and drank his. I wondered how much alcohol it took to make his little body cry uncle, and then I figured he must have worked his tolerance up pretty high by now. When you don't know how many bottles you've got, it isn't because you haven't been drinking.

My drug of choice was different, of course, and my eye was still on the pile of make. My bloodstream was crying for some addictol, the one ingredient no blend left out. And maybe, too, there was a part of me that wanted, finally, to let go and buy into the generic reality.

I swept the little pile of standard-issue Forgettol back into the envelope, folded the flap over, and put it in my pocket. I'd need it to bluff with, like Surface said. If the shakes got too bad, I might need it to snort, and to hell with the consequences.

Surface put down his glass. "Goddamn, Metcalf," he said. "You know, I haven't talked this much in years."

"We weren't talking, just now."

He waved my sarcasm away. "I mean today, since picking you up."

I felt a surge of impatience. I wanted to tell him he'd talked just fine two days ago. But of course that was irrational. Surface had been gentle with me, but I had to be just as gentle with him. Because in effect I'd escaped the decline that hit while I was in the freezer. I'd have to take care not to remind people of how much was missing now as compared to before.

"Okay," I said. "I can take a hint. Thanks for the drink." I polished off what was left in my glass.

"Don't take it too hard," he said. "Keep your eyes open and your mouth shut. You'll learn the rules."

"I'll have my lips removed as soon as I learn a way to whistle out my asshole."

"That's the idea."

I guess I was making him happy. He'd set out to save me some trouble, and I was acting like I'd gotten the message. I didn't know whether or not to tell him the bad news—that a casual remark he'd dropped a moment ago triggered an insight, which made the whole case, six years dead or not, seem tantalizingly close to a solution. I might not have a license, but that wouldn't stop me from finishing what I'd started.

I was pretty sure the defeated old ape across the table from me didn't want to hear it. But the other Surface, the grizzled veteran private inquisitor I'd known six years or two days ago, might feel a different way about it, might like to think I was still on the job.

I didn't think about it long. The Surface who would have liked to know was six years gone. I was going to have to start making the adjustment. I got up and put on my coat.

"Don't take it too hard, Metcalf," said Surface again.

"Sure," I said. I wanted to get out of there, on the chance that what he had might be contagious. Besides, sitting still was making me nervous. I was thinking about the make in my pocket, and my hands were trembling.

I didn't tell Surface to stay in touch, or take care, or anything like that. I thought he'd appreciate me keeping my mouth shut, so I just turned around and put my hand up when I got to the door. He nodded at me, and I went out and downstairs to the street. The sun was in the afternoon half of the sky now, and my stomach was beginning to chew on itself. It was about a ten-block walk to a place where I used to like to get a sandwich. Maybe it was still there. I started walking.

CHAPTER 3

THE PLACE I HAD IN MIND WAS GONE, BUT THERE WAS another one just like it down the block. Apparently people still ate sandwiches. I broke the inquisitor's fifty-dollar bill on a ten-dollar heap of bread and mayonnaise and a three-dollar cup of soda, and when the cash register opened up for my money, it performed a little burst of orchestral music that lasted until the drawer was shut again. The guy behind the counter smiled like it was the most natural thing in the world. I wanted to smile back, but the smile wouldn't come.

"I suppose your jukebox makes change," I said.

The guy frowned like he didn't understand. He took a little mechanical box out of his pocket and spoke into a microphone grille on the side of it. "That thing about the jukebox, just now," he said.

"Just a joke," said a voice from the box.

"Oh, yeah," the guy said, and he looked at me and laughed.

I wanted him to be kidding, but he wasn't. I decided it must have been what Surface meant about people talking into their sleeves, and it made me shudder. I took the sandwich to a table in the back, but my appetite was gone. I ate it anyway. When I was done, I took the cup and the wrapper and put them in the can by the door. It rewarded me with a miniature flourish of trumpets, but this time I didn't say anything. I went outside instead and spent a quiet minute on the sidewalk putting the incident carefully out of my mind. My hands were trembling, so I put them in my pockets.

The next step, as I saw it, was to acquire some kind of housing and some kind of transportation, and in my situation that meant only one thing. You can sleep in a car, but you can't drive a room in a flophouse. I located a rental agency and forked over the hundred-dollar bill to a fat guy in a lawn chair as the deposit on a weather-beaten dutiframe with half a tank of gas. I made sure to flash the stuff that looked like a pocketful of hundreds when I handed him the intact bill.

"I need your card," he grunted.

It was new to me to hand it over to anyone but an inquisitor, but I remembered what Surface said about keeping my mouth shut and learning the rules, and took it out. I had the funny idea he was going to bill me points, but he just looked it over and wrote down the serial number, then handed it back. I looked at the new card for the first time. It had my name on it but it didn't feel like mine. It was too clean. Mine had the pawprints of a thousand chumps all over it, and I missed it.

That done, the guy let me sign a few forms and drive the wreck away. The hundred was my last real money, which left me with the car, the half tank of gas, and the clothes I was wearing. Plus the packet of make if I wanted to do some fast forgetting. It was looking better and better.

I drove the car up into the hills until I found a view I liked. Then I got out and looked at it. There was a wind coming up off the bay, and it brought with it a smell of salt. It made me think of the ocean, and I entertained a brief fantasy of taking the car and driving down the peninsula to find a beach where I could throw my make and the stuff that looked like money and maybe even my seventy-five points of karma into the surf and then stretch out on the sand and wait to see what happened. I played with it the way you can when you know you'll never do it. Then I started thinking about the case again.

I got back in the car and drove to the house on Cranberry Street. I didn't have any particular reason—I just wanted to. The case had started there, with me hired to peer in the windows at Celeste, and maybe I had the idea it would end there too. For all I knew the place was torn down by now, but I was willing to chance a little of my gasoline to find out.

The house was there. I can't say if I was glad or not. I parked the car and walked around the back, just for the sake of nostalgia. The lot in the backyard was still empty; whoever had the blueprints drawn up six years ago had changed his mind about spending the money. I walked most of the way around the house, but didn't bother to look in the windows. Nothing on the outside was any different.

Encouraged, I went up to the front and rang the bell. The wait was long enough that I was turning away when the door opened. It was Pansy Greenleaf, or Patricia Angwine. I didn't know which name was righter. She looked considerably more than six years older, but I recognized her immediately. She didn't recognize me. I hadn't aged a day—well, maybe a day—but she stood blinking in the sunlight, drawing a blank.

"My name is Conrad Metcalf," I said.

The name didn't make any more of an impression than my face had. I waited, but she just stared.

"I want to talk to you," I said.

"Oh," she said. "Come in. I'll consult my memory."

She led me through the foyer. The house wasn't kept up the way it had been or could have been, but when I walked into the living room to face the sun through that big bay window, it didn't matter. The architect had designed the room to make you feel small and out of place, and it worked. Pansy still crept through the house like a burglar, and by now she'd lived here at least eight years, so I knew it worked on her too. She brought me in, pointed to a seat on the couch, and stood for a minute studying my features, knitting her brow in a parody of thought.

"I'll be right back," she said. Her voice was light. She looked twenty years older, yet the pall of guilt and sorrow she had carried with her everywhere before seemed completely lifted.

I sat back on the couch and waited while she went into the kitchen. As far as I could tell we were alone in the house. The spot where I was sitting was warm, and spread out on the table in front of me was the last of what looked to have been a bunch of lines of make, and a razor and a straw. I didn't have to guess what Pansy had been doing when I rang the bell. The only thing I felt was a vague jealousy.

When she came back, she sat down across from me and put what looked like a pocket calculator with a microphone on the table between us.

"Conrad Metcalf," she said into the microphone.

I almost responded, but I was cut off by the sound of her own voice coming out of the device on the table. "I'm sorry," the voice said. "You don't remember that."

She looked up at me and smiled, puzzled. I tried not to

stare like too much of an idiot. "I don't recognize your name," she said. "Perhaps you should check your memory. This could be the wrong house."

I thought fast. "You got my name wrong," I said. "Maynard Stanhunt. Try it again."

"Oh," she said, chagrined. She depressed a button on the microphone and said the new name.

"Maynard Stanhunt," repeated the machine. "That nice doctor. He and Celeste were so nice to you, before. They've been away."

"You're that nice doctor," she said guilelessly, as if the words hadn't been spoken in her voice just seconds ago by the thing on the table. "It's been such a long time. It's nice to see you."

I was dumbfounded, but I worked double time to cover it up. "Yes," I said. "It's nice to be back."

"Well," she said. "I'm so glad."

"That's nice," I said. The word was like an infection. "It's nice to be glad."

"Yes," she said.

"I want to ask you a few questions," I said.

"Oh," she said again. "Questions."

I guess her hand was on the button, because the thing on the table said: "Only if it's completely necessary."

"It's completely necessary," I said before she got a chance to repeat it.

She looked in confusion at the machine and then up at me. She was unsettled by my responding to the recorded voice. I guess it was impolite to admit that it was there.

"Oh," she said. "I suppose it's all right. If it's completely necessary."

"Tell me how you can afford to keep the house," I said.

She knit her brow like a housewife whose cake has fallen in the oven. "The money for the house," she said into the mike.

"Joey gives it to you," came her voice right back.

"Joey gives me the money," she said. "He's so nice to me."

"Joey," I repeated. "What happened to Danny?"

"Danny," she said to the machine.

The thing said in her voice: "Danny Phoneblum. He's so big and fat. He used to be your best friend, practically. He got tired and went to live in the rest home. He's very good to Joey. Treats him like the son he never had. A whiskey and soda with just a twist of lemon, that's what he likes."

"I guess I didn't understand the question," said Pansy haplessly.

I was beginning to get it. Memory was permissible when it was externalized, and rigorously edited. That left you with more room in your head for the latest pop tune—which was sure to be coming out of the nearest water fountain or cigarette machine.

"Forget it," I said. "Tell me who got pinned with the rap for Celeste's murder."

"Celeste's murder," echoed Pansy.

"Celeste went away for a while," replied the voice.

"Celeste went away," said Pansy. "That's not the same as being murdered."

"No," I admitted. "It's not the same."

"You must have made a mistake," she said. "Consult your memory."

"It's okay," I said. "I made a mistake. Tell me about your brother. Is he out of the freezer?"

"My brother," she said.

"You don't remember your brother," said her memory. She looked at me and shrugged.

"Orton Angwine," I said.

"Orton Angwine," she said.

"The name just doesn't mean anything to you," said her memory.

"The name just doesn't mean anything to me," she said. "I'm sorry."

"No problem," I said. I was getting tired of the conversation. The ratio of redundancy to information was a little on the high side. I'd been playing with the idea that it might be the memory machine and not Pansy herself that I ought to interrogate. Now I changed my mind. The memory had too many gaps in it. Not as many as Pansy, but too many.

"You're so full of funny questions, Dr. Stanhunt," said Pansy. "I wish I understood."

"I'm sorry, Pansy. I wouldn't ask if it wasn't completely necessary."

"You ought to use a memory."

"I have the new kind of memory," I said. "It's a cranial implant. You don't have to speak out loud. You just think, and it talks to you in a quiet little voice in your head."

"Oh," she said. She thought about that for a minute. "It sounds very convenient."

"It's great," I said. "And I really appreciate your helping me fill in a few blank spots here and there. I've been away, and I guess I've got some catching up to do."

"You and Celeste," she said brightly. "You've been on a trip."

"That's right. Now tell me about Dr. Testafer. Do you remember him?"

"Dr. Testafer," she said into the mike.

"Old Dr. Testafer," said the memory. It sounded like the beginning of a nursery rhyme. "He lives on the hill. He was Dr. Stanhunt's partner, but he retired. A gin and tonic on the rocks."

"He's your partner," she said to me. "I'm surprised you're not in touch."

"I would like to be," I said. "Is he still living in the same place?"

"That's enough," came a voice from behind me. Barry Phoneblum was standing in the foyer.

"Barry," said Pansy, her voice warm and real for the first time since I'd rung the bell. "You must remember Dr. Stanhunt. Dr. Stanhunt, this is my son Barry."

"We've met," said Barry sarcastically. He was dressed pretty simply, in a neat little shirt and a pair of striped pants, and he wasn't wearing a wig this time. He wasn't any taller, but his face now was that of a teenager, and his vast forehead was six years more wrinkled. Veins stood out like worms under the skin at his temples.

"I want you to go upstairs, Pansy," he said firmly. "Dr. Stanhunt and I need to talk." He was talking to her, but he kept his eyes on me the whole time. It reminded me of Celeste coming home and sending the kitten away. I was always getting caught questioning people who didn't know better than to feed me the answers.

"Oh," said Pansy. She scooped the memory off the table and slipped it into the pocket of her skirt. She left the razor and the straw, but I suspected she had another set upstairs. She had new stuff to forget now.

"Okay," she said. "Good day, Doctor. Give my regards to Celeste."

I promised I would.

She tiptoed upstairs, leaving Barry and me alone in the living room. He vaulted up into the seat across from me in one neat movement, tucking his feet under his knees so they wouldn't dangle. I guess by now he'd had a lot of experience being three feet tall in a six-foot world. When he put his hand inside his coat pocket, I was expecting him to produce a memory. Instead he produced a gun. It performed a couple of bars of ominous, pulsing violin when it came out of his pocket, like the occasional music titled GUN for an old radio show.

"Metcalf," he said. "The kangaroo said you were coming back. I didn't believe him."

"It didn't take you long to come into the fold," I said. "So much for evolution therapy."

"Fuck you," he said. "My motives are beyond your comprehension." Fuck you was his motto now, or at least he delivered it like one.

"Try me."

He just sneered. The phone was on the table between us, and he leaned forward and plucked up the receiver without the muzzle of the gun ever veering out of line with my heart. I watched him push buttons. Whatever the number was, his little fingers had it memorized. He pinned the phone against his big ear with his shoulder and waited for an answer.

"It's Barry," he said after what must have been a couple of rings. "Get me the kangaroo."

The party at the other end kept him hanging a minute or so. I made amusing faces while we waited but he didn't laugh.

"Shit," he said, when the answer came. "Well, tell him I've got Metcalf here at the end of my gun. He'll know what it means."

They talked a little more, and then he put the receiver

back and looked at me sourly, his vast forehead wrinkled all the way up over his skull.

"You must really be a glutton for punishment," he said.

"A gourmet, actually," I said. "If it isn't perfect, I send it back."

He didn't laugh. "What did Pansy tell you?" he asked.

"Nothing I couldn't have learned from a brick wall. We tried to play tic-tac-toe, but she kept forgetting if she was X's or O's."

Barry didn't like that. I guess he still had some kind of proprietary interest in Pansy. His jaw tightened and his face got red where the skin wasn't stretched white with tension. "Fuck you, Metcalf." His voice shook. "I could blow you away right now if I didn't mind cleaning up the mess. You wouldn't be missed."

"Fuck you, Phoneblum. You pull that trigger now, and the recoil's gonna break your nose."

He moved the gun from in front of his face. "Don't call me Phoneblum," he said.

"Maybe you don't buy him ties on Father's Day," I said. "And maybe he never took you to see the World Series. But that doesn't change it."

"I'd forgotten your interest in genealogy," he said, recovering somewhat. But there was a conflict in him between the tough-guy lingo and the babyhead talk, a conflict he couldn't resolve. "It represents a pathetic inability to see beyond superficial relationships."

"I know what you mean. I'm having a real problem seeing beyond the relationship between the kangaroo's hand and the strings attached to your arms and legs." While I talked, I inched my feet forward on the carpet and slid my knees under the edge of the big glass coffee table. "I expected more of you, Barry. You were a pain in the ass, but at least you had style."

"You're making stupid guesses," he said. "I take the kangaroo's dough so I can care for my mother. That's the beginning and the end of it."

"Your mother's dead," I said. "I walked in her blood."

It was meant to make him flinch, and it worked. I jerked the coffee table up with my knees and toppled it over on him. The telephone and the razor blade slid to the floor in a cloud of make, and the table fell without breaking to create a glass wall which trapped Barry huddling in his chair. The gun was still in his hand, but he couldn't point it at me against the weight of the tabletop.

I put my shoe against the glass where his face was. "Throw me the gun, Barry. This'll make a big mess if it breaks."

He started squirming in his cage, but he didn't let go of the gun. I pushed with my foot on the glass until the chair tipped over and Barry tumbled out onto the carpet. The gun fell into a corner. The glass slid back down to rest, propped between the chair and the carpet, intact.

I went over and took Barry by the collar and shook him a little, until my anger subsided and his shirt started ripping, then I put him down. I would have hated for him to get the impression I didn't like the way he was dressed.

When I looked up, I saw Pansy watching us from halfway down the stairs, her hands folded neatly on the railing. She didn't look overly concerned. I had no idea what she thought was happening, or whether she still possessed the equipment necessary to speculate. I didn't particularly want to think about that. I was ready to go. The possible imminence of the kangaroo was not the only reason.

Barry was all balled up on the carpet, looking like nothing so much as an aborted fetus. I stepped over him and picked up the gun. It played me the music again. The violins didn't know the action was over. I put it in my pocket, smoothed down my jacket, and stepped out into the foyer. Pansy didn't say anything.

"You ought to buy your little boy a coloring book or a stamp album or something," I said. "He's got way too much time on his hands. He's liable to take up masturbation."

As I went out the door, I heard Pansy utter "masturbation" into her little microphone, but I was gone before I could hear the answer.

CHAPTER 4

I RAN INTO A CHECKPOINT IN THE HILLS ON MY WAY TO
Testafer's place. They were idling in a narrow spot on the
road, and I didn't see them until it was too late. An inquisitor
waved me over, walked up, and leaned into my window.

"Card," he said.

I gave it to him.

"This looks pretty clean," he said.

"It's new," I said. I looked him in the eye and hoped he
didn't see my hands shaking on the wheel. They were shaking
for a few reasons. The gun in my pocket was one of them.
The make not in my bloodstream was another.

He motioned another guy to come over to my car. "Take
a look," he said. "Rip Van Winkle." He flipped him my card.
It was funny: I hadn't felt much attachment to it before, but I
experienced a sudden fondness for it seeing it in the hands of
two boys from the Office.

"Beautiful," said Number Two. "Wish I saw more like
this."

I restrained my urge to comment.

"You got papers for the car?" said Number One.

"Rental," I said. The receipt was in the glove compartment and I got it out.

He glanced at it and handed it back.

"Where you headed?" he said.

I shrugged. "Taking a look at the old neighborhood."

"Got plans?"

I thought about it. I wondered how hard they'd laugh if I told them I was a private inquisitor on a case six years old. "I'm still getting my bearings," I said.

It made him smile. He turned to Number Two. "Hear that? He's getting his bearings."

Number Two smiled and stepped up to my car. "What did you do, Metcalf?"

"Nothing, really," I said. "Stepped on some toes. It's ancient history."

"Who sent you up?"

I thought fast. In all likelihood these were Kornfeld's boys. "Morgenlander," I said.

They traded a look.

"That's a tough break," said Number Two, and there was honest sympathy in his voice. He handed me back my card. I'd said the right thing.

"Damn shame," said Number One. "They should have sprung the last of his guys years ago."

I put my card in my back pocket and kept my mouth shut. I was suddenly okay in their book, which didn't mean good things for Morgenlander. It gave me a sinking feeling, one I wouldn't have expected to feel. I shouldn't have been surprised; Morgenlander's days were obviously numbered even six years ago. But I guess some stupid optimistic part of me had been hoping he'd squeak through.

"Okay," said Number Two. "Just don't use up all your money driving around in a rental car and reminiscing. You're a young guy. Get a job."

I thanked them and said so long. They went back to their roadblock, and I rolled up my window and drove away.

I thought about Kornfeld, and decided I didn't mind if a rematch occurred. I had a lot less to lose this time. I owed the guy a punch in the stomach if nothing else, and if his underbelly turned out to be six years softer, all the better.

Yes, Kornfeld had earned a spot in my mental appointment book, but Dr. Testafer came first. I wanted Grover's help, voluntary or not, with a couple of missing pieces. I found his street and parked in the clearing at the end of the driveway. Standing in the clearing brought back memories. I'd snorted make here three days or six years ago, depending on how you counted, and it made my nose itch to think of it. I tried to put make out of my mind as I walked up to Testafer's house, but it was tough. The issue was like a jack-in-the-box with an overanxious spring; it jumped out at the slightest prompting.

The house looked pretty much the same—the main house, that is. The little house on the left didn't look occupied. I guess Testafer had sworn off sheep after Dulcie. I rang the bell, and after a minute Testafer came to the door.

He'd always looked to me like he'd been fifty years old since adolescence, and six more years didn't really make him look any older. He was still red in the face, as if he'd been running up stairs, and there might have been fewer of the wisps of white that were trying to pass for hair, but given what little he was working with, he looked good, surprisingly good. Last I'd seen him, he was hiding between two parked cars, dodging bullets, a fish out of water. Up here in the doorway of his house, he looked more comfortable.

"Hello, Grover," I said.

He looked at me blankly.

I felt a fist of sudden anger curl in my stomach. He was going to pull a Pansy on me.

"Inside," I said, growling it. I put my hands on his chest and pushed him backwards into the house, and kicked the door shut behind me. "Get the memory."

His eyebrows arched incredulously. "Go," I said. I pushed him, and he stumbled ahead of me into the living room. The whole thing stank to me all of a sudden, stank terribly. I wanted to hit him, but he was too old to hit, so I reached down and swept my arm across a table covered with glass and ceramic baubles, and they crashed into a thousand pieces on the floor. Testafer just kept backing up until he fell into the couch. I turned to pull down the shelf of old magazines, but it wasn't there anymore.

"Where's the memory?" I said. "Get it out."

The door to the kitchen swung open and a guy came out with a drink in each hand—gin and tonic, if Pansy's memory had it right. He was about as old as Testafer, but he was as thin and white as Grover was fat and red. It didn't take me any time to figure it out. Testafer had a boyfriend. It wasn't a surprise. After he quit the practice, he must have missed handling penises. In a funny way I understood.

I stepped up and took the drinks. "Take a walk," I said.

The guy let go of the drinks like he'd made them for me. Grover spoke, and it came out a whisper.

"You'd better go, David," he said. "I'll be fine."

David picked his way quietly through the broken glass and pottery strewn across the doorway and obediently disappeared. Grover had switched from sheep that walked like men to men that walked like sheep.

When I turned back to him, he had his memory out on the couch beside him, the mike cord in his hand. I'd learned fast to despise the sight of the things. He looked at me with desperate eyes, and for an odd moment my anger abated and I felt sorry for him, but it didn't last.

"Metcalf," I said.

He knew what I wanted. He said it into the memory. His voice came back out quiet and slow, as if he'd spent a lot of time on this particular entry.

"The detective," it went. "A dangerous, impulsive man. Maynard made the mistake of bringing him in, and he wouldn't go away. Danny Phoneblum's oppositional double, and a fundamentally undesirable presence."

Testafer looked up at me blankly, his mouth tight, while his voice poured out of the machine. I found myself smiling. I sort of liked the description. At the very least it was reassuring to find some trace of my work left somewhere. I handed Testafer one of the drinks, and he sipped at it nervously while we waited to see if the entry was exhausted. It was.

"That's a very old memory," he said softly, his eyes full of fear. I studied him for some sign of genuine recollection, some hint of hostility or guilt, but it wasn't there.

"That's okay," I said. "It's up to date."

He didn't get it, or maybe he did and it scared him. Either way the effect was the same: he sat staring at me, blankly astonished, like a baby when you make faces at it. I sat down in the chair across from him and took a pull at the drink in my hand. Gin and tonic, all right. I was running out of steam, and the liquor tasted awfully good. I couldn't feel my anger anymore, and I wasn't particularly trying. It seemed too much to stay angry at a guy who didn't have the faintest idea what I was talking about. I felt the weight of the past like ballast, something only I was stupid enough to keep carrying, and I began to wonder if it was time to cut loose. Testafer made it look sort of good. For a moment I envied him, and began patting the pockets of my coat to locate the little envelope of make.

For a moment. Then I thought about what I was thinking, and took a deep breath and put the drink on the floor and licked my lips clean of the taste of alcohol and forgot about the make. I carefully curled the fingers of the fist of my anger, got up from the chair, and went over and picked up Testafer's memory. The cord to the mike stretched out between us. Testafer looked up at me, eyes wide, his mouth a little open. I felt my anger now, felt it clear and cold, and I wanted him to feel it too. I hoped it made him feel vulnerable to see his memory in the palm of my hand.

"Dulcie the sheep," I said through my teeth.

His eyes showed maybe the first glimmer of something more than funhouse fear.

"Say it," I said.

He said it.

"Your steadfast companion," came his voice out of the memory. "Her life was tragically cut short. The murder remains unsolved."

"That's a lie," I said. "Orton Angwine was pinned with the sheep's killing."

Testafer looked extremely uncomfortable. The hand that held the mike was shaking. "Angwine was convicted of killing Maynard only," he said.

"Who killed the sheep?" I said.

His eyes closed.

"Who killed the sheep?" I said again.

He leaned over and pursed his lips into the microphone.

With his eyes closed he looked like he was praying into the device. "Who killed the sheep?" he repeated.

"The murder remains unsolved," said the memory.

"The murder remains unsolved," he said to me, but he didn't open his eyes.

"I solved it, Grover. Open your eyes and tell me who killed the sheep." I reached down and gripped his hand hard until he dropped the mike. This time he opened his eyes, but he didn't speak.

"You don't need this," I said, showing him the memory. "You had me going for a minute there, but you blew it when you closed your eyes. Who killed the sheep?" I dropped the box and the microphone on the floor and crushed them under my shoe. It was all plastic and wire and chips, and it crumbled pretty easily even on the soft pile of the carpet. I kicked it, spread it with my toe, until it was mixed with the first mess I'd made there. Testafer got redder and spilled his drink trying to put it down, and I think his eyes were getting wet around the edges before he caught himself and reeled it all back in.

"I killed her," he said when he could without choking. "Tell me how you knew."

"That wasn't hard," I said. "I ruled you out at first because you hit the intestine. You didn't need to, to kill her, and someone who knew enough would avoid making such a mess. But you're no surgeon, and you're certainly no veterinarian. If hitting it was clever, it almost worked, and if it was stupid, you almost got lucky. Almost."

He didn't tell me which it was. I guessed stupid and lucky.

"Dulcie knew things that could have broken the case open," I said. "I didn't get them out of her, but you didn't know that. I left you there feeling violent and frustrated and panicked. Even at the time I wondered if you would hit her. It wasn't too big a jump to pin you with the killing."

I watched Testafer crumble and age on the couch in front of me. For six years he'd kept these memories from himself. It was obvious he'd been using the Forgettol and the memory device as a public front. But it was equally obvious, from the way he was deflating, that he was living through the visceral part of the memory now for the first time.

"For God's sake," he said through his hands. "Don't dig it all up again." He sounded as if he were being confronted with the carcass, literally.

"Relax," I said. "I'm not such a stickler for animal rights. You can buy me off with the answers to a couple of questions."

I meant it. Not that I thought he'd suffered enough—I wouldn't presume to weigh suffering against sins. But from here on I was in this game for my own satisfaction, and as far as Testafer was concerned, I was satisfied.

I gave him a minute to dry himself up.

"Celeste didn't go out of town eight years ago," I said. "She came here to stay with you. You were the family doctor. You delivered Barry, and she trusted you. Phoneblum was getting abusive and she needed out."

He nodded confirmation.

"Phoneblum didn't introduce Maynard to Celeste—you did. You were training him into your practice, and they met and the sparks flew, despite your warnings."

"That's pretty much right," he said.

"Celeste and the sheep were pals from when they lived up here together, during Celeste's hideaway. Dulcie knew all about Phoneblum, and you thought I'd squeezed it out of her. You didn't believe it when she said she'd kept her little black lips zippered, and you were angry at both of us, and you took it out on her."

He only nodded.

"She did all right by you, Grover. She didn't squeal. Maybe you would have preferred it if she never let me in the door, but she didn't volunteer anything important."

He was quiet. He'd sobbed once and he wasn't going to sob again. He was going to put up a good front and answer my questions. Except I was done. That was the last piece of the puzzle. I didn't need any more information out of Testafer, and I didn't need to sit there looking at his fat red face while he sorted out his misery. I needed to move on, to finish the job—and I needed make, badly. I was out of my seat and about to leave, when I suddenly had an idea. The idea went like this: Testafer was a doctor and Testafer was a rich man and Testafer was a man who liked to snort something better than Office make, or had, six years ago.

"You don't have any old make sitting around, do you?" I asked. "Something just a little less crude than the standard issue? Something without so much Forgettol in it?"

He smiled.

"I was about to ask you the same thing," he said.

CHAPTER 5

I SAT IN MY CAR WITH THE DOOR OPEN, PUT MY HANDS ON the wheel, and watched them tremble. It wasn't stopping. I needed addictol and I needed it soon.

I drove to the makery. The lights were on, and some tainted analog of hope stirred dimly in my heart. It didn't seem too far-fetched that the maker might have a few old ingredients sitting around that he could cobble together into some semblance of my blend. If not, I'd be happy enough to take some addictol straight, nothing on the side, thanks, see you later. When I went in, the hope faded like it was bleached. A guy was feeding his card into a vending machine on the far wall. There was no counter, no wall of little white bottles, no friendly old maker. Nothing. The machines covered the walls like urinals in a train station bathroom, and I didn't have to watch him get a packet to know what they were for.

I went out, feeling sick. The complimentary packet of make was burning a hole in my pocket, but it wasn't a commodity. I could obviously help myself to as much as I liked, anytime I liked. I had a funny idea about only snorting a little, but I knew that was a joke. If I got started, I wouldn't stop for a while.

I drove up into the hills towards Phoneblum's old place. Night was falling over the trees and rooftops, and I tried to let it ease me out of my funk, but it was no go. My gut was clenched with need. I pulled the car over to the side of the road and tossed the packet of make into the woods so I wouldn't be tempted. If I wanted it later, the stuff was available, but I had work to do now. And I had more than my own memory to worry about. It was obvious I was going to have to do a lot of other people's remembering for them.

At first I didn't recognize Phoneblum's place. The big fake house was gone, leaving the stairwell naked on the crest of the hill. I parked anyway, feeling pretty sure I had business at this address no matter what it looked like on top. It wasn't the kind of property that changed hands too often.

The difference no doubt mirrored the transfer of power that had obviously taken place while I was away, from Phoneblum to the kangaroo. Phoneblum was the big fake house projected on the top of the hill, all bluff and ornament, concerned with cloaking his evil in style. And the kangaroo—when I realized I was comparing a kangaroo to a stairwell I had a laugh at myself, and let it go.

I wanted to draw a bead on the kangaroo, but I wasn't ready to tangle with him, not yet. So I turned off the engine and the lights and watched the moon come up. My hands were in motion again, the thumbs twitching, but I was getting used to it.

I always get bored on a stakeout, and this time it was no different. I thought about Maynard and Celeste and the hotel room, and I thought about Walter Surface, and I thought about the kangaroo. I thought about Catherine Teleprompter, wondered where she was and how she looked now. I thought about a lot of things. Eventually I thought about make, and I thought about it a lot, and I thought about a lot of it. Big piles. I'd laughed at plenty of junkies in my day, all the while making damn sure I had a straw for my nose when I needed it, and now I went back and apologized to each and every one of them. My system was trying to run without the fuel that had made it go for years, and it was hell. I could feel my bloodstream panhandling my fat reserves for whatever last traces of the vital addictol they had stored away, and I could feel my fat cells turning out their pockets and saying sorry pal, there's nothing left.

I don't know how long I sat there like that. I certainly didn't keep my eyes on the stairwell door very long. My hands slipped off the wheel and into my lap, and I fell asleep. My dreams were murky, incomprehensible, like babyhead talk. I didn't wake up until the sun was out again, but it wasn't the sun that woke me up. It was the voice of the kangaroo, unmistakable, and jarringly close to my window.

I started to reach for the gun in my pocket when I realized he wasn't talking to me.

"Get in the car," he was saying. I poked my head up enough to see he was saying it to Barry Phoneblum and a couple of strong-arm louts from central casting. The kangaroo unlocked the passenger seat in the car in front of mine, and the babyhead clambered in. The louts got in the back, and one of them pulled out a gun and checked its load. I put my hand on Barry's gun in my pocket and laid low.

"I told you he wouldn't come here," said Barry.

The kangaroo went around and got in behind the wheel. His window was up, and when he said something, I didn't catch it.

"He's probably got better things to do," Barry went on.

I wished like hell I did.

The kangaroo started the car, and they drove away. It was obvious they were looking for me. I cursed myself for falling asleep in Joey's front yard, then offered up a quick improvisational prayer to the patron saint of dumb luck and trembling junkies. I was stupid for coming here at all. When I'd waltzed in on Phoneblum, I'd had the double insurance of his concern for his various "loved ones" and his peculiar sense of class and sportsmanship. With the kangaroo I had neither. I was lucky to still be alive.

When I was sure the coast was clear, I straightened up and took a quick inventory. Both legs were asleep from being wedged under the dashboard, there was a taste like puke in my mouth, and when I unclenched my hand from around the gun in my pocket, it started shaking again. Otherwise, I was intact. I drove down the hill and found a pay phone and called Surface, collect.

It was time to stop fucking around.

CHAPTER 6

THE OLD APE DIDN'T SOUND TOO ENTHUSIASTIC ON THE telephone. But when I arrived at the Office, he was waiting in front of the building, and he fell into step with me as I went up the stairs to the lobby.

"Thanks for showing, Walter," I said.

"Don't mention it," he grunted.

We went in. The Office always seems caught off guard at people walking in on their own steam. They don't have a reception area so much as they have a sort of ramp for tossing people out of the building from, and a long, clear lane for picking up speed before they get to the ramp. As for going in, they expect to have to drag you struggling through the back entrance, or unconscious on the floor of an Office van. You walk in the door, and every head turns. It was no different now.

We strolled up to what passed for a reception desk, though the guy sitting at it surely hadn't received anything more elaborate than a delivery pizza for the boys upstairs.

"I want to talk to Inquisitor Kornfeld," I said.

The guy surprised me by tapping the name into his console.

"Not available," he said.

"Okay," I said. "Inquisitor Morgenlander."

We came up against the same dead end.

I got a funny feeling. Those had been the two factions when I checked out, and Kornfeld seemed a shoo-in to run things in the Office his way for a while to come. It wasn't that they weren't in the building that bothered me—it was that the guy needed to consult his computer for the names.

"Inquisitor Teleprompter," I said.

His hands came off the keyboard. "I'll see if she's here," he said, and for the first time looked me and the ape over carefully. I smiled for him, and after a minute he picked up the intercom and hit a couple of buttons.

"Ms. Teleprompter," he said. "There's a guy here at the door says he wants to talk to you." He listened, then turned back to me. "What's your name?"

I told him, and he said it to her.

"Stay right here," he said, a little wide-eyed. I guess he was surprised.

Surface and I were just stepping back from the desk to cool our heels when a cloud of Office hoods came stiff-shouldered and scowling, and bunched around us like an elastic waistband.

"Mr. Metcalf?" said one of them.

"Metcalf and Surface," I said. "We're traveling together." The ape didn't look exactly grateful, but he didn't contradict me. The inquisitors took us each by the arms and steered us to the elevator. I didn't think we could all get on, and was about to suggest that Surface and I catch the next one, but they insisted, and we managed it. The fat ones sucked in their gut, and up we went.

When the elevator stopped, on the third floor, they

walked us to one of the executive offices. I was impressed, but I knew better than to think it was a good sign Catherine had moved upstairs. The game upstairs was no cleaner than the game on the streets, last I knew. Our escorts punched in a code at the door and pushed us inside, and a couple of them followed while the rest camped in the hall.

It was one of the nice offices, with a big picture window facing the bay, and a lot of pretty photographs and memorabilia pinned to the walls. Catherine was behind a desk as big as they come, looking six years older and not a day worse. The same hair was pulled back to expose the same throat, and I got lost there for a minute before I noticed her eyes were hard.

"Clean them up," she said.

The boys worked us over. They located the gun on me and a little notebook on Surface, and they handed them to Catherine along with both our cards. She tossed the stuff in a drawer and told the muscle to wait outside.

"Sit down," she said. We did.

"You were supposed to get out of town, Metcalf," she said. "You know the way it works."

I went up against her eyes, but it was a dead end. She didn't budge. She didn't even blink, or if she did, she timed the blinks to go with mine. The effect was impressive.

"I'm two days old, Catherine," I said. "Give me a break."

"Don't call me Catherine," she said. "By letting you and your monkey into my office, I already gave you one break too many." Her voice was like a dentist's drill.

Our eyes met again. I was looking at the woman I'd climbed into bed with two nights ago, but I had to remind myself she hadn't spent six years in bed waiting for me to return from the bathroom. The deeper I buried those memories, the better.

"Okay," I said. "I get it. You're on the inside now. Congratulations, and I'm sorry. Where's Kornfeld?"

She didn't flinch at the question. There was still that much between us. "Long gone," she said. "He pushed it too far, and now he's spending time in the freezer." She made it sound like she'd done the job herself, and maybe she had. "If you've got business with Kornfeld, don't wait underwater."

"I've got a punch in the stomach that belongs to him," I said. "It'll keep. Who stepped into his shoes—or am I looking at her?"

"That might be accurate," she said.

I looked over at Surface. He shot me his sourest look.

"Then you're the one I want to talk to," I said. "Nothing to do with before."

"You have five minutes of my time."

"I'm sure you'll lose track of the time," I said. "It gets good at the end."

"I've got a short attention span," she said.

"It's pretty simple. There's some murders nobody ever bothered to solve right, and a guy in the freezer who doesn't belong there."

"If you say the name Stanhunt, you have three minutes."

"How about six minutes for two Stanhunts?"

"Get on with it."

"I'll talk fast and in a high-pitched voice, and you can record it and slow it down later. I solved the Stanhunt case. Both of them."

Surface groaned like he was on her side.

"It's a beauty," I said. "A carefully balanced mechanism that faltered and collapsed in on itself. And it begins and ends with Danny Phoneblum."

"You were obsessed with Phoneblum," said Catherine. "I

looked into it. It was hopeless. You can't shoehorn him into the case."

"I was obsessed with the truth," I said. "Phoneblum is the case. Phoneblum and Celeste. The first time I met her, I could see she was trying to shake a past that wouldn't shake. It took a while, but I figured it out. She was Phoneblum's moll, for I don't know how long, but for a while. He loved her, and she might have loved him back. She gave him a son. Testafer was the doctor who handled the delivery."

"You're straining my credulity already," said Catherine.

"Give me a minute. The boy's name was Barry. Phoneblum was looking for an heir, and he wanted Celeste to stick around and bring the kid up. But he was abusive, a wife-slapper, and Celeste ran away to stay with the doctor. I confirmed as much with Testafer yesterday afternoon."

She made a face.

"She took the baby with her, and she didn't leave Phoneblum a forwarding address. Dr. Testafer was grooming a new boy named Maynard Stanhunt for his practice, and when Stanhunt and Celeste met, the sparks flew. Testafer advised Celeste against it in private, but he didn't bother to let his golden boy know he was romancing the estranged girl-friend of an angry gangster."

"This is pretty tired stuff, Metcalf."

"Get ready," I said. "This is where the Office comes in. When Phoneblum locates his wayward madonna and child, he's pretty steamed. He wants her back but she says no, and he gets ready to put boyfriend Maynard out of the picture. Only the fat man suddenly gets an idea. He runs a business where he defrosts karma-defunct bodies, courtesy of your old pal Kornfeld, to populate a little slavebox bordello. And he needs doctors to tend to the frostbite. So he takes the kid back and blackmails Stanhunt and Testafer into running his medical facility."

I took a deep breath and went on. "Phoneblum has a junkie girl working for him running drugs. He buys her the house on Cranberry Street and converts her to a nanny for the kid."

"Pansy Greenleaf," said Surface.

"Right. So Phoneblum's got his heir, he's got his doctors, and he's got Celeste back under his screws. Which by this time in their relationship is probably all he requires."

Both Catherine and Surface were suddenly quiet and still. I had them going. I had myself going, for that matter, and now all I had to do was bring it off. I hoped I wouldn't disappoint all three of us.

"Only problem," I continued, "is Celeste has a habit of bailing out. She packs her bags and leaves the doctor, which makes Stanhunt and Phoneblum both pretty antsy. She's what balances the equation between them. They put their heads together and start hiring detectives to keep tabs on her, to try and keep their little triangle intact."

"You and me," said Surface.

"You and me," I said. "Only Celeste doesn't turn out to be the leg of the triangle that gets permanently missing. When Stanhunt turns up dead in the hotel room, the balance is thrown in the other direction. Phoneblum no longer has a reason to keep away from Celeste. She knows it, and gets nervous, and mistakes everybody who looks at her funny for one of Phoneblum's goons—me included. When she figures out I'm an independent operator, she tries to hire me for protection, and I nibble, but I don't bite. It's too bad too. The night she died, I ran into Testafer and the kangaroo creeping around town together on Phoneblum's orders, looking for Celeste."

"Celeste Stanhunt was killed by a stranger she picked up in a sex club," said Catherine. "He raped her and killed her. She'd been asking for it and it finally happened."

"Phoneblum found her that night and paid her back for leaving him," I said. "There was nothing in his way once he lost the doctor. He'd been holding his rage in reserve, because of the beauty of their arrangement. And with Kornfeld and the Office in his pocket, he didn't have to fear punishment. I can't prove it, but that's the way it went."

"This case is starting to come back to me," said Catherine. "The junkie girl had a brother. He came up from L.A. and killed Stanhunt in the hotel. He's still guilty. The rest of this material is irrelevant."

"Orton Angwine couldn't have less to do with the case if he'd never come to town," I said. "The stuff in that hotel room bugged me until yesterday morning. I didn't spend six years thinking about it, but I might have and still not come up with the answer."

I pointed at Surface. "It was something you said in your kitchen yesterday that did it. All the clues were in place, but I needed a little push to make the conceptual leap."

"Jesus Christ, Metcalf," said Surface. "You sure do like to talk."

I didn't tell him I was sweating out my addiction. I had too much pride. But if I'd stopped talking, I probably would have passed out.

"The two of you had my head spinning with theories," I said. I looked at Catherine. "You had Stanhunt having the affair in the hotel, and you"—I looked at Surface—"you had Celeste doing the same thing." I laughed. "You were both half right."

"Let's hear it," said Catherine. She wanted to rush me.

My five minutes must have been over by now, but I knew I had all the time in the world.

"I'll get there. But first I have to backtrack. There was a progression in the way Stanhunt and Phoneblum hired their private inquisitors, and it's important. I came first, and I dealt with Stanhunt, and all he wanted me to do was lean on Celeste and suggest she go home. But hiring gumshoes wasn't Stanhunt's strength, and when I didn't pan out, he turned the job over to Phoneblum. The fat man hired Walter here." I gestured at Surface. "When the report came back that Celeste was getting some on the side, Phoneblum offered Surface good money to find the new boyfriend and put him in the ground. But Walter said no. And he left the job without ever having met Stanhunt. Isn't that right?"

Surface grunted confirmation.

"Phoneblum was having trouble on another front. His son and protégé had gone babyhead, run away to Telegraph Avenue to sip whiskey and talk gibberish. Phoneblum still had hopes of reclaiming his flesh-and-blood heir—he was investing in a babyhead quarters for the backyard at Cranberry Street—but he was also looking around for another candidate. He found one in a young kangaroo named Joey Castle. Joey was an all-too-willing pupil."

"I'll buy that," said Surface. He must have been thinking of his ribs.

"So picture this," I said. "After Surface and me, Phoneblum is sour on the idea of outside help. He's got a new kangaroo gunman with an itchy trigger finger. Phoneblum gives him the assignment of tailing Celeste, the same way he hired Walter—*without the kangaroo ever meeting Maynard Stanhunt.* And the orders were the same: Take the new boyfriend out of the picture."

I paused for effect, and they both shot arrows at me with their eyes.

"Maynard Stanhunt was a pretty heavy Forgettol addict—at least by the standards of six years ago. The first time I tried to call him at home, he didn't know who I was. I'd warned Angwine of the danger of tangling with people with huge gaps in their day-to-day memory, but I hadn't really thought through the implications myself. Maynard and Celeste were both having affairs in the Bayview Motel, in the same room, in fact. With each other."

I turned to Surface. "Walter, you saw Stanhunt, only you didn't know it. He was the guy you spotted at the motel. Sure, Celeste had left him, but there was slippage in her resolve, as there so often is. She agreed to meet him for quiet afternoons in the motel—but his morning self, the one that hired the detectives, didn't know about the arrangement."

Surface just gaped.

"Yesterday you told me it was illegal now in L.A. to know what you did for a living, and that was when it clicked for me. Stanhunt was an early prototype of that. The part of him that wasn't getting any action with Celeste was murderously jealous of whoever she was seeing in the Bayview Motel, and he told Phoneblum to have his boys blow the guy away. The kangaroo didn't know what Stanhunt looked like any more than you did, Walter. He just did as he was told and killed the boyfriend. Stanhunt hired his own hit."

I stopped talking and gave them some time to sort it out. Catherine's face went through a brief series of expressions, most of them skeptical, but in the end she was too smart to pretend it didn't have the satisfying weight of something inevitable and true. I watched her get to that point, and then I watched her remind herself that she had my card in her drawer, and that nothing necessarily had to get out of this room if she didn't want it to. She hardened quickly—I guess she'd had a lot of practice in the intervening years. She was more changed than Barry, or Surface, or Testafer, or anyone else I'd dealt with since coming back. She went with the desk and the office with the big window now.

"It's an interesting story," she said. "What are you hoping it'll get you?"

"I want to see Angwine defrosted," I said. "I'll make your job hell with this if he isn't."

She just smiled.

"Humor me, Teleprompter," I said. "Let me think I'm a threat. It's no skin off your nose. The guy's harmless—and innocent."

She punched something into her desktop monitor. I guessed it was Angwine's file, but it could have been anything, really. Maybe just a stall for time. She squinted at it for a minute, and I remembered how she wouldn't let me see her in glasses the first time we met.

"I'll see what I can do," she said.

I thought about it. I'd come a long way on Angwine's fourteen hundred dollars. "That's not good enough," I said. "I need more."

She looked me dead in the eye. This time it was me who didn't blink.

"Okay," she said. "Tomorrow. You've got my word."

"Thanks."

"Don't thank me," she said. "Thank your lucky fucking stars. Take your stuff and get out of here." She opened her drawer and gave Surface his card and his pad back, and then she gave me my card and put my gun out on top of her desk. I reached for it, but her hand was still over it, and she looked at me and I looked at her and I think possibly I saw the faintest hint of a smile cross her face. The moment passed, and she let me pick up the gun and put it back in the pocket of my coat.

She leaned on the button of her intercom and spoke to the muscle waiting outside her office. "Get them out of here," she said. "Put them on the street."

They took it literally, bless their hearts.

CHAPTER 7

THE PARKING METER OUTSIDE THE WHITE WALNUT REST Home played me a couple of bars of Hawaiian bottleneck guitar when I dropped in the quarter, but I didn't stick around to hear out the tune. It had been a long drive up into the hills and my head didn't feel so good. My bloodstream wouldn't quit asking and I was running out of ways of saying no. Cold turkey was a merry-go-round I couldn't get off, and instead of a wooden horse I was riding a porcupine.

I went inside. The place was nice and quiet, all rosewood antiques and bunches of flowers. I found the office. The woman at the desk seemed frightened by my presence, but I don't know whether it was my red eyes and pasty complexion or the fact of who I was asking to see. Both, probably.

They had him in a dayroom, a pretty one, with windows on three sides and a collection of wicker furniture for putting glasses of lemonade on. He was watching television, or maybe I should say they had him facing the television, because when I moved around his wheelchair and stood in his line of sight, he didn't notice, though his eyes were open. Except for the deadness in what had once been exceptionally lively eyes, he looked pretty much the same. His beard was unkempt, but he still had a full head of hair. I waved the attendant out of the room and sat down in one of the armchairs.

We sat like that for a while, me watching motes of dust float through the sunlight, him supposedly watching the television. The only sound was the rasp of his breathing. Then I reached over and turned off the picture.

"Phoneblum," I said.

He murmured like he was asleep.

I got out of my chair and took the collar of his robe in my hands. His eyes brightened considerably. "Wake up," I said. He put his big clubby hands over mine and pushed me away.

I watched as he blinked away his stupor. His forehead wrinkled like a question mark as he looked me over.

"You're an inquisitor," he said. The voice rolled out of him like secondhand thunder, acquired cheap. It was a voice from the past, and I was impressed at the way he could still summon it up.

"That's right," I said.

"Very good." He curled a finger and rubbed at his nose with the knuckle. "Do questions make you uncomfortable? I prefer to relax the conventional strictures."

He was running on empty, but the old routines died hard. I had to tip my hat to him. It was a bluff, but his junk was better than most guys' fastballs. In another setting, minus the television and the wheelchair and the layer of dust, I might have bought it, might have believed he was still in the saddle. But the bright hard intelligence behind his eyes was missing. He didn't know who he was talking to.

"Questions are my bread and butter," I said.

He didn't remember the answer. He just nodded and said: "Good. What can I do for you?"

"I want to ask you about Celeste," I said.

I watched him chew it over. He obviously knew the name. It seemed to lull him back a step towards dreamland.

"You remember Celeste?" I said.

"Why, yes," he answered. He wasn't looking at me anymore. "I remember Celeste. Of course."

"I've been working on her murder," I said.

His eyes shot back to mine. "That's a long time ago," he said.

"Couple of days, to me. I've still got her blood on my shoes."

I said it casually, but I could see it was having an effect. His forehead lifted.

"Yes," he said softly. "So do I."

"You killed her," I suggested.

"I don't remember," he said. "I killed a lot of people."

"You loved her."

He clouded up. I waited.

"I don't remember," he concluded. His face fell slack.

"Try harder," I said. "This one was special. You loved her and you killed her." I took hold of his robe again.

His eyes cleared and his jaw set. "I suppose I did," he said. "The two sometimes go together." He smiled through his beard. "Women are already split in two from the floor halfway up, you know. I just finished the job."

That did it. I'd been arguing with myself, but now he was making it easy. I let go of his robe and stepped back and took Barry's gun out of my coat pocket. It played the creepy violin music as it came into my hand. I opened up the safety and leveled the muzzle at Phoneblum's big chest. He made a good target.

I watched him struggle to focus on the gun. He had to

cross his eyes to do it. His fingers tightened a little on the arms of his wheelchair, but his face showed no fear.

"Are you going to kill me?" he asked.

"I might," I said. I wanted to. I didn't know what was stopping me.

He squinted into my eyes. "Do I know you, sir?"

There was a long, rough minute while I tried to get myself to squeeze the trigger. The motes of dust in the air seemed to slow down and hover, glowing, in the space between the end of the gun and the beginning of Phoneblum's giant chest. Eventually I saw that it wasn't going to happen. I closed the safety and put the gun away.

"No," I said, disgusted. "There was a mix-up. I've got the wrong guy."

Phoneblum didn't say anything. He didn't even look relieved. I reached down and turned the television back on, straightened my coat, and went out into the hallway.

I passed through the lobby but I didn't sign my name in the guest register. I wasn't in the mood. I went out to the car and sat. It had enough fuel in it for one more trip, but I wasn't sure I did. I thought about the little packet of make I'd thrown into the woods, and I thought about the makery. The vending machines didn't seem so bad from this distance. I tried to tell myself the job was finished, that it was okay to let it go. I tried hard, and I got as far as starting the engine and pointing the car down the hill to the makery. But it wouldn't take. The job wasn't finished. I screwed the wheels around and drove across the ridge to the Fickle Muse.

I was early. I had to park in the lot and watch the sun set and wait for them to open the place. The sky looked like a bruise. When the guy showed up, I went inside and ordered a drink on the chance it might fool my nerves for half an hour.

Beyond that I didn't care. I didn't recognize the bartender, but I didn't have to. The face had changed but the type hadn't.

He brought me the drink. "First customer of the night," he said, as if it meant something.

"Guess so," I said back.

When I got my change, I went to the corner and used the pay phone, then I finished my drink at the bar and went back out to the lot to wait. It didn't take long. The kangaroo looked like he was alone, but I couldn't tell for sure. He wasn't riding a scooter anymore.

He got out of his car behind a gun. I wasn't surprised, and I didn't care. He wouldn't kill me until he found out what I knew and what I wanted. I just had to draw it out. He walked across the lot and came up to the window of my car.

"Get in," I said.

He sat down beside me and put the gun hand across his lap. It was more than a little reminiscent of the first time we talked, in the lot of the Bayview Motel. I knew now that he was a neophyte gunsel that night, making a pilgrimage to the scene of his first killing. Running into me must have been his worst nightmare come true. But all I had to do was look to know that the kangaroo had come a long way since then. There wasn't any great physical change—he might have been a little thicker around the collar, or a little yellower around the teeth—but he was different. I could read it in his eyes.

"Metcalf—," he started.

"Don't talk," I said. "I know how it'll come out. You're the big man now, and you know how to sweet-talk. It's your job. You'll tell me the past is the past, that it isn't worth it anymore. You'll tell me idealism went out of style while I was away. You'll mix your threats and your enticements into a nice little cocktail and pour it down my ear. I know all about it. You're Phoneblum now."

He curled his black lips in a practiced smile. It wasn't part of his former repertoire, and I took it as confirmation of my guesses. "Me Phoneblum?" he said. "I guess that's about right."

"I've got this conversation memorized in advance," I said. "You feel me out about my price tag, about what it'll take to get me to disappear. I tell you I don't buy. You remind me you didn't have to come and hear me out, you could have sent over a carload of your boys instead."

"That's good," he said. "I like that."

"Okay," I said. "I said your part. You tell me mine."

He thought it over. "You tell me you've got dirt on me that counts," he said. "I listen patiently, and break it to you slowly that you and your information are six years dead." He paused. "See, you're a funny kind of ghost, Metcalf. You can't hurt me, but I can hurt you, bad. You're insubstantial one way, the wrong way."

"That's pretty good too," I said. "Except you got it all wrong."

"Wrong how?"

"It's more like this," I said. "I tell you it was a big mistake putting me in the freezer. The events of six years ago are yesterday to me."

I watched his hand tighten around the gun again. I didn't care. He was mine now. He'd think twice about a messy murder in the parking lot of his club, and he wasn't going to get a chance to think twice.

"I tell you that you just made the biggest fucking mistake of your life not sending those boys," I went on. "And then I break your face."

He brought the gun up, but I brought it back down again, hard, and pinned it in his lap. I butted his nose with the top of my head, and he panicked and tried to stand up. The rental car wasn't big enough. I used my weight to mash him back into the seat, and pried with both hands on his trigger finger. He didn't want it to go off in his lap, so he let go, and the gun clattered down between his legs and tail to the floor of the car.

He hit me in the jaw, but his heart wasn't in it. He probably hadn't been in a fistfight since our last waltz six years back, whereas my only problem was that my hands still hurt from breaking them on his jaw two nights ago. His main weapon had always been his big legs and feet, but those were wedged under the dash. It was my show. When my hands wouldn't ball up anymore, I picked up his gun and hit him across the mouth with it a couple of times. Then I rolled down the window and tossed it out onto the gravel.

I tried to talk, but there was too much blood in my mouth. I guess he'd landed a couple of good ones. I cleared it out with my finger. Joey didn't look so hot either. His head was flopped back over the seat as if his neck didn't work. But when I started talking, I could see him listen.

"There's a reason Phoneblum was frantic for an heir," I said. "There's always got to be someone in his role, just like there's always got to be someone like me."

I wiped more blood from my mouth, then took out Barry's gun. It played me the Danger Theme, but for once that seemed appropriate. "Don't think this is for the Stanhunt murder," I said. "You were suckered into pulling the trigger. I took that into account."

Joey's eyes were big with fear. He understood every word.

"This is because you picked up the reins," I said. "It's for the girls upstairs in the back room of the Fickle Muse. It's for the six years of wrecked lives I couldn't do anything about because of the freezer. It's for things only you know you did, things you did because you let yourself step into the fat man's shoes."

"Metcalf," said Joey. "For God's sake."

"I had Phoneblum in the same spot this afternoon," I said, ignoring him. "But I was years too late. With you I'm right on schedule. Besides, I wanted to kill somebody who remembered who I was."

I squeezed the trigger. The first shot spread his face out across the top of the seat, but his legs kept moving. I had a lot of respect for those legs. I emptied the clip into his middle, and one of the bullets found his spinal column and put an end to it. Then I got his keys and left him there, and took his car for a drive. It handled a lot better than the rental job.

CHAPTER 8

THE NEXT MORNING I WAS SITTING IN JOEY'S CAR IN FRONT of the Office. I felt okay. I'd spent most of the night in the hills, looking at the moon, working the kinks out of my fingers, and apparently I'd dried out in the interval. My system was clean. I rolled down the window of the car, leaned back in the seat, and listened to the noise the new day made. I didn't mind waiting. For some reason everything looked good to me all of a sudden. I even found myself admiring the buildings they'd thrown up while I was away.

After about half an hour Angwine came out blinking into the sunlight, fingering his new card and trying to get his bearings. I didn't feel too bad for him. He was no more out of place here than he'd been six years ago. But I hunkered down in my seat as he passed. I didn't have anything to say to him when it came down to it. I just wanted to have a look.

Then I locked up Joey's car and went inside. I found an inquisitor and handed him my card and Barry's gun, which played the Danger Theme one more time. I'd come to like it, almost.

"My name is Conrad Metcalf," I said. "You're probably looking for me."

Now that I'd been cut loose, so to speak, the freeze wasn't much of a punishment. I was like a hobo tossing bricks through shop windows to get a place to sleep for the night. If I didn't like where I woke up next time, I'd get myself in trouble again, until I found a place where I fit in or they stopped offering me the free ride. In the meantime maybe I'd run across Kornfeld and deliver that punch in the stomach I was carrying around.

When I was in the holding area getting ready for the freezer, one of the inquisitors got friendly, the way they tend to do at that stage, and offered me a line of some make he was sniffing.

"Forgettol?" I said.

He shook his head no, indulging my question. "My personal blend," he said. "Give it a try."

So the makers still worked, in-house. It figured. I took the straw from him. It meant waking up with the monkey on my back, but hell, it was my monkey.

It was that rarity, an easy decision.